The Ponson Case

Freeman Wills Crofts

Must Have Books
503 Deerfield Place
Victoria, BC
V9B 6G5
Canada

ISBN: 9781773237800

Copyright 2021 – Must Have Books

Chapter 1
Mystery at Luce Manor

The dying sun of a July evening shone rosily on the old Georgian house of Luce Manor, mellowing the cold grey of the masonry, bringing out with soft shadow its cornices and mouldings, and softening and blurring its hard outlines. A fine old house, finely set on the summit of a low hill, and surrounded by wonderful old trees, it seemed to stand symbolical of the peace, security, and solid comfort of upper-class rural England.

This impression was not lessened by the outlook from the terrace in front. Below, and already shadowed by the trees beyond from the sun's rays, was a small Dutch garden, its walks and beds showing up faintly in the gathering gloom. To the right the drive swept off in an easy curve until it disappeared between two rows of beeches, celebrated in all the county round for their age and size. At the side of the house, and reached through a rose pergola, was the walled English garden, with its masses of colour, its laden bushes, and its range of glass houses. In front, beyond the lawn, whose oaks and elms stood singly like sentinels guarding the house, the country rolled away to a line of distant hills, while to the left, an opening in the trees gave a glimpse of the Cranshaw River, with behind a near horizon of tree-covered slopes.

Within, in a large room panelled in black oak, the master of the house sat at dinner. He was alone, the only other members of the household, his wife and his daughter Enid, being from home on a visit. Sir William Ponson, a self-made man, had retired from business some ten years before our story opens and, selling his interest in the large ironworks of which he was head, had bought Luce Manor and settled down to end his days in the role of a country squire. Though obviously a *nouveau riche*, and still retaining the somewhat brusque manners of his hard, northern upbringing, he had nevertheless been received with more cordiality into the local society than usually happens in such cases. For Sir William, though he had thus risen in the social scale, remained a simple, honourable, kindly old man, a little headstrong and short tempered perhaps, but anxious to be just, and quick to apologise if he found himself in the wrong.

It was seldom that Sir William partook of a solitary meal. He was fond of society, and kept open house for all who cared to visit him. He had rented some shooting, and though the fishing in the river was not good, it at least was fishing. The tennis courts were always in perfect condition, and there was a sporting golf course at the neighbouring town of Halford. But it spoke well for Sir William that, of all his acquaintances, those whom he liked best to welcome were his old, somewhat unpolished business friends from the north, by few of whom these pursuits were properly appreciated. In this he had the full sympathy of his wife, a stout, placid lady of uncertain age, who ruled over his household with leisurely, easy-going sway.

3

Enid Ponson, their only daughter, a young woman of some thirty summers, was a favourite everywhere. Not exactly beautiful, she was yet good to look at, with her pale complexion, dark eyes, and winning smile. But it was her wonderful charm that endeared her to those with whom she came in contact, as well as the sweetness and kindliness of her disposition. That she was unmarried was only explained by the fact that the man to whom she had been engaged had been killed during the Great War. Enid and her father were close comrades and allies. She adored him, while Sir William's chief thought was centred in his daughter, upon whom he thought the sun rose and set.

When the family were alone it was Sir William's custom after dinner to join his wife and Enid in the music room, where for hours the latter would sing and play, while her father smoked cigar after cigar, and the elder woman placidly knitted or crocheted. But tonight, being entirely alone, he retired at once from the table to his library, where he would sit, reading and smoking, till about ten or later he would ring for Parkes, the butler, to bring him his nightly tumbler of hot punch.

But ten came, and half past ten, and eleven, and there was no ring.

'Boss is late tonight, Mr Parkes,' said Innes, Sir William's valet, as he and the butler sat in the latter's room over a bottle of Sir William's old port, and a couple of Sir William's three and sixpenny cigars.

'Sir William *is* behind his usual hour,' admitted the butler in a slightly chilly tone. Innes had followed his master from the north and was, as Mr Parkes put it, 'well in' with him. The butler therefore thought it politic to be 'well in' with Innes, and was usually affable in a condescending way. But the latter's habit of speaking of Sir William as 'the boss,' grated on Parkes's sensitive ears.

The two chatted amicably enough, and under the influence of wine and tobacco time passed unnoticed until once again the clock struck.

'That's half-past eleven,' said Parkes. 'I have never known Sir William so late before. He is usually in bed by now.'

' "Early to bed, early to rise," ' quoted the valet. 'There's no accounting for tastes, Mr Parkes. I'd like to see you or me going to bed at ten-thirty and getting up at six when we needn't.'

'I don't hold with unnecessarily early hours myself,' the other agreed, and then, after a pause: 'I think I'll go and see if he wants anything. It's not like him to retire without having his punch.'

'Whatever you think, Mr Parkes, but for me, I could do here well enough for another hour or more.'

Without replying, Parkes left the room. Reaching the library door, he knocked discreetly and then entered. The electric lights were switched on and everything looked as usual, but the room was empty. The butler moved on, and opening a door which led to the smoking room, passed in. The lights were off here, as they were also in the billiard room, which he next visited.

'He must have gone up to bed,' thought Parkes, and returning to his room, spoke to Innes.

'I can't find Sir William about anywhere below stairs, and he hasn't had his punch. I wish you'd have a look whether he hasn't gone to bed.'

The valet left the room.

'He's not upstairs, Mr Parkes,' he said, returning a few moments later. 'And he's not been either so far as I can see. The lights are off and nothing's been touched.'

'But where is he? He's never been so late ringing for his punch before.'

'I'm blessed if I know. Maybe, Mr Parkes, we should have another look round?'

'It might be as well.'

The two men returned to the library. It was still empty, and they decided to make a tour of the lower rooms. In each they switched on the lights and had a look round, but without result. Sir William had disappeared.

'Come upstairs,' said Parkes.

They repeated their search through music room, bedrooms, dressing-rooms, and passages, but all to no purpose. They could find no trace of their master.

Mr Parkes was slightly perturbed. An idea had recurred to him which had entered his mind on various previous occasions. He glanced inquiringly at the valet, as if uncertain whether or not to unburden his mind. Finally he said in a low tone:

'Has it ever struck you, Innes, that Sir William was apoplectic?'

'Apoplectic?' returned the other. 'Why, no, I don't think it has.'

'Well, it has me, and more than once. If he's annoyed he gets that red. I've thought to myself when he has got into a temper about something, "Maybe," I've thought, "maybe some of these days you'll pop off in a fit if you're not careful." '

'You don't say, Mr Parkes,' exclaimed Innes, in a tone of thrilled interest.

'I do. I've thought it. And I've thought too,' the butler went on impressively, 'that maybe something like this would happen: that we'd miss him, and go and look, and find him lying somewhere unconscious.'

'Bless my soul, Mr Parkes, I hope not.'

'I hope not too. But I've thought it.' Mr Parkes shook his head gravely. 'And what's more,' he went on after a few moments, 'keeping this idea in view, I doubt if our search was sufficiently comprehensive. If Sir William had fallen behind a piece of furniture we might not have seen him.'

'We could go round again, Mr Parkes, if you think that.'

This proposition appealing favourably to the butler, a second and more thorough search was made. But it was as fruitless as before. There was no trace of Sir William.

And then the valet made a discovery. Off the passage leading to the library was a small cloakroom. Innes, who had looked into the latter, now returned to the butler.

'He's gone out, Mr Parkes. A soft felt hat and his loose black cape are missing out of the cloakroom.'

'Gone out, is he? That's not like him either. Are you sure of that?'

'Certain. I saw the coat and hat no longer ago than this evening just before dinner. They were hanging in that room then. They're gone now.'

5

The passage in which they were standing, and off which opened the smoking room, library, billiard room and this cloakroom, ran on past the doors of these rooms, and ended in a small conservatory, from which an outer door led into the grounds. The two men walked to this door and tried it. It was closed, but not fastened.

'He's gone out sure enough,' said Parkes. 'I locked that door myself when I went round after dinner.'

They stepped outside. The night was fine, but very dark. There was no moon, and the sky was overcast. A faint air was stirring, but hardly enough to move the leaves. Everything was very still, except for the low, muffled roar of the Cranshaw waterfall, some half mile or more away.

'I expect he's stepped over to Hawksworth's,' said Parkes at last. 'He sometimes drops in of an evening. But he's never been so late as this.'

'Maybe there's a party of some kind on, and when he turned up they've had him stay.'

'It may be,' Parkes admitted. 'We may as well go in anyway.'

They returned to the butler's room, and resumed their interrupted discussion.

Twelve struck, then half-past, then one.

Innes yawned.

'I wouldn't mind how soon I went to bed, Mr Parkes. What do you feel like?'

'I don't feel sleepy,' the other returned, and then, after a pause: 'I don't mind confessing I am not quite easy about Sir William. I would be glad he had returned.'

'You're afraid—of what you were saying?'

'I am. I don't deny it. I feel apprehensive.'

'Supposing we were to get a couple of lanterns and have a walk round outside?'

The butler considered this suggestion.

'I am of opinion better not,' he said at last. 'If Sir William found us so engaged, he would be very annoyed.'

'Maybe you're right, Mr Parkes. What do you suggest?'

'I think we had better wait as we are a while longer. Take another cigar, and make yourself comfortable.'

As both men settled themselves in easy chairs, the conversation began to wane, and before the clock struck again their steady breathing showed that each had adopted the most efficient known way of passing monotonous time.

About six o'clock the butler awoke with a start. He felt cold and stiff, and for a moment could not recall what had happened. Then, remembering, he woke the valet.

'Six o'clock, Innes. We had better go and see if Sir William has returned.'

They retraced their round of the previous night, but everything was as before. They could find no trace of their master.

'It's daylight,' went on Parkes, when their search was complete. 'We might have a walk out now, I think.'

Leaving by the small conservatory door at the side of the billiard-room wing,

6

they walked down the drive. The sun had just risen—a glorious, ruddy ball in the clearest of blue skies, giving promise of a perfect day. Everything was delightfully fresh. The sparkling dew-drops made the scene fairylike, and the clean, aromatic smell of the trees and earth was in their nostrils. Not a breath of wind stirred, and the air was full of the songs of birds, with, like a mighty but subdued dominant pedal, the sullen roar of the distant fall.

After passing between the two rows of magnificent beeches, whose branches met over the drive, they reached the massive iron gates leading on to the road. These, as was usual at night, were closed, but not locked.

There being no sign of the missing man, they retraced their steps and took a narrow path which led, through a door in the wall surrounding the grounds, to the same road. This door was also closed, but unlocked. Here again their quest was fruitless.

Returning to the house they made a more general survey, visiting the terrace and formal Dutch garden below, the rose pergola, the glass house, and the various arbours—all those places in which a sudden whim might have induced the master of these delights to smoke or stroll in the pleasant evening air. But all to no purpose. Sir William Ponson had vanished.

Parkes looked at his watch. It was twenty-five minutes past seven. He was beginning a remark to Innes when the latter suddenly slapped his thigh and interrupted.

'I'll lay you a sovereign to five bob, Mr Parkes, I know where the boss is. He's gone in to Mr Austin's, and he's kept him all night.'

Austin Ponson was Sir William's son. In many ways he was a disappointment to his father. On leaving Cambridge he had moved to chambers in London, ostensibly to read for the bar. But though he had read, it was not law, and after a couple of years of wasted time, and a scene with his father, he had dropped the pretence of legal work and turned himself openly to the pursuit of his own special interests. Finding the boy was determined to go his own way, Sir William had decided discretion was the better part of valour, and withdrawing his opposition to Austin's plans, had instead enabled him to carry them out, increasing his allowance to £1000 a year. Austin was extremely clever and versatile. Something of a dreamer, his opinions and ideals irritated his practical father almost beyond endurance. He was a Socialist in politics, and held heterodox views on the relations of capital and labour. He read deeply on these subjects, and wrote thoughtful articles on them for the better class papers. He had produced a couple of social problem novels which, though they had had small sales, had been well reviewed. But his chief study and interest was natural history, or rather that branch of it relating to the life and habits of disease-bearing insects. To facilitate research work in this direction, he had thrown up his London chambers and, partly because his relations with his father were too strained to live with him with any pleasure, and partly because the latter's residence in Gateshead was unsuitable for his hobby, he had taken a house with a good garden near Halford. That was eleven years ago, and he had lived there with an elderly couple—butler and housekeeper—ever since. Though caring nothing for society, he was not unpopular among his neighbours, being unassuming in manner, as well as kindly and generous in disposition. When his father had signified his intention of retiring, Austin had suggested the former's taking Luce Manor, which was then for sale. The two had agreed to sink their differences, and by avoiding controversial subjects, they continued on good though not very cordial terms. When, therefore, Innes suggested Sir William had gone to visit his son, Parkes could not but agree this might be the truth.

'It's not like him all the same,' the butler went on, 'he never would walk two miles at night when he could have had a car by just ringing for it.'

'He's done it, I bet, all the same,' returned Innes, 'I'll lay you what you like. There was something on between them.'

'What do you mean?' Parkes asked sharply.

'Why, this. I didn't tell you what I heard—it wasn't no business of mine—but I'll tell you now. You remember Mr Austin dining here last Sunday evening? The boss, as you know, had the hump all day, but Mr Austin when he came first was as sweet as you please. After dinner they went to the library. Well, sir, I was passing the door about half-past nine or maybe later, and I heard their voices inside. I judged they were having a bit of a row. I heard Mr Austin shouting, "My God, sir, she isn't!" and then I heard the mumble of Sir William's voice, but I couldn't hear what he said. Well, that was all of that. Then about half-past ten, when Mr Austin was leaving, I was in the hall, and got him his coat, and he was just sort of green about the gills, as if he had been laid out in the ring. He's always pleasant enough, but that night he took his coat and hat as if I was a blooming hat-stand, and out to the car without a word, and a look on his face as if he'd seen death. And Sir William hasn't been the same since either. Oh yes! I guess they've had some sort of a dust up.'

Parkes whistled.

'About the girl?' he said, with a sharp glance.

'So I thought. Miss Lois Drew may be a very nice young lady, and I don't say she's not, but she's hardly the kind of daughter-in-law the old man would be looking out for.'

'It's a fact, Innes. You're right. Now if it had been my Lady Evelyn, things would have been different.'

'You bet,' said the valet.

The men's allusion was to a subject of common gossip in Halford. Austin Ponson was universally believed to be in love with the daughter of the local bookseller. And as universally, it was assumed that such a match would have the determined opposition of Sir William.

'I think we might send in to Mr Austin's, and find out,' went on Parkes after a pause. 'If he's there no harm's done, and if not, why, it might be just as well to tell Mr Austin.'

'Well, I'll go in and see him if you think so.'

'I would be glad. Hughes can run you in in the small car.'

Some twenty minutes later Innes rang at the door of a pleasant looking little villa on the outskirts of Halford.

'Is Mr Austin about yet, Mrs Currie?' he asked, as an elderly woman, with a kindly, dependable face, answered.

'He's not down yet, Mr Innes. Will you come in?'

The valet answered her question with another.

'Sir William didn't call last night, I suppose?'

'Sir William? No, Mr Innes, I haven't seen Sir William for over a month.'

'Well, I'll come in, thank you, and when Mr Austin's ready I'd like to see him.'

'I'll tell him you're waiting.'

When some twenty minutes later Austin Ponson came into the room, Innes looked at him in some surprise. As a rule Austin was a man of easy and leisurely manners, suave, polished, and unhurried. He had an air of comfortable and good-humoured contentment, that made him a pleasant and soothing companion. But this morning he was strangely different. His face was pale, and dark circles below his eyes pointed to his having passed a sleepless night. His manner was nervous, and Innes noticed his hand shaking. When he spoke it was abruptly and as if he were upset.

'Good morning, Innes. You wanted to see me?'

'Sorry for troubling you so early, sir, but Mr Parkes sent me in with a message.'

'Yes?'

'It was to ask if you knew anything of Sir William, sir. He went out late last night without saying anything about it, and he has not turned up since, and Mr Parkes was a little anxious about him in case he might have met with an accident.'

A look almost of fear appeared in the other's eyes.

'And how should I know anything about him?' he answered quickly, and Innes noticed that his lips were dry. 'He did not come here. Have you tried at Mr Hawksworth's or Lord Eastmere's? He has dropped in to see them often in the evening, hasn't he?'

'That is so, sir, but we thought we had better consult you before raising an alarm. As you say, sir, Sir William has often gone over to these places in the evening, but never without saying he would be late, and he never stopped all night.'

'Oh well, I expect he's done it this time. But you had better go round and see. Stay, I'll go with you myself. Wait a few minutes while I get some breakfast.'

Twenty minutes later they were on the road. They called at the two houses mentioned, but at neither had anything been heard of Sir William. It was nearly nine when they reached Luce Manor. Parkes hurried to meet them.

'Any news, Parkes?' asked Austin as he entered the house. He had recovered his composure, and seemed more at ease.

'No, sir,' replied the butler, 'but we've made a discovery—just before you came.'

Again the flash of something like fear showed in the other's eyes. He did not speak, and Parkes went on:

'About ten minutes ago, sir, Smith, the under-gardener, who is boatman also,

9

came up here asking for Sir William. I saw him, and he said he had just discovered that one of the boats was missing—stolen, he said. I kept him, sir, in case if you came back with Innes you might like to speak to him.'

Austin Ponson's face paled as if this news was a shock.

'Good Heavens! Parkes,' he stammered, 'you don't mean to suggest—'

'I thought, sir,' resumed the butler smoothly, 'that maybe Sir William had taken a sudden notion to go over and see Dr Graham. Sometimes, as you know, sir, gentlemen like to consult a medical man privately. He might have rowed himself across the river for a short cut.'

Austin seemed relieved.

'Yes, yes, quite possible,' he said. 'But we ought to make sure. Run round, Innes, will you, in the car and find out.'

'Will you see Smith, sir?' asked the butler when Innes had gone.

Austin seemed to awake out of a reverie.

'Yes—oh yes, I suppose so,' he answered. 'Yes certainly. Bring him in.'

A small, stout man, with a short brown beard stepped up. He was, he explained, boatman as well as under-gardener, and it was his custom each morning to visit the boathouse, give the boats a run over with a cloth, brush the cushions, and leave everything ready in case a boat might be required during the day. On this morning he had reached the boathouse as usual, and was surprised to find the door unlocked. Entering, he had at once noticed that the water gate connecting the basin in the house with the river was fully open, and then he saw that the *Alice*, the smallest of the skiffs, was missing. A glance at the rack had shown that the oars and rowlocks had also gone. He had looked round generally, but could not find any other trace of disturbance. He had immediately come up to the house to inform Sir William.

Austin Ponson had listened carefully to the man's statement, and he now asked a question:

'You say you were surprised to find the boathouse door unlocked. I have been at the boathouse scores of times, and I never knew it to be locked. Why should it have been locked then?'

'I lock it, sir,' the man replied, 'every night at dusk. Every morning I open it, and it stays open through the day.'

'And did you lock it last night?'

'Yes, sir.'

'About what time?'

'About 8.00 or 8.30, I should think.'

'Who else has a key?'

'No one but Sir William, sir.'

Austin turned to the butler.

'Do you know where he keeps this key?'

'In the drawer of his writing table, sir.'

'See if you can find it now.'

In a few moments Parkes returned. Several keys, each attached to its neatly lettered block of wood, were in the drawer, but that of the boathouse door was missing.

'That will do, thank you, Smith,' Austin went on, then, when the man had withdrawn, he turned to the butler. He still seemed nervous and upset.

'It seems pretty clear Sir William has gone out on the river; now what on earth would he do that for? I wish that man would come back from the doctor's.'

'He won't be long, sir. Say ten minutes there and ten back, and five to make inquiries. He should be here in five or six minutes.'

In about that time Innes returned. Sir William had not called at Dr Graham's.

Austin and Parkes exchanged troubled glances. The same terrible idea which had been in their minds since the discovery of the missing boat was forcing itself to the front.

The River Cranshaw was a broad and sluggish stream at Halford, and for the two miles or so of its course to the point where it passed Luce Manor. But just below Sir William's grounds there was a curious outcrop of rock, and the waters had cut for themselves a narrow channel down which, when the river was full, they raced at ever increasing speed till they reached the Cranshaw Falls. Here they leaped over a ledge of rock, not very deep—not, in fact, more than four or five feet—but the river bed at the foot, and for some distance downstream, was so full of huge boulders that the waters danced and swirled, and were churned into a mass of foam as great as might have been expected from a fall of five or six times the height. A dangerous place at which there had been more than one accident. On the last occasion, some twenty years earlier, a party of a man and two girls had allowed themselves to drift into the narrow channel, and in spite of their frantic efforts, their boat had been carried over and all were drowned. The bodies, two of them frightfully disfigured, were found in the smooth water below the rapids. As at the present time, there had just been a severe thunderstorm followed by torrential rain over the whole country, the river was in flood, and the fear that a similar fate might have overtaken Sir William was only too reasonable.

For a few moments none of the men spoke. Then Austin, pulling himself together with an effort, said in a low tone, 'We must go down the river, I'm afraid. Better bring Smith.'

The four men walked to the boathouse, and then turning downstream, continued their course along the bank. Soon they came to the rocky ground where, from 300 feet or more in width, the river narrowed in to about sixty. There was a strong fresh, and the water seethed and eddied as its speed increased, while the roar of the fall grew louder.

Just above the fall a two-arched bridge carried a road across the river, a huge rock in midstream parting the current, and bearing the masonry pier. Here the men divided, the butler and Smith crossing to the opposite bank, and Austin and the valet remaining on the Luce Manor side. Then they pushed on till they reached the fall itself.

The river was even higher than they had realised, almost as high as during the winter rains. It went over the ledge in a smoothly-burnished curve, then plunging into the mass of boulders, was broken into a thousand whirling eddies, all seething

11

beneath leaping masses of foam. As the men looked at it their hearts sank. A skilful Canadian lumberman on a raft or in a strong, seaworthy boat might have negotiated the place in safety, but for an elderly business man like Sir William, in a frail skiff, only one end seemed possible.

Slowly they walked on, examining with anxious eyes the swirling flood. And then at last they saw what they were in search of. Near the end of the rapids, where the river had quieted down to a more even flow, the bow of a boat was sticking up out of the water against a rock. Hastening forward they caught their breath as they saw a little farther downstream a dark shapeless object, lying almost submerged in a backwater. It was the body of a man.

It was obvious that nothing in the nature of help could be given, as the man must have been dead long since. The body was on the Luce Manor side of the river, and Parkes and Smith hurrying round, the four stepped into the pool, and with reverent care lifted it out and laid it on the grass. One glance at the face was enough. It was that of Sir William Ponson.

Chapter 2
A Sinister Suggestion

For some moments the men stood, reverent, and bareheaded, looking down at the motionless form. The face was disfigured, the left cheek from the ear to the mouth being cut and bruised, evidently from contact with a boulder. The left arm also was broken, and lay twisted at an unnatural angle with the body.

At last Austin made a move. Taking out his handkerchief, he stooped and reverently covered the dead face.

'We must send for the police, I'm afraid.' He spoke in a low tone, and seemed deeply affected. 'You go, Innes, will you? Take the large car and run them back to the bridge. You had better bring Dr Ames too, I suppose, and a stretcher. Also send this wire to Mr Cosgrove. We'll wait here till you come.'

He scribbled a telegram on a leaf of his pocket book:

'To Cosgrove Ponson, 174B Knightsbridge, London.—Terrible accident. My father drowned in river. Tell my mother at Lancaster Gate, then come.—AUSTIN.'

Cosgrove Ponson was the only son of Sir William's younger brother, and was consequently cousin to Austin and Enid. These three with Lady Ponson were now the only living members of the family. Cosgrove was a man of about five-and-thirty who had inherited some money from his father, and lived the careless life of a man about town. Though he had never got on well with Austin, he had been a favourite of Sir William's, and had spent a good deal of time, on and off, at Luce Manor.

When the valet had gone Austin sat down on a rock and, leaning his head in his hands, seemed to give himself up to profound meditation. The others, uncertain what to do, withdrew to a short distance, not liking either to intrude, or, after what Austin had said, to leave altogether. So they waited until after about an hour Innes reappeared, and with him Dr Ames, a sergeant of police, and two constables carrying a stretcher.

'Innes has told us, Mr Ponson. A truly terrible affair!' said the doctor, with real sympathy in his voice. He shook hands with Austin, while the sergeant saluted respectfully.

'I'm afraid, doctor, you can do nothing. He was dead when we found him.'

'Ah, I imagined so from what your man said.' Dr Ames knelt down and lifted the handkerchief from the battered features. 'Yes, you are right. He has been dead for some hours.' He replaced the handkerchief, and rose to his feet. 'I suppose, Mr Ponson, you will have him taken to Luce Manor? There is no reason why that should not be done at once.'

'I was only waiting for the stretcher.'

The doctor nodded and took charge.

'Your stretcher, sergeant,' he said.

The remains were lifted on, and slowly the melancholy little procession started. Before they left, the sergeant asked who had made the tragic discovery, and was shown exactly where the body had been found. One constable was left with instructions to see that no one touched the boat, and the sergeant and the other policeman walked with the party, taking their turns in carrying the sad burden. After Austin had instructed the butler to hurry on and prepare for them at the house, no one spoke.

When the body had been laid on the bed in Sir William's room, and the little excitement caused by the arrival had subsided, the sergeant approached Austin Ponson.

'Beg pardon, Mr Ponson,' he said. 'I'm very sorry, but I'll have to make a report about this, and I'm bound to ask a few questions. I hope, sir, you won't mind?'

'Of course not, sergeant. I understand you must do your duty.'

'Thank you, sir. May I ask then if you can explain how this accident occurred?'

'No more than you can, sergeant. I only know that Innes, Sir William's valet, came to my house when I was dressing this morning, to know if Sir William was with me. He said he had gone out after dinner last night without leaving any message, and they didn't know where he was. I came back with Innes, and they had just then learnt that the boat was missing. We thought perhaps my father had rowed across the river to see Dr Graham, and I sent round to inquire, but when we learnt he hadn't been there we began to fear the worst. We therefore went down the river to see if we could find anything.'

'And when, sir, did you see him last?'

'On Sunday evening—three days ago. I dined here, and left about ten or later.'

'And was he in his usual health and spirits then?'

'Yes, I noticed nothing out of the common.'

'And he said nothing then, or indeed at any time, that would explain the matter?'

'Not a thing. He seemed perfectly normal in every way.'

'Very strange affair, sir, where he could have been going to. Was he skilful with a boat?'

'No, I should say not. He could row a little, but not well. He did not specially care for it. I rarely knew him to go out for pleasure.'

'Thank you, sir. With your permission I will see now what Mr Parkes and the other men can tell me.'

He heard the butler's story, then Innes's and lastly Smith's. He was a young and intelligent officer, and was anxious to send in a complete explanation of the tragedy in his report, but he was almost equally desirous not to inconvenience or offend Austin Ponson, whom he supposed would succeed Sir William and become a magistrate and a leading man in the district. Though he had admired Sir William and was genuinely shocked and sorry about the accident, yet he was human, and he could not but recognise the affair gave him a chance of coming under the special notice of his superiors.

Up to a certain point he was clear in his own mind what had occurred. Sir William had left his house sometime between 8.45 and 11.30 the previous evening, and had gone down to the boathouse with his key, entered, opened the water gate and taken out the *Alice*. In the darkness, and probably underestimating the amount of fresh in the river, he had allowed himself to be carried into the narrow channel. Once there he had practically no chance. The place was notoriously dangerous.

So much was plain enough, but the sergeant was bothered by the question, what had Sir William gone out for? No one had as yet thrown any light on this.

Calling Dr Ames, who, not having had any breakfast, was just finishing a somewhat substantial snack in the dining-room, the sergeant explained that he wished to go through Sir William's pockets, if the doctor would come and assist him. They accordingly made their way upstairs and began their search.

The pockets contained just those articles which a man in Sir William's position would naturally be expected to carry, with one exception. Besides the bunch of keys, handkerchief, watch, cigar-case, money and such like, there was a very singular object—nothing more nor less than a small-sized six-chambered Colt's revolver, unloaded. There were no shells, either full or empty, and the barrel was clean, showing it had not been fired.

'By Jove! Sergeant,' Dr Ames exclaimed in a low tone. 'That's surprising.'

'Surprising, sir? I should just think so! You never know, sir, about *anybody*. Sir William was the last man, I should have said, to go about armed.'

'But he wasn't armed, sergeant,' rejoined the doctor. 'A man with a revolver is not armed unless he has something to fire out of it. That's no more an arm than any other bit of old iron.'

The sergeant hesitated.

'That's so, sir, in a way, of course. Still—you can hardly think of anyone carrying an empty revolver. I expect he must have had the habit of carrying shells, but by some oversight forgot them yesterday.'

'Possibly. There doesn't seem to be much else of interest anyway.'

'No, sir, that's a fact.' The sergeant, having emptied all the pockets, began laboriously to make a list of the articles he had found. Dr Ames had taken up a small diary or engagement book, and was rather aimlessly turning over the sodden leaves. Suddenly he gave an exclamation.

'Look here, sergeant,' he whispered. 'Here's what you have been wanting.'

There was a division in the book for each day of the year, with notes of engagements or other matters in most. At the bottom of the space for the previous day—the portion which would probably refer to the evening—was written the words: 'Graham, 9.00 p.m.'

'There it is,' went on Dr Ames. 'That's where he was going last night. He evidently intended to consult Dr Graham privately. As it was too far to walk round by the road, and he didn't want to get a car out, he thought he would take a short cut by rowing across the river.'

The sergeant made a gesture of satisfaction.

'You have it, sir. That's just what he's done. I don't mind saying that was bothering me badly. But now, thanks to you, sir, the whole thing is cleared up. I'll go over to Dr Graham's directly, and see if I can't learn something about it from him.'

'I have an operation in an hour and I must go back to Halford, but I'll come out again in the afternoon, and have another look at the body. If you call in with me tonight I'll let you have the certificate.'

'There'll have to be an inquest, of course, sir.'

'Of course. It should be arranged for tomorrow.'

'It'll be for the coroner to fix the time, but I would suggest eleven or twelve. I'll call round tonight anyway sir, and let you know.'

Taking Smith, the gardener-boatman, and the constable who had helped to carry the body, the sergeant returned to the site of the accident. The river was falling rapidly, and with some trouble the four men succeeded in getting the damaged boat ashore. Smith identified it immediately as the *Alice*. A careful search in the neighbourhood brought to light the rudder and bottom boards—each split and torn from the rocks. But there was no sign of the oars or rowlocks.

It was useless, the sergeant thought, to look for the rowlocks. They would be at the bottom of the river. But the oars should be recoverable. Sending the two men downstream to search for them, he himself took the Argyle, which Austin had left for the convenience of the police, and drove to Dr Graham's. That gentleman had not heard the news and was profoundly shocked, but when the sergeant went on to ask his question, he denied emphatically that there had been any appointment for the previous evening. Sir William, he stated, was a personal and valued friend, and they had often visited at each other's houses, but he had never met the deceased in a professional capacity. He believed Dr Ames was Sir William's medical adviser.

'But, of course,' Dr Graham concluded, 'it is quite possible he may have wished to consult privately. He knows I am usually to be found in my study about nine, and he may have intended to walk up unobserved by the path through the shrubbery, come to the study direct, and enter by the French window.'

'Very likely, sir,' returned the sergeant, as he thanked Dr Graham and took his leave.

His next visit was to the coroner, who also was much shocked at the news. After some discussion the inquest was arranged for twelve o'clock the following morning, provided this would suit the chief constable of the district, who might wish to be present.

'It will be a purely formal business, I suppose, sergeant?' the coroner observed as the other rose to take his leave. 'There are no doubtful or suspicious circumstances?'

'None, sir. The affair is as clear as day. But, sir, I have been thinking the question may arise as to whether boating should not be prohibited altogether on that stretch of the river.'

'Possibly it should, but I think we may leave that to the jury.' The sergeant saluted and withdrew. Again taking the car, he reached the police station as the clocks were striking half-past two. Going to the telephone, he rang up the chief constable—

to whom he had telephoned immediately on hearing of the accident—and reported what he had learnt. The official replied that he would be over in time for the inquest.

An hour later the two constables who had been sent to search the lower reaches of the river arrived at the police station. They had found the missing oars, and had taken them to Luce Manor, where they had been identified by Smith, the boatman. They had, it appeared, gone ashore close beside each other nearly a mile below the falls, and two points about the affair had interested the men. First, the oars had been washed up on the left bank, while the other things had been deposited on the right, and second, while all the latter were torn and damaged by the rocks, neither oar was injured or even marked.

'What do you make of that, Cowan?' the sergeant asked when these facts had been put before him.

'Well, I'll tell you what the boatman says, and it seems right enough. You know that there road bridge above the falls? There's two arches in it. Well, Smith says he'll lay ten bob the boat went through one arch and the oars the other. That would look right enough to me too, because the right side is more shallow and more rocky than the other, and more likely for to break anything up. The left side is the main channel, as you might say, and the oars might get down it without damage. At least, that's what Smith says, and it looks like enough to me too.'

'H'm,' the sergeant mused, 'seems reasonable.' The sergeant knew more about sea currents than river. He had been brought up on the coast, and he had learnt that tidal currents having the same set will deposit objects at or about the same place. It seemed to him likely that a similar rule would apply to rivers. The body, boat, rudder, and bottom boards had all gone ashore at one place. The oars also were found not far apart, but they were a long way from the other things. What more likely than the boatman's suggestion that the two lots of objects had become sufficiently divided in the upper reach to pass through different arches of the bridge? This would separate them completely enough to account for the positions in which they were found. Yes, it certainly seemed reasonable.

And then another idea struck him, and he slapped his thigh.

'By Jehosaphat, Cowan!' he cried, 'that's just what's happened, and it explains the only thing we didn't know about the whole affair. Those oars went through the other arch right enough. And why? Why, because Sir William had lost them coming down the river. That's why he was lost himself. I'll lay you anything those oars got overboard, and he couldn't find them in the dark.'

To the sergeant, who was not without imagination, there came the dim vision of an old, grey-haired man, adrift, alone and at night, in a light skiff on the swirling flood—borne silently and resistlessly onward, while he struggled desperately in the shrouding darkness to recover the oars which had slipped from his grasp, and which were floating somewhere close by. He could almost see the man's frantic, unavailing efforts to reach the bank, almost hear his despairing cries rising above the rush of the waters and the roar of the fall, as more and more swiftly he was swept on to his doom. Almost he could visualise the tossing, spinning boat disappear under the bridge, emerge, hang poised as if breathless for the fraction of a second above the fall, then with an unhurried, remorseless swoop, plunge into the boiling cauldron below. . . . A horrible fantasy truly, but to the sergeant it seemed a picture of the actual happening.

But why, he wondered, had both the oars taken the other arch? It would have been easier to explain the loss of one. With an unskilful boatman such a thing not unfrequently occurred. But to lose both involved some special cause. Possibly, he thought, Sir William had had some sudden start, had moved sharply, almost capsizing the boat, and in making an involuntary effort to right it had let go with both hands.

He was still puzzling over the problem when a note was handed him which, when he had read it, banished the matter of the oars from his mind, and turned his thoughts into a fresh direction. It ran:

Luce Manor, Thursday.—Please come out here at once. An unfortunate development has arisen.—WALTER AMES.

Without loss of time the sergeant took his bicycle and rode out the two miles to Luce Manor. Dr Ames was waiting impatiently, and drew the officer aside.

'Look here, sergeant,' he said. 'I'm not very happy about this business. I want a post-mortem.'

'A post-mortem sir?' the other repeated in astonishment. 'Why, sir, is there anything fresh turned up, or what has happened?'

'Nothing has happened, but'—the doctor hesitated—'the fact is I'm not certain of the cause of death.'

The sergeant stared.

'But is there any doubt, sir—you'll excuse me, I hope—is there any doubt that he was drowned?'

'That's just what there is—a doubt and no more. A post-mortem will set it at rest.'

The sergeant hesitated.

'Of course, sir,' he said slowly, 'if you say that it ends the matter. But it'll be a nasty shock for Mr Austin, sir.'

'I can't help that. See here,' the doctor went on confidentially, 'some of the obvious signs of drowning are missing, and he has had a blow on the back of the head that looks as if it might have killed him. I want to make sure which it was.'

'But might he not have got that blow against a rock, sir?'

'He might, but I'm not sure. But we're only wasting time. To put the matter in a nutshell, I won't give a certificate unless there is a post-mortem, and if one is not arranged now, it will be after my evidence at the inquest.'

'Please don't think, sir, I was in any way questioning your decision,' the sergeant hastened to reply. 'But I think I should first communicate with the chief constable. You see, sir, in the case of so prominent a family—'

'You do what you think best about that, but if you take my advice you'll ask the Scotland Yard people to send down one of their doctors to act with me.'

'Bless me, sir! Is it as serious as that?'

'Of course it's serious,' rapped out the doctor. 'Sir William may have been drowned, in which case it's all right; or he may not, in which case it's all wrong—for

18

somebody.'

The sergeant's manner changed.

'I'll go immediately, sir, and phone the chief constable, and then, if he approves, Scotland Yard. Where will you be, sir?

'I have my work to attend to; I'm going home. You'll find me there any time during the evening. And look here, sergeant. I'd rather you said nothing about this. There may be nothing at all in it.'

'Trust me, sir,' and with a salute the officer withdrew.

He rode rapidly back to Halford, and once again calling up the chief constable, repeated what Dr Ames had said.

The two men discussed the matter at some length, and it was at last decided that the chief constable should ring up the Yard and ask the opinion of the Authorities about sending down a doctor. In a short time there was a reply. Dr Wilgar and Inspector Tanner were motoring down, and would be at Luce Manor about eight o'clock. The sergeant went round to tell Dr Ames, and it was arranged that the latter should meet the London men there. In the meantime the sergeant was to see Austin Ponson, and break the disagreeable news to him.

This programme was carried out, and shortly after ten o'clock five men met at the police station at Halford. There were the medical men, Inspector Tanner, the sergeant, and Chief Constable Soames, who had motored over.

'Well, gentlemen,' said the latter, when the preliminary greetings were past, 'we are met here under unusual and tragic circumstances, which may easily become more serious still.' He turned to the doctors. 'You have completed the post-mortem, I understand?'

'We have,' replied Dr Wilgar.

'And are you in agreement as to your conclusions?'

'Completely.'

'Perhaps then you would tell us what they are?'

Wilgar bowed to Dr Ames, and the latter replied:

'The first moment I glanced at the body the thought occurred to me that it had not exactly the appearance of a drowned man. But at that time I did not seriously doubt that death had so occurred. When, however, I came to make a more careful examination, the uncertainty again arose in my mind. There was none of the discolouration usual in such cases, and the wounds on the side of the face did not look as if they had been inflicted before death. But, as a result of the long continued washing they had had, I could not be certain of this. When in addition I discovered a bruise on the back of the head which might easily have caused death, I felt I would not be justified in giving a certificate without further examination.'

The chief constable bowed and Dr Wilgar took up the story.

'When I saw the corpse I quite agreed with my colleague's views, and we decided the post-mortem must be carried out. As a result of it we find the man was not drowned.'

His hearers stared at him, but without interrupting.

'There was no water in the lungs or stomach,' went on Dr Wilgar. 'The

19

wounds on the face occurred after death, and were doubtless caused by the boulders in the river, but the cause of death was undoubtedly the blow on the back of the head to which my colleague has referred.'

'You amaze me, gentlemen,' the chief constable remarked, and a similar emotion showed on the sergeant's expressive face. Inspector Tanner, a fair haired, blue eyed, clean-shaven man of about forty, merely looked keenly interested.

'Do I understand you to say that the late Sir William was killed before falling into the river?' went on Mr Soames.

'There is no doubt of it.'

'That means, I take it, that he was flung out of the boat in such a way that the back of his head struck a rock, killing him before he dropped into the stream?'

'We do not think so, sir,' Dr Wilgar answered. 'In that case he would certainly have swallowed water. Besides, the blow was struck square on with a blunt, smooth-surfaced implement. The skin was not cut as a boulder would have cut it. No, we regret to say so, but the only hypothesis which seems to meet the facts is that Sir William was deliberately murdered.'

'Good gracious, gentlemen, you don't say so!' The chief constable seemed shocked, while the sergeant actually gasped.

'I am afraid, and Dr Ames agrees with me, that there is no alternative. The blow on the back of the head was struck while Sir William was alive, and it could not have been self inflicted. It would have been sufficient to kill him. The other injuries occurred after death, and it is certain he was not drowned. There is no escape from the conclusion that I have stated. On the contrary, there is every reason to believe a deliberate and carefully thought out crime has been committed. Though it is hardly our province, it seemed to us the whole episode of the boat and the river was merely an attempt to hide the true facts by providing the suggestion of an accident. And I may perhaps be permitted to say that had a less observant and conscientious man than my colleague been called in, the ruse might easily have succeeded.'

'You amaze me, sir,' exclaimed Mr Soames. 'A terrible business! I knew the poor fellow well. I met him in Gateshead before he moved to these parts, and we have been good friends ever since. A sterling, good fellow as ever breathed! I cannot imagine anyone wishing him harm. However, it shows how little we know' . . . He turned to Inspector Tanner. 'I presume, Inspector, you came here prepared to take over the case?'

'Certainly, sir; I was sent for that purpose.'

'Well, the sooner you get to work the better. And now about the inquest. With the medical evidence there can be but one verdict.'

'I think, sir,' observed Tanner, 'that with your approval it might be wiser to hold that evidence back. It might put some one on his guard, who would otherwise give himself away. I should suggest formal evidence of identification, and an adjournment.'

'Very possibly you are right, Inspector. What reason would you give for that procedure?'

'I would say, sir, that it is desirable on technical grounds that some motive for Sir William's taking out the boat should be discovered, and that the inquest is being adjourned to enable inquiries on this point to be made.'

'Very well. I shall see the coroner and arrange it with him. It is not of course necessary for me to remind you of the importance of secrecy,' and with a bow Chief Constable Soames took his leave, and the meeting broke up.

'Come along round and have some supper at the George,' Inspector Tanner invited the sergeant. 'I've got a private room, and I want a talk over this business.'

The sergeant, flushed with the honour, and delighting in his feeling of importance, accepted, and the two went out together.

An hour later they lit up their pipes, and Tanner listened while the sergeant told him in detail all he knew of the affair. Then the Inspector unrolled a large-scale map he had brought, and spread it on the table.

'I want,' he said, 'to learn my way about. Just come and point out the places on the map. Here,' he pointed as he spoke, 'is Halford, a place of, I suppose, 3000 inhabitants.' The sergeant nodded and the other resumed. 'This road running through the town from north to south is the main road from Bedford to London. Now, let's see. Going towards London it crosses the Cranshaw River at the London side of Halford, and for about a mile both run nearly parallel. Then at the end of the mile, what's this? A lane leading from the road to the river?'

'Yes, that's what we call the Old Ferry. It's a grass-grown lane through trees, and there's a broken-down pier at the end of it.'

'H'm. Then the river bears away towards the south-east; while the road continues almost due south. Luce Manor is here in this vee between them?'

'Yes, that's it, sir.'

'I see. Then at the end of Luce Manor, a cross road runs from the Bedford-London road eastwards, crossing the river just above the falls and leading to Hitchin?'

'Yes, sir. That's right.'

'So that the Luce Manor grounds make a triangle bounded by the main London road, the cross road to Hitchin and the river.'

The Inspector smoked in silence for some minutes. Then, rolling up the map, he went on:

'Now I want to learn my dates, and also what weather you have been having. This is Thursday night, and it was, therefore, Wednesday night or early this morning the affair happened. Now what about the weather?'

'We've had a lot of rain lately. It was wet up to last Monday. In the afternoon it cleared up, and it has been fine since—that is, here. But farther up the country there has been a lot of thunder and heavy rain. That has left the river full for this time of year.'

'Wet up till Monday afternoon, and fine since, I see. Well, sergeant, I think that's about all we can do tonight. By the way, could you lend me a bicycle for the morning?'

'Certainly, I'll leave it round now,' and with an exchange of good-nights the men separated.

As soon as it was light next morning Inspector Tanner let himself out of the hotel, and taking the sergeant's bicycle, rode out along the London Road. It was again a perfect morning, everything giving promise of a spell of settled weather. The dew lay thick on the ground, sparkling in the rays of the rising sun, which cast long, thin shadows across the road. Not a cloud was in the sky, and though a few traces of mist still lingered on the river, they were rapidly disappearing in the growing heat. From the trees came the ceaseless twittering of birds, while from some unseen height a lark poured down its glorious song. The roads had dried up after the recent rains, but were not yet dusty, and as the Inspector pedalled along he congratulated himself on the pleasant respite he was likely to have from London in July.

He crossed the Cranshaw River, and gradually diverging from it, rose briskly through the smiling, well-wooded country. About a mile from the town a grass-grown lane branched off to the left, leading, he presumed, back to the river at the Old Ferry. From it began the stone wall which bounded the Luce Manor grounds, and he passed first the small door at the end of the footpath from the house, and then the main entrance. A little farther, some two miles from the town, he reached the cross roads and, turning to the left and still skirting the Manor lands, arrived after a few minutes at the two-arched bridge which crossed the Cranshaw immediately above the falls. Here he hid the bicycle among some bushes, then stepping on to the bridge, he looked around.

The river had greatly fallen, as he could see from the high water mark along the banks. But even now it was running fast, and swirled and eddied as it raced through the archways beneath. Below the falls the two distinct channels were visible, and Tanner could understand how objects passing through the right arch would almost inevitably get among the boulders and be smashed up, while those carried through the other might slip downstream uninjured.

In the opposite direction the river curved away between thinly-wooded banks, and on those banks the Inspector decided his work must begin. From the medical evidence it had seemed clear to him that Sir William Ponson had first been murdered, the body afterwards being placed in the boat. With the ground in the soft condition produced by the recent rains, this could hardly have been done without leaving traces. He must therefore search for those traces in the hope of finding with them some clue to the murderer's identity.

Not far from the bridge there was a gate in the Luce Manor wall, leading from the road into the plantation of small trees which fringed the river. He passed through, and getting down near the water's edge, began to walk upstream, scrutinising the ground for footprints. As he expected, most of the bank was still soft from the rain, but where he came to hard or grassy portions or where the rock outcropped, he made little detours till he reached more plastic ground beyond. It was during one of these deviations, some quarter of a mile from the bridge, that he made his first discovery.

At this point a small stream entered the river, and the ground for some distance on each side had been trampled over by cattle coming to drink. The brook, which was not more than a couple of yards wide by a few inches deep, was crossed by a line of rough stepping-stones. The Inspector, looking about, saw that several persons had recently passed over. Their tracks converged like a fan at each end of the stones. Here, he thought, is where Austin Ponson and the butler, valet and boatman walked when searching for the body.

But Tanner was a painstaking and conscientious man. He never took probabilities for granted and, therefore, at the approaches to the stepping-stones, he set himself to check his theory by separating out the four prints for future identification. It gave him some trouble, but he presently found himself rewarded. Instead of there being four different prints, there were five. Four men had walked together down the river; the fifth had crossed slightly diagonally to the others, and had gone upstream. In all cases where the steps of this fifth man coincided with others the former were the lower, showing that their owner had passed up before the others came down. He had worn boots with nailed soles, and his steps were smaller and closer together than any of the others. Tanner deduced a small-sized man of the working classes.

He was about to move on, when, looking up the little tributary, he saw another line of steps crossing it some thirty yards above the stones. These were heading downstream, and the owner had evidently not troubled to diverge to the stones, but had walked right through the water. The soil at the place was spongy, and the tracks were not clear, but Tanner, by following them back, was able to identify them as those of this same fifth man.

The Inspector at first was somewhat puzzled by the neglect of the stepping-stones. Then it occurred to him that one of two things would account for it. Either the downward journey had been made at night when the unknown could not see the stones, or he had been too perturbed or excited to consider where he was going. And Tanner could not help recognising that anyone hastening from the scene of the murder would in all probability show traces of just such agitation.

He continued his search of the bank, seeing no traces of an approach to the river, but finding here and there prints of the four men going downstream, and of the fifth leading in both directions.

About a hundred yards before he reached the boathouse a paling went up at right angles to the river, separating the rough, uncared for bank along which he had passed from the well-kept lawn he was approaching. The grass on this latter was cut short, and looking up under the fine oaks and beeches studded about, he could see the façade of the house. A gravel path connected the two buildings, leading from the Dutch garden in front of the terrace straight down to the door of the boathouse. From the latter point another path branched off at right angles to the first, running upstream along the river bank. This, Tanner remembered from his examination of the map, afterwards curved round to the left, and joined the narrow walk from the house at the road gate. A third short path ran round the boathouse, and terminated in a flight of broad landing steps, leading down into the river.

A careful search of the ground near the boathouse revealed occasional impressions on the closely cut sward. The Inspector spent over an hour moving from point to point, and was at last satisfied as to what had taken place. The four men whom he had assumed were Austin and the servants, had evidently come down the path from the direction of the house. They had turned to the right before reaching the boathouse, thus approaching the river diagonally, and had crossed the paling bounding the lawn close to the water's edge. These men had walked together and the tracks were exactly in accordance with the statement of their movements they had made to the sergeant.

The fifth man had crossed the paling almost at the same place as the others —it was the obviously suitable place—but instead of turning up towards the house, his steps led direct to the boathouse! Another line of the same steps led back from the boathouse to the fence—in neither case continuously, but here and there, where the grass was thin. And at two points along these tracks the Inspector gave a chuckle of satisfaction. At one there was a perfect impression of part of the right sole, and at another of the remainder and the heel. Tanner decided he must take plaster casts of these prints before they became blurred.

Passing the boathouse—he felt that marks in it, if any, would keep—he continued his careful search of the bank above flood level. Very painstaking and thorough he was as he gradually worked his way up, but no further traces could he find. At last after a good hour's work he reached the Old Ferry. Here the track approaching the ruined pier was hard; and he recognised that, shut in as it was by trees, it would have made an ideal place for disposing of the body. He thought he need hardly expect traces above this, but, as he wished to cross the river, and he could do so no nearer than the London road bridge at Halford, he continued along the bank, still searching. Then, reaching the bridge, he crossed and worked in the same way down the left bank till he reached the other bridge at the Cranshaw Falls. When the work was completed, he felt positive the body could only have been set adrift at either the boathouse or the Old Ferry.

It was now eleven o'clock, and he had been at it for over five hours. Taking the bicycle, he rode back into Halford, where he had a hurried meal. Then he left again to attend the inquest at Luce Manor.

A long, narrow room, with oak-panelled walls, and three deep windows, had been set aside for the occasion. Round the table, which ran down the centre, sat the jury, looking self-conscious and important. At the head was the Coroner, and near him, but a little back from the table, were Austin and Cosgrove Ponson, Dr Ames, the butler, valet, boatman, sergeant, and a few other persons. As Tanner entered and slipped quietly to a seat, the Coroner was just rising to open the proceedings.

He made a brief speech deploring the unhappy event which had robbed their neighbourhood of so worthy and so useful a man as Sir William, and expressing on his own behalf and that of those present the sympathy which they felt for the surviving members of the family. Then he lamented the fact that the law required an inquest, and promised that on his part at least the proceedings should be conducted so as to give the least possible amount of annoyance and pain. Partly on that account, and partly because the authorities for technical reasons required some information which there had not as yet been time to obtain, he did not propose to complete the inquest that day, but after formal evidence of identification had been taken he would adjourn the proceedings to a more convenient date.

The speech was cleverly worded. While it stated nothing explicitly, its whole suggestion was that as every one knew an accident had happened, further inquiry must be mere waste of time. He touched but slightly on the adjournment, proceeding at once to call the roll and swear in the jury.

While he was speaking Tanner ran his sharp eyes over the faces of those present, memorising their features, and noting their demeanour. There sat Parkes, the butler, solemn and ponderous, surveying the scene with grave and decorous interest. Innes, sharp-eyed and alert, seemed to be watching the proceedings with an eye for flaws in the Coroner's law. Smith, the gardener-boatman, somewhat overawed with his surroundings, was evidently there, a plain man, to tell a plain man's tale. After registering a mental picture of each, Tanner's gaze passed on, but when it reached Austin Ponson it halted and remained steady.

The son and nephew were seated together. There was a considerable similarity in their appearance. Of middle height, both had blue eyes, clear complexions, and clean-shaven chins. Their features were not unlike, but Austin was stouter, and seemed younger, and more easy going. Cosgrove looked as if he had lived hard. He was thin, and lines radiated from the corners of his eyes while the hair near his temples showed slightly grey. He had the indefinable stamp of a society man, which Austin lacked. But both were well looking enough, and would have passed unnoticed among any crowd of well-dressed Englishmen of the upper classes.

But it was not on these points of superficial resemblance that Tanner's gaze rested. He was a reader, so far as he was able, of hearts. And it was the expressions of the cousins which had specially attracted his attention.

That both were shocked and upset by the tragedy there could be no doubt. But, while this seemed the sum total of Cosgrove's emotion, the detective's keen eye recognised something more in Austin's face and bearing. He was anxious—unquestionably anxious—and he was trying to hide it. And when the Coroner mentioned the adjournment he started, and a look of undoubted fear showed for a moment in his eyes. Inspector Tanner's interest was keenly aroused. That Austin knew something he felt sure, and he decided his first business must be to learn what it was.

Accordingly, when the body had been viewed and formally identified, and the proceedings had come to an end, he sought out his victim, and quietly introduced himself.

'I am exceedingly sorry, Mr Ponson,' he said politely, 'to intrude myself upon you at such a moment, but I have been sent here by Scotland Yard to make certain inquiries into this unhappy occurrence, and I have no option but to carry out my instructions. Could you spare me a few moments?'

Austin's face paled as the other made his occupation known, and again the look of fear showed in his eyes. But he answered readily enough:

'Certainly, Inspector. I am at your service. Come in here; we shall not be disturbed.'

He led the way into a small study or office on the left of the hall, plainly furnished in mahogany, with dark red leather upholstering. Drawing forward two arm-chairs he motioned his visitor to a seat.

'I should feel greatly obliged, sir,' began Tanner, as he accepted a cigarette from the case the other held out, 'if you would tell me all you can about this unhappy affair. I have practically only arrived, and I have not heard the details.'

'There's not much I can tell you, I'm afraid,' Austin answered, and then he repeated almost word for word the statement he had made to the sergeant. He spoke calmly, but the Inspector could see that he was ill at ease.

'It seemed to my people,' went on Tanner, 'that a good deal hinged on the motive Sir William had for taking out the boat. You cannot form any theory about that?'

'None whatever. It was the last thing I should have expected him to do.'

'There is no one whom he might have wished to visit?'

'The butler suggested that,' and Austin mentioned Dr Graham. 'But,' he

26

ended up, 'we could find nothing to bear out that theory.'

'Can you tell me if Sir William had anything on his mind recently?'

Austin hesitated and moved uneasily.

'No,' he said, 'not to my knowledge.' But his voice changed, and the Inspector felt he was not speaking the truth.

'When did you see him last, Mr Ponson?'

'On Sunday. I dined here and spent the evening.'

'And you noticed nothing unusual in his manner then?'

'Nothing.'

'You will be wondering what is the point of all these questions. I am sorry to tell you, Mr Ponson, that my superiors have got an exceedingly unpleasant suspicion into their minds. I hardly like to mention it to you.'

The Inspector paused, watching the other keenly. He was evidently on tenterhooks. Seemingly unable to remain quiet, he threw his cigarette away, and then with quick, jerky movements lit another. But he controlled himself and spoke calmly.

'Yes? What do they think?'

'They are not satisfied,' went on Tanner, slowly watching all the time the effect of his words, 'that the affair was an accident at all.' Austin paled still further and tiny drops of sweat appeared on his forehead.

'In the Lord's name,' he cried hoarsely, 'what do you mean?

'They fear suicide, Mr Ponson.'

'Suicide?' There was horror in the man's eyes, but to the Inspector there was relief also. 'What infernal drivel! They did not know my father.'

'That is so, of course, sir. I'm only telling you what the Chief said. That's the reason they postponed the inquest, and that's the reason I was sent down.'

'I tell you, Inspector, the thing's absurd. Ask anybody that knew him. They will all tell you the same thing.'

'I dare say, sir, and probably correctly. But might I ask you when you go home to turn the matter over in your mind, and if you think of anything bearing on it to let me know?'

'Of course,' assented Austin, and the relief in his manner was now unmistakable.

There's just one other point,' Tanner continued. 'I have to ask a question I deeply regret, but I can only assure you it is one asked invariably, and as a matter of routine in such cases. I trust you will not mind. It is this. Will you please let me have a statement of your own movements on last Wednesday night?'

Austin Ponson threw up his hands.

'I have been afraid of that question, Inspector, ever since I first heard the news, and now you've asked it, by Jove, I'm glad! I have been trying to make up my mind to tell the police since—since it happened, and it'll be a huge relief to do so now. I tell you, Inspector, I've been actually *afraid* when I thought of it. Here goes for the whole thing.'

He spoke with excitement, but soon calmed down and went on in ordinary tones.

'On Wednesday night I was the victim of what I then thought was a stupid and rather unkind hoax, but what since this affair I have looked on in a more sinister light. At the same time I confess I am entirely puzzled as to its meaning. In order that you may understand it I must tell you a few facts about myself.

'I have lived, as you perhaps know, alone in Halford for several years. I have some private means, and I pass my time in research work in connection with certain disease-carrying insects, besides writing on scientific and social subjects. Recently I became deeply attached to a young lady living close by—a Miss Lois Drew—and on last Saturday I put fate to the test, and asked her to marry me. She consented, but wished our engagement kept a secret for a few days. I only mention her name to you, Inspector, on her own authority, indeed at her express direction, but at the same time I trust you will respect my confidence in the matter.'

Tanner bowed without speaking.

'About six o'clock on Wednesday evening, my butler handed me a note. He had found it, as I afterwards learnt, in the letter box of the hall door, and as it had not come through the post, it must have been delivered by private messenger. But there had been no ring, nor had he seen anyone approaching the house.

'The note was in Miss Drew's handwriting, and it said that she and her sister were going that evening to call on a Mrs Franklyn, who lived a mile or more from the town along the London road. They would be returning about nine, and if I liked to take a boat down to the Old Ferry and wait for them there, I could row them home.

'I need hardly say I was delighted, and I went to the Club to get a boat, intending to be down at the Old Ferry in good time. But there was a delay in getting the boat I wanted, and in spite of rowing hard it was a little past the hour when I reached the place. There was no one there, but I had not waited more than five or ten minutes when a girl came walking up. It was getting dusk, and I thought at first it was Miss Drew's sister, but when she got nearer I saw she was a stranger. She was below medium height, dark, and badly dressed, with a thin muffler up round her face, as if she had toothache. I could not see her features distinctly, though I think I should know her again. She asked me if I was Mr Austin Ponson.

' "I am Mrs Franklyn's housemaid," she said, "and I was sent to give you this note."

'It was a pencil scrawl from Miss Drew, saying that she and her sister had gone with Tom and Evelyn Franklyn, the two younger members of the family, to the Abbey, where the ghost was reported to be abroad. I was to follow, and the girl, Mrs Franklyn's housemaid, would watch the boat till we returned.

'The Abbey, I should explain, is an old ruin, a little farther away than Mrs Franklyn's house—about two miles from the town. It is reached by a narrow and little used path from the London road, perhaps half a mile or less long. According to the local tradition it is haunted, and every now and then the ghost is supposed to walk. I don't know the exact details of the superstition, but as the place is interesting, and the walk there pleasant enough, to look for the ghost is often made the joking excuse for paying the old place an evening visit.

' "You will watch the boat till I come back?" I said to the maid, and she answered:

' "Yes sir, Mrs Franklyn told me so."

'I set off to walk the mile or more to the Abbey, reaching it in about twenty minutes. I was a little surprised by the whole business, for though the Abbey would have been a likely enough walk for Miss Drew and the others to take under ordinary circumstances, the path that night was a good deal wetter and muddier than I thought any of the ladies would have cared for. As you know, the weather only cleared up that morning after a long spell of rain. However, I pressed on till I reached the Abbey. Inspector, there was no one there!

'I searched the whole place, and called aloud, but not a creature did I find. Quite mystified, and a good deal annoyed, I turned and hurried back.

' "I have been hoaxed by those four," I thought, and I decided to go round to the Franklyns' and enjoy the joke with them. But when I reached the house it was in darkness, and the door was shut. I knocked, and rang, and walked round it, but nowhere was there any lights, and I had to conclude it was empty. I returned to the Old Ferry and found the boat still there, but Mrs Franklyn's servant was gone. Sorely puzzled, I rowed back up the river. By the time I reached the boat club it was quarter to eleven, and the place was closed. I had to root out the caretaker to get the boat in. Then I walked on to the Drews', arriving about eleven, just as they were preparing for bed; I apologised, of course, for turning up at such a time, but when I explained the reason, Miss Drew cried out that the whole thing was a hoax. She hadn't been out that evening, and she hadn't written any notes. Furthermore, she knew the Franklyns had been called away unexpectedly the previous day to see their son who was ill, and had sent their servants home, and closed the house.

'So there, Inspector, you have the whole thing. At the time, as I said, I thought it merely a stupid practical joke, but since I heard of this affair I cannot but wonder if there is no connection. I recognise anyway that I am in an exceedingly unpleasant position, for I am quite unable to prove what I have told you.'

Beyond a murmured acknowledgment, Inspector Tanner did not reply for some moments, as he thought over what he had just heard. There were obviously two theories about it. First, if the story were true it cleared Austin, not merely as an alibi, but it accounted for his suspicious manner. And the Inspector could see no reason why it should not be true. Such a plant on the part of the murderer, with the object of throwing suspicion on Austin, and therefore off himself, would be quite possible. It would be proved that Austin took a boat, and went down the river, and was away long enough for him to have reached the Luce Manor boathouse and committed the murder. And the ruined Abbey was just the place the inventor of such a plant would choose, a deserted spot where Austin would be unlikely to meet anyone who could confirm his story.

On the other hand, Austin might really know the truth, even if he was not himself the actual murderer. If so, the story was a clever invention on his part, well designed and thought out. But whichever of these theories were true, it was obvious to Tanner that he must test the whole thing as thoroughly as he possibly could.

'If you will allow me to say it, sir,' he observed, 'you did a wise thing in telling me this story. Had you not done so, and had I found out about your using the boat, I should have taken a very different view of the affair. And now for your own sake, as well as mine, I feel sure you won't object to my testing your statement. You say the path to this ruin was muddy. There has been no rain since Wednesday. Your footprints will therefore be clear. Come into Halford with me now, and lend me the shoes you wore that night, and I will go out to the place and see the marks with my own eyes.'

Austin slapped his thigh.

'Capital, Inspector!' he cried. 'The more you test it the better I'll be pleased. It will be no end of a weight off my mind. I don't deny I have been horribly worried.'

His manner did not belie his statement. As a few minutes later he drove Tanner and the sergeant into Halford, he seemed to have thrown off his depression, and chatted easily and almost gaily.

They drew up at the door of his small villa. It was opened by a butler rather resembling Parkes, but younger and slighter.

'Come in, Inspector, and I'll give you what you want. Will you wait here a moment?'

Austin led the way into a cheerful room fitted up as a study and workroom. A large table in the corner was littered with papers and manuscripts, there was a fine microscope in the window, while everywhere were strewn books and periodicals. The Inspector moved about noting and memorising what he saw, till Austin returned.

'There you are,' the latter exclaimed, holding out a pair of tan shoes, 'and here's a bag to put them in.'

'New?' queried Tanner as he took the shoes, and glanced at their soles.

'Quite. I got them on Monday, and I have only worn them once.'

The Inspector nodded.

'Thanks, Mr Ponson,' he said, as he took his leave, 'I'll keep you advised how I get on.'

Remaining in the town only long enough to hire a car and buy some plaster of Paris, Inspector Tanner and the sergeant drove out once more along the London road. The weather had come in hot, and the air hung heavy and motionless beneath the trees. The cattle had moved into the shade, and except for an occasional impatient switch of their tails, remained standing rigid, the embodiment of placid unintelligence. Aromatic scents floated across the road, and masses of colour blazed out from the adjoining gardens. In the distance the hills showed faint and nebulous in the haze, while objects closer at hand quivered in the heated atmosphere. The car slid rapidly along, its rubber treads purring in a companionable way on the smooth road. On the left the sergeant pointed out the lane leading to the Old Ferry, then on the right the entrance to Mrs Franklyn's villa. On the left again were the large gates of Luce Manor, and quarter of a mile past them, and on the opposite side, a grass-grown path branched off. At this the motor pulled up.

'Abbey Lane,' the sergeant explained, and having arranged for the car to wait, the two men dismounted and passed down the path.

At first the surface was hard, some traces of old macadam remaining. But as they went farther it grew softer and more grassy. They examined the ground, and for a long way could find no marks. But later they came on what they wanted. Not far from the ruins the path crossed a shallow valley where, the water having run down from each side, the bottom was soft and muddy. Here clear and distinct were two lines of footprints, one going and one returning. Tanner compared Austin's shoes with the impressions. They fitted exactly.

Notwithstanding this discovery, the officers continued till they reached the ruins. Here a careful search revealed three prints of Austin's shoes, but there were no traces of other visitors.

To check another point in Austin's statement, Tanner noted the time it took them to walk quickly from the Abbey to Mrs Franklyn's house. Here they made another search, with the result that at several points close to the building they found prints of Austin's shoes. That he had been there also was beyond question, and his story was therefore true so far.

Having ascertained the time, occupied in walking from Mrs Franklyn's to the Old Ferry, the two men were driven back to Luce Manor. Here they took plaster casts of the various footprints on the river bank. Then, re-entering the car, they returned to Halford, tired out from their day's work.

Inspector Tanner was an early bird. Though on the next morning he did not attempt to emulate his performance of the day before, half-past eight o'clock saw him cycling out to the Luce Manor boathouse to undertake the examination which had been postponed from the previous evening. Leaving his bicycle among the shrubs at the entrance gate, he walked down the path which ran along the river bank, and which he had not yet examined. But here he found nothing of interest.

The boathouse was a modern structure in the Old English style, with brick sides, half-timbered gables, and a red tiled roof. The door was in the wall opposite the river, and the Inspector unlocked it, and entered a chamber of about thirty feet square, lighted from a louvre in the roof. The water basin occupied about half the floor area, and was in one corner, leaving an L-shaped wharf, laid down in granolithic. Along the walls were racks for oars and presses for rowlocks and fishing tackle. An archway at the end of the basin led out to the river, and was closed by a grill or portcullis raised by chains from a small windlass. Two boats were floating in the basin.

For some minutes Tanner stood motionless, noting these details, and looking round in the hope of seeing something that might help him. This cursory inspection proving fruitless, he settled down to make a methodical examination of the entire building.

If, as seemed likely, the man who had made the fifth set of tracks on the river bank had really entered the house, his muddy boots must surely have left traces. Tanner therefore began with the floor, and crawling on his hands and knees backwards and forwards, scrutinised the cement-coloured surface. It was tiresome work, but at last he found what he thought looked like footprints. On the quay not far from the corner of the basin were a number of tiny mud-coloured spots. At first he could not connect these to make a complete whole, but by lying down on his face and using a lens he was able to find several other patches of coagulated sand, which he marked with a pencil; and when he had finished there showed out on the granolithic the nail patterns of two clearly marked heels with the corresponding middle portion of the soles in front. It was evident a man had stood with his back to the door, and facing the basin, and had remained there long enough to allow the moisture from the soles of his shoes to run down the nail heads, and settle on the floor.

It was the work of a few seconds for Tanner to compare these marks with those of the fifth man on the river bank. They were identical.

He resumed his search. There were no more footmarks, and he made but one other discovery. In the left-hand corner of the quay, at the very edge of the basin, and hidden behind the mooring rope of one of the boats, lay the stump of a cigarette. Clearly the intention had been to throw it into the basin, but it had just missed going down, and had fallen unnoticed. Tanner had a good working knowledge of cigarettes, but this one he could not place. The paper was yellow, and the tobacco very dark in colour. He thought it looked South American. But he was pleased with his find, for it seemed to have been but recently smoked, and as he put it away in his pocket, he thought he had perhaps gained a clue.

An examination of the door handles and styles, winch handle, backs of chairs and similar objects with a powdering apparatus revealed several finger prints, but, alas! all too smudged and blurred to be of use. Nor could he find anything else of interest.

He was disappointed that the boathouse had yielded so little. It was true that either the footprint or the cigarette end might prove valuable, but on the other hand neither were necessarily connected with the murder. Both might have got there in a perfectly ordinary and legitimate manner.

He sat down on one of the chairs to consider his next step. There were three lines of inquiry open to him, and he hesitated as to that on which to begin. First, there was the general investigation, the interviewing of the servants, Lady Ponson, Miss Enid, and any others from whom he might gain information, the examination of Sir William's papers, the tracing of his movements for some time previous to his death, the consideration of his finances, the ascertaining whether anyone might benefit by his death—all routine details, each step of which was suggested by his training, and his experience in similar cases. This work he knew he would have to carry out some time, and obviously the sooner it was done the better.

Next came the testing of Austin's alibi. Though he had made a beginning with this, a great deal remained to be done before he could feel satisfied as to its truth. And satisfied he must be. The circumstances were too suspicious for anything less than utter certainty to suffice.

As he turned the matter over in his mind he slowly came to the conclusion that he could work on these two points simultaneously. The same information would, to some extent at least, be required for both, and the same people would have to be interviewed.

But there was a third point which, equally urgently, required attention. The man who had made the fifth line of footsteps must be traced. And here, again, no time should be lost in getting to work.

Tanner felt he could not take on this inquiry with the others. There was work in it alone for another man. He therefore decided he would wire for an assistant to whom he could hand over this portion of the case.

But as he was here he might as well begin the interviewing of the Manor servants. He therefore left the boathouse, and walked slowly up to the terrace under the great trees of the lawn, past long herbaceous borders, and through the Dutch garden with its geometrically shaped beds, its boxwood edgings, and its masses of rich colour. Approached from the front, the old house looked its best. Though somewhat heavy and formal in detail, its proportion was admirable, and it had an air of security and comfort strangely at variance with the tragic happening which had overtaken its owner. Tanner labelled it one of the 'stately homes of England' as he crossed the terrace to the ornate porch and pulled the bell.

Parkes opened the door. The Inspector introduced himself, and courteously asked for an interview. With equal politeness, and an evident desire to help, Parkes brought his visitor to his own sanctum and told his story. But to Tanner most of it was already known. Indeed, on a very few points only did he add to his knowledge of the case.

The first was that on the previous Friday, five days before his death, Sir William had become depressed and irritable, as if some trouble was weighing on his mind. The change had occurred quite suddenly between breakfast and lunch and had continued until the end. To Parkes the cause was unknown.

The second matter was more interesting and suggestive, but less tangible. When Tanner was interrogating the butler about Austin Ponson he noticed that certain of the latter's replies were not so spontaneous as those to earlier questions. In particular, when he asked whether during his call at Luce Manor on Sunday evening Austin had seemed worried or depressed, Parkes, though he replied in the negative, seemed so uncomfortable that the Inspector began to doubt if he was speaking the truth. He was not certain, but the thought crossed his mind that the butler knew something which he was holding back. At this stage Tanner was anxious not to arouse suspicion that he was interested in Austin. He therefore changed the subject and made inquiries about Cosgrove. But of him he learnt nothing except that he had not been at Luce Manor for over a month.

From the butler Tanner found out also that neither Austin Ponson nor anyone at Luce Manor smoked dark-coloured cigarettes.

The Inspector next interviewed Innes. Having heard the valet's statement, which was almost identical with Parkes's, he began to question him in the hope of learning something further.

'I wonder, Mr Innes,' he asked, 'if you can tell me what upset Sir William between breakfast and lunch this day week?'

The valet stared.

'You weren't long getting hold of that,' he commented. 'Yes, I can tell you; or partly at least. He got a letter with the morning delivery. I bring them up to him when they come about half-nine. There were about half a dozen, and he took them and looked over the envelopes as usual. When he saw one he sort of scowled, and he tore it open and read it. I don't know what was in it, but it fairly gave him the pip and he didn't get over it. He was kind of worried right up to the end.'

'You didn't notice the handwriting or the postmark?'

'No.'

'What letters come by that delivery?'

'London, but that means all parts.'

'That was Friday of last week. Now can you tell me Sir William's movements since?'

'Friday there was a dinner party on—about half a dozen people—and bridge afterwards. Then Saturday Sir William went up to town. Sunday was a quiet day. Mr Austin dined and stayed the evening. Monday Sir William went up to town again.

34

Tuesday and Wednesday he stayed here alone. He was quite alone, for her ladyship and Miss Enid went up to town on Tuesday.'

'Were all these things in accordance with Sir William's custom? To go to London two days running, for example?'

'He went now and again; I can't remember him going two days running.' The valet hesitated, then went on: 'There was another thing struck me about that, but I don't know if there's anything in it. When he did go, it was nearly always in the car. I only remember him going by train when the car was out of order, and then he groused about it. But these two days he went by train though the car was there and the chauffeur doing nothing.'

'It is curious, that,' Tanner agreed. 'Now, Mr Austin's coming on Sunday. You saw him, I suppose?'

'Yes, both when he was coming and leaving.'

'Ah, that is fortunate. You could tell, then, if he seemed just in his ordinary humour, or if anything had upset him?'

'I only saw him for just a moment. It would be hard to form an opinion in the time.'

Inspector Tanner was keenly interested. He thought he recognised a sudden reserve in the man's tone and manner, and he remembered that he had had the same impression about Parkes, when the butler was asked a similar question. He suspected both men were withholding information. Something apparently had occurred on that Sunday night. He decided to bluff.

'It would be a kindness, Mr Innes, if you would tell me just what happened on that night.'

The valet started, and an uneasy expression passed over his face. Neither were lost on the Inspector.

'I don't know of anything special,' Innes answered. 'Just what are you getting at?'

The Inspector bluffed again.

'Mr Austin was upset too? Come now, Mr Innes, you'll agree to that, surely?'

'Well, he may have been a bit.'

'Was that when he was going or on arrival and departure both?'

'He seemed a bit absent-minded when he was going, but, Lord! Mr Tanner, what's that? He may have been feeling a bit seedy, or had a headache, or half a dozen things.'

The man seemed nervous and ill at ease. More strongly than ever Inspector Tanner felt there was more to come. He racked his brains to guess what might have happened, and to frame leading questions. Suddenly an idea occurred to him. He bent forward and tapped the valet on the knee.

'Now, Mr Innes, about the trouble they had that night. You might tell me what you know.'

The valet gave his questioner a sour look.

'I suppose Parkes told you about that,' he grumbled, 'but I think he might have kept his mouth shut. It's no business of yours, or mine either.'

'Tell me anyway.'

'I heard them in the study. Their voices were raised, and that's all there's of it.'

'And what did they say?'

'I only heard a word or two. I didn't wait to listen.'

'Of course not, Mr Innes. But people can't help overhearing things. What was it you heard?'

The valet seemed to be considering his answer. At last he replied:

'I heard Mr Austin say, "My God, sir, she's not." That's every blessed word, so now you know it all.'

His manner had altered, and Tanner felt this was the truth.

So the father and son had been quarrelling that Sunday evening about a woman! That was a suggestive fact, and it was evident from his hesitation that Innes thought so too. Then Tanner remembered that Austin had told him it was on the previous day that he had proposed to Miss Lois Drew, and been accepted. Could he have been telling Sir William, and could the latter have objected to the match? He continued his questions.

'Thank you, Mr Innes. I'm sorry to be such a nuisance. But I don't see that it helps us very much after all. Now about Sir William's visits to town. Can you give me any hint of his business there?'

'No.'

'You've been up with him, I suppose?'

'Lord, yes. Scores of times.'

'Where does he usually lunch?'

'Sometimes the Savoy, but usually at one of his clubs, the St George or the Empire.'

'I have done at last, Mr Innes. Could you just tell me in conclusion the trains Sir William travelled up and down by on Saturday and Monday, and also how he was dressed on each occasion?'

The deceased gentleman, it appeared, had gone by the same train on each occasion, the 10.55 from Halford. He had motored to the station direct on the Saturday, but on the Monday had on his way made a call at the local branch of the Midland Counties Bank. On Saturday, he had returned comparatively early, but on Monday he had not reached home till close on dinner time.

Having received this information, the Inspector expressed his indebtedness to the other's forbearance and good nature. Innes, who had seemed rather ruffled by the catechism, was mollified.

'I'm afraid,' Tanner went on, 'I shall have to have a look over Sir William's papers, but not now. I'll come on Sunday, and take a long quiet day at it. Now I wonder could I see Mr Smith, your boatman?'

'Why, certainly. Let's see; it's quarter-past one. He'll be at his dinner. I'll show you his house if you come along.'

They went to a trim, clematis-covered cottage at the back of the yard, and there found the boatman-gardener. Tanner questioned him in detail, but without learning anything fresh.

On his return to Halford for lunch Tanner telephoned to Scotland Yard for assistance, and it was arranged that Detective-Sergeant Longwell should be sent down by the first train. The Inspector met him on his arrival, and explained what he wanted done, showing him the casts of the fifth man's footsteps.

'I want you,' he said 'to find the man who made those tracks. You need not mind about the Manor people, I shall attend to them. Get round the country, and make inquiries in the neighbouring towns and villages. Particularly work the railway stations and garages. The man will be small, and of the working classes in all probability, and he will certainly have had very wet and muddy boots and trousers on account of walking through the stream. It's not conclusive, but the fact that he missed the stepping-stones by so great a distance, points to his being a stranger to the locality. But in any case he shouldn't be hard to trace. Keep in touch with me through the Halford police station.'

That afternoon and the next morning the Inspector saw all the other servants at Luce Manor, both indoor and out, but here again without result. In the case of the men he took prints from their boots to compare with those he had found on the river bank. This was a tedious operation, involving troublesome explanations and reassurances, but at last it was done, and Tanner was able to say with certainty that three of the four men who had walked together were the butler, the valet, and the gardener, while the tracks of the fifth man, who had stood in the boathouse, were not made by anyone belonging to the estate. It was probable, therefore, that this fifth man was concerned in the tragedy, and Tanner was glad he had lost no time in setting Sergeant Longwell to work to trace him.

In the afternoon the Inspector called at Austin's villa, and interviewed first Lady Ponson, and secondly Enid. Apologising courteously for his intrusion, he questioned both ladies on all the points about which he was in doubt, but once more without gaining any fresh information. Both had noticed Sir William had not been quite up to his usual form for a few days before their departure for London, but both had put it down to some trifling physical indisposition, and neither could throw light on any possible cause of worry to him. Asked if he had an enemy who might have been giving him annoyance, they emphatically negatived the suggestion, saying that as far as they knew Sir William had been universally beloved. As they had been in London on the night in question, they of course knew nothing of the actual details of the tragedy.

Inspector Tanner was sure from the bearing and manner of both ladies that they were telling him the absolute truth, and really were ignorant of anything which might have been at the bottom of the affair. They clearly were terribly shocked and distressed, and he made his interview as short as possible.

The next day was Sunday, and, as he had mentioned to the valet, Tanner determined to spend it in going over the late Sir William's papers. He brought the sergeant out to help him, and they were soon settled in the library, immersed in their work. Tanner, seated at the big roll top desk, went through paper after paper, while the sergeant, with the keys found on the body, unlocked drawers and carried their contents to the desk for his superior's inspection. The work was tedious, but they kept hard at it, and when after some time Parkes came into the room, they found with surprise that it was nearly two o'clock.

'What about a bite of lunch, gentlemen?' the butler invited them. 'I should be pleased if you would join me.'

'Very good of you, I'm sure, Mr Parkes,' Tanner answered. 'We'll be through in ten minutes.'

'And have you found anything to help you?' went on Parkes, running his eye over the open safe and drawers.

'Not a blessed thing. There's not the slightest hint of anything out of the common that I can see.'

'Well, come to my room when you're ready.'

On the previous day Parkes had shown the Inspector over the house, and among other things Tanner had noticed large framed photographs of Sir William, Austin, and Cosgrove. Before following the butler he slipped up to the room in which these were hanging and, deftly removing the frames, noted the photographer's name. Then locking up the library they went to lunch, soon afterwards taking their leave.

Though Tanner's statement to Parkes that he had made no helpful discovery among Sir William's papers was true, he had noticed one thing which had puzzled him. He had been turning over the blocks of the dead man's cheque book, and he had found that on the previous Monday and Tuesday—the two days before the tragedy—Sir William had written two cheques, both payable to self. That dated for the Monday was for £100, and that for the Tuesday for no less a sum than £3000. That the deceased should have required such sums immediately prior to his murder was interesting and suggestive enough, but that was not all. What had specially intrigued the Inspector's imagination was the fact that below the word 'self' was in each case one letter only—a capital X. He looked back through the book, and in every other instance found below the name the purpose for which the money was required. These two sums must therefore have been for something so private that it could be designated only by a sign. It was evidently something quite definite, as the blocks of other cheques payable to self bore such legends as 'personal expenses,' 'visit to Edinburgh,' and so on. What, the Inspector wondered, could it be?

Considerably interested, he went back through some of the completed books, and at intervals he found other cheques bearing the same mysterious sign. Without a real hope that it would lead him anywhere he had set the sergeant to go back over all the blocks he could find, and make a list of these X cheques, noting the date, number, and amount. He found they had been drawn during a period of four years, were all made out to self, and were all for even hundreds, all excepting the last, varying from £400 down to £100. In all £4600 had been paid.

It seemed to Inspector Tanner that there was here some secret in Sir William's life which might or might not be important. Was it gambling, he wondered, or perhaps women? From what he had heard of the deceased's life and character both these suppositions seemed unlikely, but, as he said to himself, you never know. He remembered that Innes had stated Sir William had called at the bank on his way to the train on the Monday morning, and he wondered if this was to cash the cheques. He thought that some inquiries there would do no harm.

He went to the bank as soon as it opened next morning and saw the manager. The cashier recollected Sir William's visit on the previous Monday. The deceased gentleman had, it appeared, cashed a cheque for £100, and on comparing the number, Tanner found it was that belonging to the X-marked block. He had been paid in Bank of England fives—twenty of them. None of the officials could tell anything about the £3000 cheque which apparently had not been cashed, nor indeed about any of the other X cheques.

Tanner was anxious to learn something of the dead man's history, see his will, find out who would benefit by his death, and who, if anyone, might have a grudge against him. He had discovered when going through the papers on the previous day that Sir William's lawyers were Messrs Greer, Arbuthnot & Greer, of Lincoln's Inn. To call on them, therefore, seemed his next step. From the station he telephoned making an appointment for two o'clock, then, taking the 10.55 a.m. train, he went up to town.

He saw Mr Arbuthnot, a tall, rather stooped man with strongly marked, clean-shaven features, a thick crop of lightish hair slightly shot with grey, and a pair of very keen blue eyes. He bowed his visitor to a chair.

'We had your message, Inspector,' he said. 'I hope there is nothing wrong. We look on you Scotland Yard gentlemen rather as stormy petrels, you know.' His face as he smiled lit up and became friendly and human. Tanner took an instinctive liking to him.

'I dare say you can guess my business, Mr Arbuthnot,' he began. 'It is in connection with the sad death of Sir William Ponson.'

'Yes?'

Tanner hesitated for a moment.

'I think, sir,' he said at last, 'if you will treat what I am about to say as confidential, I had better tell you the complication which has arisen.'

Mr Arbuthnot nodded, and the Inspector went on.

'You know the circumstances, of course, of Sir William's death? Everything seemed to point to an accident. Well, we are not so sure about it. I am sorry to say there is a suspicion of foul play.'

The lawyer looked up sharply.

'Foul play?' he repeated. 'Good Lord, I hope not!'

'I'm afraid, sir, there is little doubt of it. The medical evidence points in that direction at any rate.'

Mr Arbuthnot, it seemed, had been more than merely legal adviser to the deceased gentleman. They had been close personal friends, and the solicitor was profoundly shocked by Tanner's news. It had the effect of eliciting his warm sympathy with the Inspector's efforts, and he hastened to assure the latter of his cordial help and co-operation. 'Tell me now,' he concluded, 'what I can do for you.'

Tanner thanked him, and went on:

'I want you, sir, if you will be so kind, to tell me what you can about Sir William—his history, his family, his money affairs, and so on. May I ask first if you act for the remainder of the family?'

'For Lady Ponson only.'

Tanner bowed, and Mr Arbuthnot, going to a press, took out a despatch box labelled 'Sir William Ponson,' from which he removed some papers. Consulting these from time to time for dates and names, he told the Inspector the following history:

Sir William's wealth and position, it appeared, had come from very small beginnings. His father and mother, Mr Arbuthnot believed, had died while he was quite young, leaving him and his brother John alone in the world. He had got work as an office boy in a small iron-foundry at Gateshead, where, owing to his extraordinary industry and energy, he had worked himself up to the position of manager at the comparatively early age of twenty-nine. Under his guidance the concern, which for years had been moribund, had prospered amazingly, and thirteen years later he was taken into partnership. This consummation had been reached in only six years when the former owner died, leaving him in sole control. William then sought out his brother John, who also had prospered, having worked himself up to the chief-engineership of one of the large Cunarders. William took John into partnership with the result that, the mechanical side of the work being reorganised, the firm advanced still more rapidly, the two brothers becoming wealthy men. William next turned his attention to civic affairs. He was elected a member of Newcastle Corporation, and during his time of office as mayor, he received his knighthood on the occasion of a royal visit to the town. When Sir William was some sixty years old his brother John died suddenly, and he, not caring to work on alone, sold his interest in the firm, and moving south, purchased Luce Manor, where he devoted his still abundant energies to experiments in the application of machinery to farming.

With regard to his home life, Sir William, thought Mr Arbuthnot, had been, in his later years at all events, a happy man. He had at the age of thirty married a widow, a Mrs Ethel Dale. It was believed, though Mr Arbuthnot could not vouch for it, that there had been quite a romance about it. According to the generally accepted story, William Ponson, then a clerk in the iron works, and Tom Dale, a traveller for the same concern, had both loved the pretty Ethel Osborne, the daughter of a doctor in the neighbourhood. Dale was outwardly a rather fascinating personality, good looking, always well dressed, and with attractive manners, though at heart he was a rotter. But the serious and somewhat pompous young Ponson had failed to bring his more sterling merits into prominence, with the result that the lady had preferred his rival. She married Dale, and regretted it from the first evening, when he returned drunk to the small seaside hotel at which they were spending their honeymoon. Things went rapidly from bad to worse. Dale continued drinking, they got into debt, and Ethel began to fear her husband's dismissal, and consequent poverty. Then, after some three years of unhappiness, Dale was sent to Canada on the business of the firm. He sailed on the *Numidian*, but off Newfoundland the ship struck an iceberg, and turning turtle, went to the bottom in thirteen minutes. There was an appalling casualty list, but to Mrs Dale it meant release, for her husband's name was among the drowned.

The lady was left in absolute destitution. Ponson managed to help her anonymously, then after a couple of years he renewed his suit, and some time later she capitulated and they were married. There had been no children to her previous marriage, but now Austin and Enid Ponson were born.

The two children were very different in disposition. While Enid, sweet-tempered and charming, was beloved by all, and was her father's life and soul, Austin was somewhat difficult. When first he went to a boarding school, it was a relief to all at home. From Rugby he progressed to Cambridge, then, as the Inspector had already learnt, he threw up his studies there and devoted himself to social and entomological subjects. He had gone back at this time to his father's house at Gateshead, but the two rubbed each other up the wrong way, and Sir William, making his son a handsome allowance, advised him to live elsewhere. Austin had then taken the villa at Halford, amid surroundings suitable to the pursuit of his hobbies.

'But,' explained Mr Arbuthnot, 'you must not think from this Austin is a man of bad or weak character. The separation was due purely to incompatibility of temperament. Austin, so far as I know, is an honourable, kindly man, and I have never heard of him doing a shady thing. He is a hard worker too, and I believe has carried out some quite valuable original research into the distribution of disease by insects. Sir William recognised this, hence the allowance, and the fact that, though they couldn't pull together, they never really quarreled.'

'I rather gathered that from the way the servants spoke,' Tanner answered. 'But there is another Ponson you haven't mentioned—Cosgrove.'

'Cosgrove is the only child of Sir William's brother John, consequently he and Austin are first cousins. Cosgrove is the least estimable member of the family. He was, I am afraid, a bit of a waster from the first. He did badly at school, and was all but sent down from college. His father kept some kind of control over him during his life, but on his death he inherited a large sum of money, and I fear it had the usual result. He now lives in bachelor quarters in Knightsbridge, and is reported to be in a rather fast set. I happen to know he has run through most of his money, and is now considerably pinched. But he always got on well with Sir William. The old man liked him, and passed over his follies as mere youthful indiscretions. I think his disappointment in Austin rather drove him to make a friend of Cosgrove, but of that of course I can't be sure. He left Cosgrove a good slice of his fortune at all events.'

'That was the next thing, Mr Arbuthnot, I wished to ask you—about the financial position of the various members of the family.'

'Obviously, I can give you only very approximate figures. When the death duties are paid I fancy Sir William's capital will be worth about £500,000 to his legatees. He has been up to the present allowing Austin £1000 a year, and Miss Ponson and Cosgrove £500 each. His will preserves the same proportion between them—Austin gets £150,000, and Miss Ponson and Cosgrove £75,000 each, the remainder, about £200,000, going to Lady Ponson.'

'Suppose any of these four should die intestate?'

'If that question should arise the deceased's share is to be divided between the survivors in the same proportions as was Sir William's money. It is a little complicated, but it would mean for example that if Austin were to die without leaving a will, Lady Ponson would get about £90,000 and Cosgrove and Enid £30,000 each of Austin's £150,000.'

'Has Austin any means other than this £1000 a year?'

'Not very much, I fancy. He has written a good deal on social and scientific subjects, which must bring him in something, and he had a legacy of £5000 from his Uncle John. But I don't suppose he has more than twelve or thirteen hundred a year.'

'And Cosgrove? You do not know exactly how he is fixed financially?'

'No, except that from his point of view he is in low water.'

'Do you happen to know anything about a Miss Lois Drew of Halford?'

'Yes,' the lawyer returned with a grimace, 'I do. The last day Sir William was in here he was telling me about her. It appeared Austin had been smitten by the young lady, and some rumours of it had reached Sir William. He was extremely annoyed at the idea, because, though he admitted that so far as he knew Miss Drew was personally all that could be desired, her social standing was not good. Of course, you and I may think that rather Victorian, but the old man had achieved so many of his ambitions, he could not bear to see his last—that of social position—thwarted. Indeed, he spoke of altering his will if the matter came to a head.'

'You didn't know then that they are engaged?'

The lawyer seemed considerably surprised.

'You don't say so? No, I did not know. It was a rumour only Sir William spoke of.'

'Austin told me they fixed it up on Saturday week, but it is to be kept private still.'

There seemed no question, then, about the cause of the quarrel. Indeed, the more Tanner heard, the more essential the most searching test of Austin's alibi became.

'There is just one other point, Mr Arbuthnot,' the Inspector went on, and he told the lawyer about the cheques, marked X. Upon these, however, the latter could throw no light.

'And you know of no one who had a quarrel with Sir William, or who for any reason might desire his death?'

'No one. Quite the opposite. Sir William was universally liked and respected.'

Tanner was silent for a moment, considering if he had obtained all the information he was likely to get from the solicitor. Deciding he had, he rose.

'Well, Mr Arbuthnot, let me express my gratitude for the way you have met me. I am sorry for having been such a nuisance.'

'All in the day's work, Mr Tanner,' the solicitor returned as he shook hands and bowed his visitor out.

Tanner left Lincoln's Inn, and after making a call at the Yard, took the next train back to Halford.

Chapter 5
Inspector Tanner Becomes Convinced

After dinner that same evening Inspector Tanner, having lit his pipe, and selected the most comfortable arm-chair he could find, set himself to take stock of his position, and see just where he stood with his new case.

He realised that the lawyer's communication contained food for thought. Certainly a lot of the information he had gained seemed to point in a rather unmistakable way to Austin. That the latter had murdered his father he felt it hard to believe, and yet he had known men to be convicted on slighter evidence than that he already held. Absent-mindedly pressing down the tobacco in his pipe, he closed his eyes, and tried to view the facts he had learnt in a proper perspective.

Here was a son who had never been able to get on with his father, so much so that they could not live in the same house. To the father he had been a continual disappointment, and no doubt that irritation would show in the father's manner, and could not but increase the bad blood between them. It was true they had agreed to differ, and Sir William had allowed Austin £1000 a year, but agreeing to differ did not necessarily prevent very unpleasant feelings on both sides, and as for the money, though it seemed handsome at first sight, it was very small compared to what Sir William might have paid without missing it.

From what Tanner had seen of Austin and his villa, he thought the latter must be living at the rate of well on to a thousand a year. That was to say, nearly at the rate of his income. Under these circumstances he falls in love and decides to marry. The lady would have but a small dot, if any. The two of them must therefore live on what had before been enough for Austin only. What does Austin do? He sees his father the day after the engagement, probably to tell him the news, and possibly to ask for an increased allowance. As in the ordinary course of nature a large portion of Sir William's money would soon become his in any case, this would not be an unreasonable demand. But what does Sir William answer? Tanner could only surmise, but from what the dead man had said to Mr Arbuthnot it was probable he had not only refused the increase, but had threatened altering his will adversely to Austin if the marriage took place. If, as appeared possible from the words overheard by Innes, Sir William had said anything derogatory to the lady, Austin's feelings, already considerably aroused, would probably reach white heat. At all events, whether the interview between father and son had or had not taken this course, it was bed-rock fact that they had quarrelled about some woman.

Tanner continued his surmises. Assuming he was correct so far, Austin would inevitably be faced with a very terrible temptation. If his father should die without altering his will, it would mean £150,000 to himself. £150,000! Quite a respectable sum of money! There would then be no question of love in a cottage with Miss Drew. He could give her all those things which men delight to give women.

And the irritation of the constant unpleasantness with Sir William would be gone. The more Tanner considered the matter, the more powerful he felt this temptation would have been. Many a stronger man than Austin seemed to be had succumbed to less.

Then coming down to details. The murderer had unquestionably known his way about Luce Manor. He had either gone to the library by the side door, and there committed the crime, carrying the body down to the boathouse, or, more probably, he had devised some scheme to make Sir William go there of his own accord. He had also taken the particular oars belonging to the boat used. All the knowledge necessary for this Austin of course possessed.

But more suspicious than that, Austin by his own showing had actually taken a boat down the river on that night, and the hours of leaving and returning were such that he would just have had time to reach the Luce Manor boathouse, commit the murder, and return the boat to the club. Of course, he had claimed to have an alibi for this period, but alibis could be faked, and the very readiness and apparent completeness of this seemed to Tanner slightly indicative of prearrangement.

There was then the question of the oars. This also had a suspicious look. At first Tanner had accepted without question the boatman's theory that the boat and oars had become separated in the upper channel and had passed down to the falls through different arches of the road bridge. Indeed, his own inspection of the place had led him to the same conclusion. And this losing of the oars had seemed to explain adequately enough how the accident happened.

But when it was shown that the affair was not an accident at all, the matter of the oars took on a very different complexion. Evidently it was part of the plant— deliberately arranged to create the very impression it had produced. And Tanner now saw that the murderer had overreached himself. Sir William might easily have lost one oar, but he would not have let both go. And it was very unlikely, even if he had dropped both, that they would have separated far enough from the boat to have taken the other archway. Here again one might have done so, but not both. No, Tanner was driven to the conclusion that the boat must have been sent adrift close to the Luce Manor bank of the river, while the oars were taken over to the opposite side in another boat, and there thrown overboard. And Austin had had such a boat down the river that night.

Lastly, and most suggestive of all was Austin's start and look of fear, when the Coroner had announced the adjournment of the inquest. It was true he had accounted for his apprehension. An investigation might bring up the question of the alibi in which, as he was unable to prove its truth, no credence might be placed, leaving him in an awkward position. But was this a satisfactory explanation? Were these consequences not too remote to be seen with such immediate clearness as to cause an actual start? Did it not involve too instantaneous a perception of the facts? The Inspector thought so.

But he saw as he still smoked and pondered, that it was equally possible that his whole conclusions were erroneous. Austin unquestionably might be, as he pictured himself, the innocent victim of the real murderer's plant.

His thoughts turned to Cosgrove Ponson. Here was another man who had an interest in Sir William's death. And from what Mr Arbuthnot had said, his interest might be quite as strong, or even stronger, than Austin's. When a man about town who had been living a rather fast life got into financial difficulties, he was not usually very squeamish as to how he extricated himself. £75,000 to a man perhaps faced with ruin would be worth taking a risk for. And if Cosgrove had become hardened enough to commit the crime, he would probably not have jibbed at making the plant to throw the suspicion on Austin. Tanner concluded that if Austin's alibi held, his next work must be the investigation of Cosgrove's life as well as his movements on the night of the murder.

His whole cogitations therefore simply brought him back to the point from which he had started. Before he did anything else, every point of Austin's alibi must be gone into with the most meticulous care.

Accordingly, having refilled his pipe, he set himself to go over in detail the story Austin Ponson had told him of his movements on the night of the murder. He wished not only to be clear in his own mind as to the sequence of events, but to make a list of the points upon which he could reasonably hope to obtain confirmatory evidence.

Austin, according to his own statement, left the pavilion of the Halford boat club at about ten minutes before nine. He rowed to the Old Ferry, sat there for about ten minutes, until the maid arrived with the note, then walked to the Abbey and spent a few minutes searching for Miss Drew and her friends. Failing to find them, he went to the Franklyns' house, satisfied himself it was empty, returned to the Old Ferry, and rowed back to Halford, arriving at the pavilion about quarter before eleven. There he had waked the caretaker to get the boat in. He had walked to the Drews', stayed with them some ten minutes, going on to his own house, which he reached about twenty minute past eleven. Now, first, as to the checking of these hours.

Tanner took a sheet of paper, and looking up his note of the times it had taken him to walk the various distances, and estimating for the rowing, he made a statement something like a railway time table. When he had finished he found that the total estimated time which the journeys should have taken worked out at practically that mentioned by Austin. So far, then, the story hung together.

Next with regard to outside testimony. What confirmation would it be reasonable to expect?

From the attendant at the boat club pavilion he should be able to learn if Austin did take out a boat, and if so, at what hour. Possibly other persons in the club might have been present, and could substantiate this point. The attendant would also know the hour at which he was called out on Austin's return. The Drews would certainly have remarked the time of Austin's call, and lastly, the latter's own servants would be sure to remember the hour of his return. There should be ample—indeed overwhelming—evidence of the times at which Austin set out with his boat and returned.

So far so good, but it was clear to Tanner that if he could get no further corroboration than this, the whole alibi was worthless. One point—but that a vital point—would remain unsubstantiated. Austin might have left and returned at the hours he stated, but where was he between them? Did he go to the Abbey and the Franklyns'? If he did, he could not have been to Luce Manor, and necessarily was innocent. How was this to be ascertained?

There were, of course, the footprints. That these were made by Austin's shoes was beyond question. The fact that the latter were new prevented the marks showing the individuality that might otherwise have been expected, but against that, at one point on the edge of the left sole there was a slight dint—caused possibly by striking a stone—and this dint was faithfully reproduced in the prints. It was too much to suppose that two separate pairs of similar shoes should have similar dints.

But two other points were by no means beyond question. Though it was certain that Austin's shoes had passed over that ground, how could it be proved that Austin was then wearing them? How, again, could it be known that they were made at the time stated? Could not Austin really have been at Luce Manor on that evening, and have made the tracks to the Abbey at some other time? Tanner was puzzled. He did not see how this point was to be cleared up.

Next morning he began his investigation at the pavilion of the Halford boat club. It was quite a large place, situated on a kind of bay on the river, just below the town. The house was built of red brick, with heavy overhanging eaves, and a kind of piazza in front. Before the piazza and stretching a good way past it in each direction, was the wharf wall, with several broad flights of steps leading to the river. Out on the water were moored some dozen or more boats, and others were in the railed-off space surrounding the house. Tanner pushed open the gate of this railing and entered.

At first he could see no one about, then, as he walked round the house, he came on a youngish man in a cap and a blue jersey, who was washing out one of the boats. He hailed him, and they got into conversation in a leisurely way. Tanner praised the house and general appearance of the place, and then gradually came to the object of his call.

He had no trouble in obtaining the required information. The caretaker remembered Austin taking out the boat on the Wednesday night. He confirmed the latter's statement on all points, and was quite certain of the hours he had left and returned.

'Mr Ponson was in a rare old hurry to be away,' went on the man. 'The boat he wanted was out, but it was just coming round the bend there, and I told him to wait a moment and he could have it. Well, he did wait, but he was all jumping like a hen on a hot griddle to be off. "Hang it, Stevens," he says, "are those people going to be all night?" But Mr Brocklehurst, that was him who had out the boat, was sculling in quite fast. Well, sir, I fixed up the boat, and let him have it, and he rowed off like a blooming paddle steamer. I couldn't but laugh when I watched him going down the river.'

'What time did you say that was?'

'It was ten minutes to nine. Mr Brocklehurst got ashore about the quarter, and it took me about five minutes to get the boat squared up.'

'And you say he rooted you out of bed when he got back?'

'Yes, sir. It was a quarter to eleven, and I had just put out the light.'

Tanner was nothing if not thorough. He went to the police station, learnt that Mr Brocklehurst was a solicitor with an office in the main street, and promptly called on him. In five minutes he had his information. Mr Brocklehurst had reached the pavilion about quarter before nine, for he recollected that as he had arrived at his house the town clock had struck nine.

The inspector then turned his steps to Elm Cottage, the residence of the Drews. Apart from the question of the alibi, he was anxious to meet Miss Drew and form his own conclusions as to the part she would be likely to play in the matter.

Elm Cottage was a small detached villa, set some twenty yards back from the road, and surrounded by a tiny, but well-kept garden. Tanner sent in his card, and was taken to a low and rather dark drawing-room at the back of the house, from which however there was a fine view of the river. Everything bore traces of culture and taste, but of rather straitened means. The room wanted papering, the carpet was worn, the furniture shabby. But what there was of it was good, there was everywhere neatness and spotless cleanliness, and the otherwise somewhat drab effect was met by means of flowers in bowls and vases. If the room bore the impress of Miss Drew's character, as Tanner suspected, it showed her a fine girl, bravely determined to make the best of things which she could not remedy.

In a few moments she joined him, and as the Inspector looked at her face, he felt the character he had imagined of her was there. A low, broad forehead crowned by masses of dark hair surmounted two dark, intelligent eyes, which met his own with steady directness. Her nose was small, her lips rather full but delicately modelled, and her chin firm and well-rounded. Indeed, if anything, the lower part of her face might be considered a trifle too much developed for perfect symmetry. It gave her almost too pronounced an appearance of strength and determination, and Tanner felt she would be a person to be reckoned with. But as they talked he became convinced her power would never be used except to further what she believed to be just and right.

'I have to apologise, madame, for this intrusion,' he said courteously, 'but I have been sent down by Scotland Yard to inquire into the circumstances attending the death of Sir William Ponson. Mr Austin Ponson has told me of the hoax which was played on him on the same evening, and we discussed whether there might not possibly be some connection. He mentioned your name, and I ventured to call to ask you if you would please tell me what you know about it.'

'Did Mr Ponson tell you we are engaged?'

'He did, Miss Drew, under promise of secrecy. He gave that as his excuse for mentioning your name, also saying he had your authority to do so.'

'And what precisely do you want me to tell you?'

'Anything you can about it, please. What, for example, was the first you heard of it?'

The girl did not reply for a moment. Then she answered with another question.

'Just let me understand you, if you please, Mr Inspector. Do you doubt Mr

Ponson's story, and are you looking for confirmation?'

Inspector Tanner hesitated in his turn.

'I think, Miss Drew,' he said quietly, 'that you would probably prefer me to tell you the exact truth.'

She nodded and he went on.

'The answer to your question is Yes and No. In the ordinary routine way I asked Mr Ponson where he himself was on Wednesday night. Such a question is always asked under such circumstances, and it has no unpleasant significance. In answer to it he told me about the hoax. The story seemed to me probable, and I saw no reason for doubting it. But that did not absolve me from trying in every way I could to test its truth. You must see that I was bound to do so. And I may be allowed to say that all the inquiries I have made up to the present confirm what Mr Ponson told me.'

'But why does it matter whether or not his story is true?'

Tanner felt very uncomfortable. Though hardened by a life of contact with crime, he was a good fellow at heart, and he disliked intensely giving pain, especially to women. But as he looked into the steady, truthful eyes of the girl before him, he felt he could not prevaricate.

'I would rather not tell you,' he answered, 'but if you insist, I will.'

'I insist.'

'Well, I am sorry to say we don't exactly understand how Sir William died. There is a doubt that it may have been suicide or even murder. Let me make it clear that this is by no means certain, but I am bound to say that the idea has occurred to us that the murderer, if there was one, hoaxed Mr Ponson to try to throw suspicion on him.'

The girl's face paled, but she gave no other sign of emotion.

'I dreaded it,' she replied in a low tone, 'and he dreaded it too. We talked the whole thing over on the afternoon of the day the body was found, and we couldn't see any reason why Sir William should have gone down to the boat of his own accord. And then this hoax looked as if it had been made for just what you say. But I am at least thankful you take that view and don't suspect Mr Ponson of inventing the whole thing. That, I may say now, was what I really feared.'

'I can only repeat that all the inquiries I have made up to the present have confirmed Mr Ponson's story, and I have no reason whatever to think he invented it.'

'Thank you for that at all events. Now what do you want me to do?'

'To tell me at what hours Mr Ponson came and left here on the Wednesday night, and what took place while he was here.'

'He came at eleven—almost exactly. I looked at the clock when the ring came, for we seldom had so late a call. He showed me the two notes he had received, and asked me about them. When I explained I had not written them he told us—my father was present—the whole story of the hoax. As I have said, he did not stay, leaving in about ten minutes.'

Tanner rose.

'Thank you, Miss Drew. That is all I want to know. I am sorry for having come on unpleasant business, and exceedingly grateful for the way you have met me.'

She also rose and held out her hand.

'I hope you will let me know how you get on,' she said.

'You may trust me,' he promised, and bowing low, took his leave.

As he walked slowly towards Austin's villa, Tanner thought over the interview he had just had. He felt sure that the accounts he had heard of Miss Drew —that she was 'a fine girl' and 'a real lady'—were true. He believed she was the kind of girl who would marry neither for wealth nor position, and the fact that she had consented to an engagement with Austin seemed to speak well for the latter.

His thoughts turned back to the point about the alibi which still worried him —whether Austin had really been at the Abbey at the time he said. And suddenly a way in which he might test the matter occurred to him. The shoes which made the tracks Tanner had found had, so Austin had said, been bought by him in London on the Monday. He, Tanner, had got them from Austin after the inquest on Friday. If he could trace the movements of those shoes from Monday to Friday, would light not be thrown on the problem? Tanner thought it worth while trying.

Not far from the door of Austin Ponson's house a police constable was moving slowly along his beat. The Inspector went over to him.

'Have you seen Mr Ponson lately?' he inquired.

'Yes, sir,' answered the man, 'he and Lady and Miss Ponson passed in the car about half an hour ago, going towards London.'

This was a fortunate chance, and relieved the Inspector of a possibly tedious wait, as he wished to make his call at the house when Austin was from home. He now rang at the door. The butler appeared.

'Is Mr Ponson at home?'

'No, sir. He went out about half an hour ago. I expect him back about six. What name shall I say?'

'Tanner. Inspector Tanner of New Scotland Yard. I am sorry Mr Ponson is out as I wished to ask him for a little information, but perhaps if you would be so kind you might be able to give it to me.'

The butler was obviously impressed by the occupation of his visitor, and Tanner felt sure his curiosity would also be aroused.

'If you will come in I shall be glad to do what I can.'

'Now, Mr—? I didn't hear your name?'

'Lewis. John Lewis.'

'Well, Mr Lewis, Mr Ponson told me a curious story of a hoax that had been played on him last Wednesday night. I was down, you know, about Sir William's death, and we got talking. You know about the hoax, I suppose?'

'Not a word,' the butler answered, his manner portraying keen interest.

'He didn't tell me it was any secret. He got a note on Wednesday evening asking him to go out to meet some friends that night at the Abbey ruin.'

The butler nodded several times.

'Yes, I remember that note. I found it in the hall-door letter-box. It must have been left by private messenger, for there was no postmark on it. After Mr Austin had read it he came asking me where I had found it. He seemed kind of puzzled about it.'

'That would be it,' Tanner agreed. 'He went out to the Abbey, but when he reached it there was no one there and he had his journey for nothing. Someone had hoaxed him properly.'

'Bless us all!' ejaculated the butler. 'You don't say?'

'Mr Ponson asked me when I was here to look into the thing for him and I did. I found some footsteps there that might give a clue, but the worst of it is I don't know whether they weren't made by himself. Maybe, Mr Lewis, you would help me there. I would be much obliged, I'm sure.'

'Certainly, Mr Tanner. I'd be pleased if you'd tell me how.'

'All I want is to see the shoes Mr Ponson wore on Wednesday night, so as I can compare them with the prints.'

The butler's face fell.

'That's just the one thing I can't do,' he answered. 'They're not here. I missed them on Friday, and told Mr Austin. He said they were not comfortable, and he had sent them to be stretched.'

'They were new, then?'

'Yes, he got them in town on Monday.'

'It was curious he should wear them that night if they weren't comfortable.'

'I suppose he hadn't found it out. That evening was the first time he had had them on.'

'I see.' Tanner nodded his head, then continued, 'What time did he go out, Mr Lewis?'

'About eight or a bit after.'

'And when did he get back?'

'A little before half-past eleven. I brought him some whisky, and when I was coming out of his room the clock struck the half-hour.'

'And he didn't go out again that night?'

'No, he went to bed about twelve. I heard him go up.'

'I see. And what was the next occasion he wore those shoes?'

'There wasn't no next occasion. That was the only time he had them on.'

Tanner considered. This seemed to be pretty conclusive, but he was anxious to obtain even stronger evidence. After a moment he went on again.

'I'm afraid I'm not quite clear about the thing yet. What I want to get at is whether anyone else could have got hold of those shoes and made the tracks I saw at the Abbey.'

'If that's all's worrying you, you may make your mind easy. Those shoes were in my charge from Monday evening till Mr Ponson put them on on Wednesday after dinner. Then I brought them down to clean before I went to bed that night, and they were there till he took them on Friday. I remarked them particularly because they were new, and if anyone had touched them I would have known. Besides, there was no one about that could do it.'

'What state were they in when you cleaned them?'

'Muddy—very wet and muddy. I couldn't think where Mr Austin had been to get them into such a condition.'

'One more question, Mr Lewis. You tell me the shoes were not worn except on Wednesday evening. But could someone else not have worn them then? Suppose Mr Austin went out wearing some other pair, and some one else slipped in and got hold of these and made the tracks, and then put back the shoes without your knowing?'

The butler looked at the other with an expression of pitying scorn.

'Why, Mr Inspector, I'm not altogether a fool. I tell you I saw them on Mr Austin's feet when he was going out, and I saw them on his feet when he was coming in, so they weren't in the house for anyone else to take. And what's more, if that doesn't convince you, every other pair of Mr Austin's boots and shoes were in the house that evening. I know because I happened to look over them to see if any wanted mending. So if anyone else had his new shoes he must have been going about himself in his socks.'

It was enough. This placed the affair beyond doubt, or it would if one other point were settled. Tanner rose.

'I am extremely obliged to you, Mr Lewis, and now I must beg your pardon for having played a little trick on you. I have the shoes. Mr Ponson gave them to me on Friday. Come with me to the hotel and have a drink, and tell me if the shoes I have are the ones you were speaking of, and that'll be all I'll ask you.'

That the butler was suspicious there was more in the questions than met the eye was obvious, but he made no remark, and on seeing the shoes, he identified them unhesitatingly as Austin's.

Tanner was pleased with the result of his inquiries. As he summed up the situation it stood as follows:

Austin had left Halford and returned to it at such hours as would have just enabled him to reach the Abbey in the interval. Therefore, if he did reach it he could not have been at Luce Manor, and if he was not at Luce Manor he was innocent. Footprints were made at the Abbey by a certain pair of shoes. Those shoes were at Austin's house every moment of the time from their purchase till they came into Tanner's possession, except during the particular period in question. The tracks at the Abbey must therefore have been made during this period. Further, during this period Austin himself must have been wearing the shoes, as not only had he left his house and returned to it wearing them, but he had no others to put on—the remainder were all at his house. If, therefore, Austin did not himself make the tracks at the Abbey, he must have had no shoes during the time this was being done, in which case he could hardly have been at Luce Manor committing the murder. To Tanner the alibi was complete. Short of seeing Austin at the Abbey, he could expect no stronger evidence.

Even if the truth of Austin's story were unlikely, Tanner would have felt compelled to believe it. But, as he had seen from the start, it was by no means unlikely. On the contrary the whole thing was just the kind of plant the real murderer might probably enough devise to shift suspicion from himself to Austin. That it was such a plant Tanner now felt certain.

And if so, had it not one rather suggestive point? The man who made the plant was familiar with Austin and his affairs. Who, of those who knew the affairs of both Austin and Sir William, had an interest in the latter's death?

The answer was not far to seek. One such at least was Cosgrove Ponson. He had both the knowledge and the motive. Tanner felt his next business must be with the cousin.

And then a more sinister idea entered the Inspector's mind. What if there was more in the plant than a mere attempt to shift the suspicion off the murderer? What if the plan was to encompass Austin's death as well? If Austin were convicted and executed it would make a great difference to Cosgrove apart from rendering his position safe. Tanner recalled the terms of the will. If Sir William died Cosgrove received £75,000, but if Austin also should lose his life his cousin would net another £30,000. Here was motive enough for anything.

Tanner recollected the woman who, Austin had stated, had handed him the note at the Old Ferry. As the latter's story must now be taken as true, this must be a real woman, and if Cosgrove were the guilty man she must be his accomplice.

Here was a line of inquiry which might lead to something. Tanner decided he would return to town by the next train, and start this new phase of the case.

Chapter 6
What Cosgrove Had To Tell

At three o'clock that same afternoon Inspector Tanner stepped from the train at St Pancras. He had telephoned to the Yard before leaving Halford, and, as a result, one of his men was awaiting him on the platform.

'Ah, Hilton,' the Inspector greeted him. 'I want you to go over to Knightsbridge and look up a man for me—a Mr Cosgrove Ponson who has rooms at Number 174B. All you need find out is whether or not he is at home, I'll follow you round in a couple of hours, and you can report to me there.'

This arranged, Tanner took a taxi and was driven to his house at Fulham.

Town was very hot. The sun poured down out of an almost brazen sky, taking the freshness from the air and turning the streets into canals of swimming heat. The narrow courts were stifling, the open spaces shone with a blinding glare. Dust was everywhere, a dry burning dust which parched the throat and made the eyeballs smart. As Tanner looked around him he recalled with regret the green lawns and shady trees of Luce Manor.

A couple of hours later he emerged from his house, resplendent in a silk hat and frock coat, with well-fitting gloves and a gold-headed cane. Taking another taxi, he drove to Knightsbridge. There he dismissed his vehicle, and approaching his man, Hilton, made him a slight sign. The other responded by nodding his head. Cosgrove, the Inspector understood, had gone out.

Sauntering leisurely across the road, Tanner mounted the steps of the house and rang. The door was opened by a dark, clean-shaven manservant.

'Mr Ponson is not at home, sir,' he said in reply to the Inspector's inquiry, as he reached back for a salver.

Tanner held out a card engraved 'Mr Reginald Willoughby, The Albany.'

'I rather wanted to see Mr Ponson on business,' he went on. 'Do you think he'll soon be back?'

'I think so, sir. He'll almost certainly be in before seven.'

The Inspector glanced at his watch.

'I have half an hour to spare. I think I'll come in and wait.'

'Very good, sir,' the man replied, as he led the way to a large sitting-room on the first floor.

Left to himself, Tanner began by looking carefully round the room, and noting and memorising its contents. It was furnished as a library, with huge leather-covered chairs, and a large roll-top desk. The walls were lined with bookshelves, relieved here and there by a good print. The air was heavy with the scent of innumerable roses, arranged in bowls of silver and old china. Books and papers, mostly of a sporting character, were littered on chairs and occasional tables. Cosgrove Ponson, it was evident, was not hard up in the sense in which the words are understood by the man in the street.

Tanner waited motionless for a few minutes, then rising softly, he tiptoed over to the roll-top desk and tried the lid. It was locked. Slipping a small tool from his pocket, he gently inserted it in the lock, and after a few turns he was able to push the shutter noiselessly up.

The desk was littered with papers. Tanner sat down before it and began a systematic though rapid search. He wanted to find out for himself Cosgrove's exact financial position as well as, if possible, the names of any lady friends, one of whom might have impersonated Mrs Franklyn's servant.

But he had no luck. It seemed likely Cosgrove must have some other desk or sanctum in which he kept his more private correspondence. There were here notes, invitations, bills, a few receipts, and other miscellaneous papers, but no bank-book nor anything to give a clue to his means. Nor were any of the letters from female correspondents couched in sufficiently familiar language to seem worthy of a second thought.

Considerably disappointed, Tanner pursued his search according to the regular routine he employed in such cases, ending up when he had finished with the letters by drawing a small mirror from his pocket and with it examining the blotting paper. He rapidly scanned the various sheets, and was just about to put them down as useless when his eye lit on the blurred and partial impression of an address. It consisted of three lines. The first he could not read, the second he thought was Gracechurch Street, following an undecipherable number, while the third was clear—the word 'City.' He had not noticed this address on any of the papers, and he now remarked it only because it seemed to suggest finance. Thinking it might be worth while trying to decipher the name, he slipped the page out of the blotter and secreted it in his pocket. Then silently closing the desk he tiptoed to the door. After listening for a moment at the keyhole he opened it and stepped stealthily out.

Several doors opened off the passage, and Tanner stood for a moment wondering which led to the room of which he was in search. At last he selected one, and having ascertained from the keyhole that all was quiet within, he silently turned the handle. It opened into a dining-room. Withdrawing in the same noiseless manner he tried the next, to find himself in a spare bedroom. But the third door led to his goal. It was evidently Cosgrove's dressing-room, and there at the opposite wall was what he was looking for—a long line of Cosgrove's boots and shoes. A moment's examination sufficed. Cosgrove's foot was too big to have made the tracks of the fifth man at the Luce Manor boathouse. Silently he returned to his seat in the library.

He looked at his watch. His search had lasted thirty-five minutes. He rang the bell.

'I am sorry I cannot wait for Mr Ponson,' he told the butler. 'I shall write to him.'

That evening he sat down to re-examine the sheet of blotting paper. He studied the second line for several minutes, and at last came to the conclusion his first idea had been correct. It was apparently Gracechurch Street. But the number was quite beyond him.

Taking a street directory he began to go through the Gracechurch Street names, comparing each with the blotsheet marks. He had been through about half when he came on one that seemed the correct shape—Messrs Moses Erckstein & Co. And when he saw that Messrs Erckstein were money-lenders, he felt hopeful that he was on the right track. But he was very thorough. He worked through the whole list, lest there should be some other name even more like that on the sheet. But there was none.

Next morning he called on Messrs Erckstein. He was again wearing his silk hat and frock coat, and with these clothes he put on, to some extent at least, the manners of what our friends across the pond call a club man. He had made inquiries about the firm, and he now asked for the senior partner. After a delay of a few minutes he was shown into the latter's room.

Mr Erckstein was stout and dark, with a short black beard and Semitic features. Tanner had found out that, though he had been a German before the War, he was now a Pole.

He proved an unwilling witness. It was not until Tanner had wasted over an hour, and threatened his informant with a summons to Court, where his books and his methods would be probed mercilessly in public, that he got what he required.

Cosgrove Ponson, it appeared, was, and had been for many years, heavily in the firm's debt. Including interest at the exorbitant rate charged, he now owed the money-lenders close on £30,000. Moreover, he had recently been severely pressed for part payment. Tanner, after a lot of trouble, saw copies of the letters sent, the last of which politely but unmistakably threatened proceedings and ruin unless the interest at least was immediately paid.

'Why did you lend such a large sum?' Tanner asked.

'Because of his uncle, Mr Tanner. Sir William Ponson thought a lot of Mr Cosgrove, and he would have helped him. Now that he is dead we shall get our money. We understand Mr Cosgrove comes into a handsome legacy.'

When Tanner left the office he was more than satisfied as to the strength of Cosgrove's motive for the crime. Far stronger it appeared to him than that of Austin. It looked as if he was on the right track at last.

Hailing a taxi, he handed the driver a pound in advance and instructed him in detail as to what he wished done. Then he stepped into the vehicle and was driven to Knightsbridge.

Within view of Cosgrove's chambers the car swung close to the sidewalk and the engine stopped. The driver sprang down, and opening the bonnet, became engrossed with his engine. It was obvious a slight mishap had taken place.

Tanner sat well back in the car watching the house before him. It was getting on towards one. For more than half an hour the repairs continued. Then the Inspector saw Cosgrove leave his door and hail a taxi. He called softly to his own driver, and the work at the engine being completed at just that moment, the latter mounted and started the car.

'Keep that taxi in sight,' Tanner ordered as they moved forward.

The chase was not a long one—down Piccadilly, across the Circus and into

Shaftesbury Avenue. There the quarry turned into a narrow lane and Tanner, leaping out of his taxi, saw the other stop at the stage door of the Follies Theatre. He turned back to his own car.

'Pick me up when I sign and follow it again,' he said to his driver, then, becoming absorbed in a bookseller's window immediately opposite the end of the lane in which the other car stood, he waited.

With the corner of his eye he had seen Cosgrove enter the theatre, and after some ten minutes he observed him emerge following a lady whom he handed into his taxi. Rapidly Tanner regained his own vehicle, and as the other swept out of the lane and turned west, his driver took up his former position behind it.

Once again the chase was short. Reaching the Strand, the leading car turned into the courtyard of the Savoy. As he stepped out of his taxi Tanner was in time to see his victims entering the great building. He followed quickly to the restaurant, and while they were looking for a table, slipped a couple of pounds into the head waiter's hand.

'I am from Scotland Yard,' he whispered. 'Put me beside that lady and gentleman like a good fellow.'

The head waiter led him forward and presently he found himself seated at a small table immediately behind Cosgrove. The lady was on Cosgrove's right and from where he sat the Inspector could see her without appearing to stare. He recognised her immediately as Miss Betty Belcher, one of the most talented and popular actresses in London.

She was a woman of about thirty, small, sprightly, and rather inclined to stoutness. Her features were delicate, her complexion creamy, and her eyes large and of the lightest blue. Her lips were just a trifle thin, and in repose wore the suspicion of a pout. But her glory was her hair. It was of a deep rich gold, piled up in great masses above her low forehead. Famous for her play in light, sparkling parts, her vivacity on the stage was unrivalled. But here she was not vivacious. On the contrary, both she and Cosgrove seemed ill at ease. While the waiter was serving them they discoursed on everyday topics, but when he passed on their voices dropped and Tanner could no longer overhear them.

It was evident from their expressions they were discussing some serious matter, and Tanner strained his ears to learn its nature. For a time he was unsuccessful, but at last during lulls in the general conversation he caught enough to enlighten him. Disconnectedly and without the context he heard Cosgrove use the words 'inquest adjourned,' and 'detective,' and later the lady said something very like 'suspicion aroused' and once again, unquestionably, the phrase 'the alibi should hold.'

Inspector Tanner was extremely interested. Obviously they were talking about the Luce Manor tragedy, and from the reference to the alibi they seemed to have very first-hand information of Austin's affairs. This, however, was natural enough and by no means suspicious. But the expression of anxiety on the lady's face was not so natural. Tanner wished he was sure of its cause.

After coffee Cosgrove lit a cigarette, and the Inspector was rather thrilled to notice it was of a light-brown colour. His thought turned to the end he had discovered in the Luce Manor boathouse. If Cosgrove's case contained the same unusual brand as that found at Luce Manor, his suspicions would undoubtedly be strengthened.

Cosgrove smoked quietly, while Tanner paid his bill and got ready to leave the restaurant. At last the others made a move, Cosgrove dropping the cigarette end into the saucer of his coffee cup. Tanner moved aside, and turned his back till they had passed, then returning to his table as if he had forgotten something, he rapidly picked up the cigarette end, quenched it and dropped it into one of the little boxes he always carried. Then he hurried out after his quarry, and as they took another taxi, re-entered his own.

This time they had a longer run. It was not till they reached Lyme Avenue, Chelsea, that the chase ended. There at the door of a block of flats the two dismounted. But Cosgrove did not go in. When the lady had disappeared he returned to his taxi, and started back towards London. Tanner's driver had run on towards the end of the road, but he skilfully manoeuvred for position, and soon was back in his own place behind the other.

At the door of the Huntingdon Club in Piccadilly, Cosgrove dismounted, paid off his driver and entered the building. This suiting Tanner's plans as well as anything else, he also paid his man, and after a few minutes followed Cosgrove into the club.

Handing the porter another of his false cards—Mr Percival Hepworth-Jones, The Constitutional—he asked for Cosgrove, and was shown into a waiting-room.

In about ten minutes Cosgrove appeared—a questioning, puzzled look on his thin, good-looking face.

'I must apologise, Mr Ponson,' began the Inspector, 'for sending in a card which is not my own. You are wondering where you have seen me before?'

'I confess that I am. I know your face, but I can't recall our meeting.'

'We didn't meet, but you saw me at the inquest at Luce Manor. I am Inspector Tanner of Scotland Yard, and I have been put in charge of the case.'

The Inspector, who was watching the other keenly, noticed a sudden look flash across his face and then disappear. It was not exactly a look of alarm. Rather was it that of a man brought suddenly face to face with a danger he had long recognised—a kind of bracing of himself to meet a crisis which was at last at hand. But his manner was free from any trace of anxiety as he motioned his visitor to a chair.

'Ah yes,' he said, 'of course. I remember now. My cousin, Austin Ponson, told me about you. So you fear my uncle's end might have been suicide? It is a horrible idea, and you won't mind my saying that I cannot but think you are wrong. He was not at all that kind of man.'

'So I am beginning to think, Mr Ponson. But orders are orders. I have been told to investigate and report, and I must do so.'

Cosgrove agreed and they conversed for some time. Tanner asked a good many questions, but without learning anything of interest. Then at last he came to the real object of his visit. Speaking very much as he had done to Austin, he asked

Cosgrove to state his own movements on the fatal Wednesday night. Cosgrove, unlike Austin, got on his high horse.

'Really, Inspector, I think that's a little too much. Why should I tell you anything of the kind? What has it to do with the affair?'

Tanner could be direct enough when he saw cause.

'Why this, Mr Ponson,' he answered, still watching the other keenly. 'As you must see, the possibility of suicide involves that of murder also. The question I have asked you is asked in such cases as a matter of course to every one interested.'

Cosgrove started slightly at the last words.

'Interested?' he repeated. 'What do you mean by that? Do you think I was interested?'

'Mr Ponson, as reasonable men we must both see that you were interested. You will forgive me—I don't wish to be offensive—but it is common knowledge that you are in low water financially, and that you benefit considerably under the will.'

'Good Heavens!' Ponson cried angrily, 'and do you actually mean to say you suspect me of *murdering* Sir William?'

'I mean nothing of the kind, Mr Ponson. I only want to justify myself in asking you the question to which you have just objected.'

Cosgrove did not reply. At last Tanner went on in a courteous tone:

'Obviously, I cannot force you to answer me, Mr Ponson. But it must be clear to you that should you decline you may raise suspicions which, no matter how unfounded, are bound to be unpleasant. Please don't think I am speaking threateningly. You can see the matter as clearly as I.'

The Inspector's moderation appeared to bring Cosgrove, to a decision. He moved nervously, and then replied:

'I suppose you are right, Inspector, and that I have no cause to resent your inquiries. I haven't the slightest objection to telling you where I was when you explain yourself as you have just done.'

'I am much obliged. It will save me a lot of trouble.'

Cosgrove settled himself more comfortably in his arm-chair.

'I remember that Wednesday night,' he began, 'for I did one of the silliest things that night that I have ever been guilty of, and I think I may say without bragging I am usually as wide awake as most people. But I shall tell you.

'You know, or perhaps you don't, that I go in a good deal for racing. I have a small stable not far from Bath, and I make a bit off dealing and training as well as on the course. For some time I have wanted another horse, and there was one for sale near Montrose that seemed the thing, so much so that I determined to run down and see it. I have a good many engagements, mostly of a social kind, and I found that the only day I could go was the Thursday of last week—the day after my poor Uncle disappeared. There was an "At Home" at the Duchess of Frothingham's on the Wednesday afternoon, and a ball at Lincolnshire House on Friday evening, at both of which I wished to be present, so I decided to travel to Montrose by the night train on Wednesday, see the horse on Thursday, return to London that night, and get some sleep on Friday, so as to be fresh for the evening.

58

'This programme I carried out, but not quite as I had intended. I was at the Duchess of Frothingham's till a little after five, when I returned home, dined and drove to King's Cross to catch the 7.15 for the north. This train was due at Montrose about 5.30 the next morning, and it was my intention to drive the three or four miles out to the training stables and see the horses at their early exercise, returning to town when convenient.

'I reached King's Cross in good time, found the sleeping berth which I had engaged was ready for me, deposited my things therein, and began to make myself comfortable. Wishing to smoke I drew out my cigar-case, and then I discovered it was empty. I was considerably annoyed, not only for my own sake, but because I wished to be able to offer a smoke to the man with whom I hoped to deal. I glanced at my watch. It was still ten minutes past seven. Thinking I had plenty of time I seized my hat and ran to the refreshment room, which was close by. As I was selecting some cigars I glanced up at the refreshment room clock. It was pointing to 7.15.

' "Your clock's fast, I suppose?" I said.

' "No, I don't think so," the girl answered.

'I left the cigars on the counter and ran out on the platform. But the clock was right, and all I saw was my train moving off. It was already going too fast to board, and I had to accept the fact that it was gone with my luggage in the sleeping berth.

'I looked at my watch. It was still showing two minutes to the quarter. It was usually an excellent timekeeper, but in some way which I can't account for just on the occasion that mattered, it was three minutes slow. Pretty maddening, wasn't it?'

'It's the way things happen,' said Tanner philosophically.

'Isn't, it? Well, I got my cigars, and then I went to the Stationmaster's Office and asked what I should do. It appeared there was a comparatively slow train to Dundee at 8.30, but the next to Montrose was the express at 10.30. Even by taking a car from Dundee this earlier train would not get me to the stables in time for the morning exercise, so I decided my best plan would be to take the 10.30. I then asked about a sleeping berth. But here my luck was out. All those on the 10.30 were engaged.

' "And what about my things that have gone on in the 7.15?" I asked.

' "They will be all right," the clerk answered. "The first stop of both the 7.15 and the 10.30 is Grantham, and I shall wire the agent there to have your things collected from the 7.15 and handed in to you on the 10.30."

'This seemed the best arrangement, and I thanked the man, and having telegraphed to the dealer at Montrose, I strolled out of the station, wondering how I could best put in my three hours.

'More by force of habit than otherwise I took a taxi and drove back to my rooms. But my little adventure had made me restless, and I couldn't settle down to spend a lonely evening. I would have liked to go to the Follies and see my friend Miss Betty Belcher, but I knew she was acting all the evening except during part of the second act, say from about 9.30 till 10.00. To pass the time till 9.30 I at last decided to go to the Empire. I did so. I left my rooms almost at once, drove to the Empire, sat there for an hour or so, and then went to the Follies. From about 9.30 till 10.00 I sat with Miss Belcher in her room, then when it was nearly time for her to go on again I made my adieux and returned to King's Cross. I took care not to miss the 10.30, and at Grantham I got out and found a porter looking for me with my things. I duly reached Montrose about half-past eight next morning. So I trust you won't any longer suspect me of being at Halford.'

Tanner laughed.

'How was I to know, sir, what you did until you told me? I am very greatly obliged. You have saved me an immensity of useless work.'

Cosgrove Ponson was quite mollified. He seemed like a man from whose shoulders a weight had been removed. He took out his cigar-case.

'I don't know if it will confirm my story,' he said smiling, 'but I hope in any case you will smoke one of the actual cigars I bought at King's Cross.'

The Inspector accepted. He asked a few more questions, obtained the name of the Montrose horse-dealer, and then, with further compliments and thanks, took his leave.

It was obvious to him that, if true, Cosgrove's story made a complete alibi. If he had been at King's Cross at 7.30 o'clock, at the Follies Theatre at 9.30, and had travelled from King's Cross to Montrose by the 10.30 express it was out of the question that he could have been at Luce Manor. Satisfied as Tanner was as to the soundness of Austin Ponson's alibi, Cosgrove's was even more convincing, and what was better still, it would be easier to test. Though he did not believe Cosgrove would make such a statement unless it could bear the touchstone of inquiry, Tanner felt his obvious next business would be to check what he had just heard so fully as to remove all possible doubt of Cosgrove's innocence.

Chapter 7
Cosgrove's Trip North

On leaving Cosgrove Ponson, Inspector Tanner walked slowly up the shady side of Regent Street, his mind still running on the statement to which he had just listened. To test its truth was his obvious first duty, and as he sauntered along he considered the quickest and most thorough means of doing so. From the very nature of the story he felt inclined to believe it. Too much independent testimony seemed to be available for the alibi to be a fraud.

And if this was so, he, Tanner, was on the wrong track, and was wasting time. He had already lost nearly a week over Austin, and all the time he was working on these blind alleys the real scent was getting cold. But as he reviewed the facts he had learnt, he felt he could hardly have acted otherwise than as he had.

He considered Cosgrove's statement point by point. Firstly, was it true he could only have gone to Scotland on the night in question of all others? In answer to this it should be easy to find out if he really was at the Duchess of Frothingham's on the same afternoon. Then the missing of the train at King's Cross must be known to several persons—the clerk at the stationmaster's office, the barmaid who sold the cigars, as well possibly as the sleeping-car attendant, and the telegraph-office clerk, and copies of the wires to Grantham and to Montrose should be available. He was not sure that confirmation of Cosgrove's visit to the Empire would be obtainable, though some attendant might have noticed him. But there should be ample proof of his call on Miss Belcher at the Follies Theatre. Not only would there be the testimony of Miss Belcher herself, but some of the many attendants must almost certainly have seen him. Then, if Cosgrove was not actually seen leaving London by the 10.30 p.m., he must have been observed in that train at Grantham, where his luggage was handed in to him. Finally, to ensure that he did not leave the train there and return to Luce Manor, as well as to test the genuineness of the whole journey, Tanner could see Colonel Archdale, the horse owner of Montrose.

And then another point struck him. What, he wondered, were the precise relations between Cosgrove Ponson and Miss Betty Belcher? From their demeanour at the restaurant, they were certainly on pretty intimate terms. In this case could Miss Belcher's testimony to Cosgrove's call at the theatre be relied on? Here was what undoubtedly might be a flaw in the alibi, and he felt he must handle this part of it with special care.

As he reached this point in his cogitations he arrived at the goal of his walk —a small but extremely fashionable tobacconist's in Oxford Street. Handing in his card, he asked to see the manager.

He was shown into a small, neatly-furnished office, and there after a few minutes a tall young man in a grey frock coat joined him.

'Hallo, Tony,' said the Inspector when the door had closed.

The newcomer greeted his visitor breezily.

'Why, Tanner, old son,' he cried, 'how goes it? You're a stranger, you are. And what's blown you in today?'

'Business as usual. I want your help.'

'You bet your life! And when you want help you know the right place to come. Tony B won't see you left, eh?'

'I know that. You're not as bad as you look.'

The other winked slowly.

'And what's little Albert's trouble this time?' he asked.

'Why this,' Tanner answered, taking out his two little boxes and shaking the cigarette ends on to the table. 'I want to know what kind of cigarettes these are, and when they were smoked.'

'H'm. Think I'm a blooming crystal-gazer, do you? Or one of those Zancigs —what do you call 'em?'

As he spoke he was examining the ends with a strong glass. Then he smelt them, drew out a shred of tobacco from each and tasted it, and finally picked them up and took them out of the room.

'Sit tight, Albert,' he remarked as he left, 'and keep your little hands out of mischief till daddy comes back.'

In a few minutes he re-entered and laid the ends down on the table with beside them a whole cigarette of a dark yellow colour.

'There you are, sonny,' he announced. 'All chips of the old block, those are.'

'And what are they?' Tanner queried, examining the little brown tube with interest.

'Costly rubies, rich and rare,' his friend assured him. 'They're what we call "Muriquis," and they're made in Rio by a firm called Oliveira. There ain't many in this village, I tell you. Who are you trailing now? Is it Henry Ford or only his Majesty the King?'

'Neither,' Tanner returned seriously, 'it's that Ponson case I'm on.'

'Never heard of it. But Ponson knows his way about in cigarettes anyway, you bet your life.'

'And how long since they were smoked? Can you tell me that?'

'Nope. Not Tony B. This one about an hour; this one about a week at a guess. But don't you take all you hear for gospel. I don't know, as the girl said when her lover proposed.'

Tanner, though more bored with his friend's conversation every time he met him, remained chatting for some minutes. The two men had been at school together, and the Inspector kept up the acquaintanceship because of the valuable information he frequently got on matters connected with tobacco. But as soon as possible he took his leave, breathing a sigh of relief when he found himself once more in the street.

His interest was considerably aroused by the news he had just received. The suspicions he had entertained of Cosgrove had been somewhat lulled to rest by the latter's story. But the fact that the cigarette-end found in the boathouse at Luce Manor was of that same rare kind which Cosgrove smoked revived all his doubts,

62

and made him more than ever resolved to test the alibi to the utmost limit of his ability.

Before leaving Halford, Tanner had written to the photographers whose names he had found on the prints in the drawing-room at Luce Manor, ordering copies of Sir William's, Austin's, and Cosgrove's photographs. The studio was in Regent Street, and hailing a taxi, Tanner drove there. The photographs were ready, and he put one of each in his pocket. Also he selected prints of three or four other men as like in appearance to the cousins as he could find. Then he went on to the Duchess of Frothingham's house in Park Lane.

He saw her Grace's butler, and representing himself as a reporter on the staff of a well-known society journal, asked for a list of the guests present at the 'At Home' on the Wednesday of the murder, discreetly insinuating that he was prepared to pay for the trouble given. The addendum had the desired effect, and after a considerable delay a copy of the list was in Tanner's hands. A glance at it showed Cosgrove's name among the others, and a few judicious questions established the fact that he had actually been present.

Once more in the street, Tanner looked at his watch. It was after six o'clock.

'A little dinner and then the Empire,' he said to himself as he turned into Piccadilly. He had decided his first step must be to apply to those sources of information which could not possibly be interested in Cosgrove's affairs; afterwards, if need be, hearing what Miss Belcher had to say on the same subject.

A couple of hours later he reached the Empire. Here he made exhaustive inquiries, but without finding anyone who had seen his man. But he was not greatly disappointed, as he had already realised that confirmation of this part of the alibi was problematical, if not unlikely.

Returning to his taxi, he continued his journey till he reached King's Cross. It was just nine o'clock, and the great station was partially deserted, there being a lull in the traffic about that hour. For the first time that day Tanner felt cool, and he began to realise that he was tired. But apart from the general urgency of his business, he expected the persons he wished to see were on evening duty, and he decided he must finish his inquiries then and there. He therefore went to the stationmaster's office, and sent in his card. A dark, intelligent looking young man with an alert manner received him, and to him Tanner explained his business.

'I did hear something about it,' the young man returned. 'If you will wait a moment I'll make inquiries.'

He left the room, returning presently with a clerk.

'Mr Williams here remembers the affair. He dealt with it. Tell this gentleman what you know, Williams.'

'On Wednesday evening, the 7th instant, about 7.20 or 25,' began Williams, 'a man called at the office and said he had booked a berth to Montrose on the 7.15 p.m., but that he had missed the train while in the refreshment room. He said his suitcase and waterproof had gone on in the train, and he asked what I would advise him to do.'

'That's the man,' said Tanner, nodding. 'Yes?'

'I told him the trains. The next to Montrose was the 10.30 p.m., and his mistake only meant that he would reach there at 8.24 a.m. instead of 5.25. But it seemed he wanted to arrive early, and I mentioned the 8.30 p.m. which runs from here to Dundee, suggesting he could go on by car. But on going into it he decided even this would be too late, and said he would travel on the 10.30. With regard to his luggage I offered to wire Grantham, which is the first stop of both the 7.15 p.m. and the 10.30, to have it collected from the sleeping car on the 7.15 p.m., and put into the 10.30. He agreed to this, and I sent the telegram at once.'

'Would you know the man if you saw him again?'

'Yes, I believe I should.'

'Any of these he?' and Tanner handed over the half-dozen photographs.

The clerk instantly passed over Sir William's and those of the strangers, then he examined Austin's for some moments with a puzzled expression, but when he came to Cosgrove's he hesitated no longer.

'That's the man,' he said, repeating Tanner's words of a moment before, 'I should know him anywhere.'

'So far so good,' thought Tanner as he stepped out once more on to the concourse. 'Now for the refreshment room.'

He found the platform from which the 7.15 had started on the night in question, and looked about him. There was little doubt as to where Cosgrove had gone for his cigars. On the platform itself was a large sign 'First-Class-Refreshment Room.' The Inspector pushed open the door and entered.

'Good evening,' he said, raising his hat politely to the presiding goddess. 'I want a few cigars, please.'

'I have only these,' the girl answered, placing two partially emptied boxes before him.

Tanner examined them.

'I am not much of a judge,' he informed her, 'but these look the lighter. I'll have half a dozen, please. That is,' he went on with a whimsical glance at the clock, 'if it's safe.'

The barmaid looked at him as if she thought he was crazy, but she did not speak and Tanner explained:

'A friend of mine had an experience here the other night buying cigars, so he told me. He missed his train over the head of it. I was wondering if I should do the same.'

A light seemed to dawn on the girl. She laughed.

'I remember your friend. I couldn't help smiling, but I was sorry for him too. He came in here and chose a dozen cigars, and then he looked up and saw the clock.

' "Your clock's fast," he says.

' "I *don't* think," I says, and with that he hooked it out of the door, fair running, and all the cigars lying on the counter. I couldn't but laugh at him.'

'But *he* didn't laugh, for he missed his train,' prompted Tanner.

'Oh, he missed his train right enough. He came back and showed me his watch—three minutes slow. But he got his cigars all right.'

Tanner took Austin's photograph from his pocket, and glancing at it casually, passed it to the girl.

'He's a good old sport, he is,' he announced, 'but to look at him there you wouldn't think butter would melt in his mouth. What do you say?'

The girl wrinkled her pretty eyebrows.

'But that isn't the man,' she exclaimed.

Tanner took the card.

'I'm a blooming idiot,' he said. 'I've shown you the wrong photo. This was the one I meant.' He handed over the print of Cosgrove.

'Why, yes,' the girl answered unhesitatingly. 'That's him and no mistake.'

'He's a good soul enough,' went on Tanner, 'but he was very sick about that train, I can tell you.'

They conversed for a few moments more as the Inspector lit one of his purchases. Then with a courteous 'Goodnight,' he left the bar.

Whatever else might be true or false in Cosgrove's statement, thought Tanner, it was at least bed rock that he had missed the 7.15 train as he had said. The thing now to be ascertained was whether he really had travelled by the 10.30.

By dint of persistent inquiries the Inspector found a number of the men who had been on duty when that train left. But here he was not so successful. No one so far as he could learn had seen Cosgrove.

But this was not surprising. Tanner could not and did not expect confirmation from these men. They had had no dealings with Cosgrove which would have attracted their attention to him. The point could be better tested at Grantham, where whoever gave him his luggage should remember the circumstance.

Inspector Tanner glanced at the clock. It was ten minutes to ten. Why, he thought, when he was so far, should he not carry the thing through right then? He looked up the time tables. A train left at 10.00 p.m. for Grantham, arriving at 12.28. The 10.30 p.m., following, reached the same station ten minutes later, proceeding at 12.43. If he went by the 10.00 he would have fifteen minutes at Grantham to make inquiries, and he could go on by the 10.30 to Montrose and interview Colonel Archdale. And if fifteen minutes proved insufficient for his Grantham business he could sleep there, and go on in the morning.

Five minutes later he was in the train. Though, compared to that following, it was a slow train, it only made four stops—at Hatfield, Hitchin, Huntingdon and Peterborough. A minute before time it drew up at Grantham.

Here Tanner had even less difficulty than at King's Cross. An official at the stationmaster's office remembered the episode of the telegram, and was able in a few seconds to find the porter to whom he had entrusted the matter. This man also clearly recollected the circumstances and unhesitatingly identified Cosgrove from his photograph.

'Just tell me what occurred when you met Mr Ponson, will you?' asked Tanner.

'Well, sir,' the man answered, 'I was going along the train with 'is bag and coat, and 'e comes out of a first-class carriage bare 'eaded, and when 'e sees the bag 'e says, "that's my bag, porter," 'e says, and 'e gives 'is name. "Shove it in 'ere," 'e says. 'E 'ad 'is 'at on the seat for to keep 'is place, and that's all I knows about it.'

The confirmation seemed so complete that Tanner was tempted to return to town instead of taking the long journey to Montrose. But before everything he was thorough. He had paid too dearly in the past for taking obvious things for granted. In this case every point must be tested.

Soon, therefore, he was moving slowly out of Grantham on his way north. He had not been able to get a sleeping berth, but he made himself as comfortable as possible in the corner of a first-class compartment, and there he slept almost without moving till the bustle at Edinburgh aroused him. Here a restaurant car was attached, and shortly after Tanner moved in and breakfasted.

At Montrose he went to a barber's and was shaved, then, hiring a car, he was driven out to the training stables.

Colonel Archdale was an elderly man of a school Tanner had imagined was extinct—short, red-faced and peppery, and dressed in a check suit and riding breeches. The Inspector had called at the house, a low, straggling building of the bungalow type, but had been sent on to find its master at the stables, half a mile distant.

'Mornin',' the Colonel greeted him, as Tanner handed him his card and asked for a few moments conversation. 'Certainly, I'll go up to the house with you in a minute.'

'I shouldn't, sir, dream of troubling you so far,' Tanner assured him. 'Besides, it is not necessary. A minute or two here when you are disengaged is all I want.'

'Be gad, sir, you're modest. Comin' all the way from London for a minute or two,' and calling out some directions to a groom, he led the way into a kind of small office at the end of the stable.

'Well, sir,' he said as he seated himself before a small roll top desk, and pointed to a chair, 'and what can I do for you?'

'I am engaged, sir,' Tanner answered, 'in making some confidential inquiries into the movements of a man, who, I understand, was recently here—Mr Cosgrove Ponson of London.'

'He was here'—the Colonel hesitated a moment—'this day week. And what the devil has he been doin'?'

'Nothing, sir, so far as we know. It is the case of another man altogether, but it is necessary for us to know if Mr Ponson really was out of London on that day.'

'Well I've told you he was here. Is that evidence enough?'

'Quite, sir, as far as that goes. But I would like also to know some details to assure myself if his business here was genuine. What was his business, if I might ask?'

'You may ask and I'll tell you too, be gad. He wanted to see Sir Jocelyn, that's a three-year-old I'm goin' to sell. Devilish good bit of horseflesh too. But he wouldn't stretch to my figure. I wanted seven hundred, and he would only go five fifty. So it was no deal.'

66

'He came about this time in the morning, I suppose?'

'Yes, and a confoundedly silly time it was to come. He was to have been here at six for the morning exercise, but he missed his train, so he said, in London.'

'I understood so from him. Just one question more, sir. When was the arrangement about his visit made?'

'Some days before; I think it was on Monday evening I got his wire asking would Thursday suit me.'

'This is the man you mean, I presume?' and Tanner took out Cosgrove's photograph.

The colonel nodded as he answered: 'That's he.'

'And there was nothing, sir, in the whole episode that seemed to you suspicious or otherwise than it appeared on the surface?'

'Not a thing.'

Tanner rose.

'Allow me then, sir, to express my thanks for your courtesy. That is all I want to know.'

Declining an invitation to go up to the house for a drink—'too devilish risky to keep it here, by gad'—he returned to Montrose and looked up the trains to London. There was one at 2.29 which, travelling by Edinburgh and Carlisle, reached St Pancras at 6.30 the following morning. This, he decided, would suit him admirably, and when it came in he got on board.

As he sat a little later gazing out on to the smiling Fifeshire country, he went over once more, point by point, that portion of Cosgrove's alibi which he had already checked. So far as he had gone it certainly seemed to him very complete. In the first place, not only was the journey north made with, so far as he could ascertain, a quite genuine purpose, but the selection of that particular night was reasonably accounted for. The arrangement for it had been made at least as early as the previous Monday, which, again, would be a reasonable time in advance. Tanner could see nothing in any way suspicious or suggestive of a plant about the whole business.

Then, coming to details, the missing of the train at King's Cross might of course have been faked, but there was no evidence to support such a supposition. On the contrary, everything he had learnt seemed to prove it genuine. But even if it had been a plant, it was demonstrated beyond a shadow of doubt that Cosgrove *had* missed the 7.15 p.m. as he said, and that, further, he *had* travelled to Montrose by the 10.30. Even as the case stood Tanner felt bound to accept the alibi, but if he could confirm Cosgrove's statement of his visit to his rooms at 7.45 or 8 o'clock, and to the Follies about 10.00, any last shred of doubt that might remain must be dispelled. This, he decided, would be his next task.

The following morning, therefore, he returned to Knightsbridge. Here, keeping his eye on Cosgrove's door, he strolled about for nearly an hour before he was rewarded by seeing it open and Cosgrove emerge and disappear towards Piccadilly. He allowed some ten minutes more to elapse, then he walked to the door and rang. It was opened by the same dark, clean-shaven butler who had admitted him before. The man recognised his visitor, evidently with suspicion.

'Mr Reginald Willoughby, the Albany?' he asked with sarcasm, and a thinly veiled insolence in his tone.

'That's all right,' Tanner answered easily. 'I know my name is not Willoughby. It's Tanner'—he handed over his real card—'and if you'll invite me in for a moment or two I'll show you my credentials so that you'll have no more doubt.'

The butler was evidently impressed, and proffering the suggested invitation, led the way to a small sitting room.

'Mr Ponson he phoned the Albany,' he explained, 'and they said there weren't no one of that name there, so we was wondering about your little game.'

Tanner, following his usual custom, rapidly sized up his man, and decided how he should deal with him. With the veneer of his calling removed the Inspector imagined he might prove a braggart, a bully, and a coward. He therefore took a strong line.

'I suppose you know,' he began, without heeding the other's remark, 'that Mr Cosgrove Ponson is under serious suspicion of the murder of his uncle, Sir William, at Luce Manor?'

It was evident this was the last thing the butler had expected to hear. He stared at the Inspector in amazement.

'Lord lumme!' he stammered, 'is that a fact?'

'That's a fact,' Tanner went on sharply, 'and I want some information from you. And let me advise you to give it to me correctly, for if you don't you may find yourself in the Old Bailey charged as an accessory after the fact.'

The man blenched, and Tanner felt that the estimate he had made of his character was correct.

'I don't know nothing about it,' he growled sulkily.

'Oh yes, you do. Mr Ponson told me he spent that Wednesday night here, or a part of it anyway. Is that true?'

Tanner had set his little trap to learn whether the butler had been primed with a story by Cosgrove. His victim did not answer for a time. Clearly a struggle was going on in his mind. Then at last he said, 'Has Mr Cosgrove been arrested?'

The question still further bore out the estimate Tanner had made of the man's character. The Inspector could follow the thought which had prompted it. If the butler was to continue uninterruptedly in his master's service, he would rather not have the latter know he had given him away, but if Cosgrove was already in custody he would keep on the safe side and tell the truth. Tanner did not assist him to a conclusion.

'Never you mind that. You concentrate on avoiding arrest yourself. Now, will you answer my question?'

After some further urging the statement came. Cosgrove had not spent the evening in his rooms. He had left about 6.45 to catch the 7.15 at King's Cross, but he had returned unexpectedly in about an hour. He told the butler he had missed his train, and was travelling by a later one. He had gone out again, almost at once, and the butler had not seen him for two days.

Tanner asked several searching questions, and ended up completely satisfied that the man was telling the truth. There was no doubt whatever that Cosgrove's story was true in this particular also.

There now remained to be checked only the matter of his visit to the Follies, and though Tanner was not certain of the necessity for this, his habit of thoroughness again asserted itself, and he drove to the theatre. There he learnt that there was no rehearsal that forenoon, and he went straight on to Chelsea. His ring at the actress's flat was answered by a smartly dressed maid, to whom he handed his card, asking for an interview with her mistress.

The girl disappeared and in a few moments returned.

'Miss Belcher will see you now, sir.'

He was ushered into a small drawing-room, charmingly furnished in pale blue, with white enamelled woodwork. The chairs were deep and luxurious though elegant, the walls panelled with silk and bearing a few good monochrome drawings, while on the dark polished floor were thick and, as the Inspector knew, costly rugs. But though everything in the room was dainty, its outstanding feature was its roses. Roses were everywhere, massed in great silver bowls and rare old cut-glass vases.

'It's a rose case,' thought the Inspector whimsically, as he recalled that in two other sitting rooms he had had to visit—those of Miss Lois Drew and Cosgrove Ponson—he had found the same decoration, though in neither case with the same prodigal liberality as here.

He waited for over half an hour and then the door opened and Miss Belcher appeared.

Seeing her full face in the light from the window, he realised her beauty as he had not done in the restaurant. Though she was slightly—Tanner thought comfortable looking, though jealous people might have used the word stout—her features were so delicately moulded, her little, pouting mouth so daintily suggestive of dimples, her light blue eyes so large and appealing, her complexion so creamy, and above all and crowning all, her hair, so luxuriant and of so glorious a shade of red gold, that he began to understand the position she held in the popular favour. She was dressed in a garment which Tanner imagined was a *négligé*, a flowing robe of light-blue silk trimmed with the finest lace, beneath which peeped out the tiny toe of a gilt slipper.

Tanner bowed low.

'I beg you to pardon this intrusion, madame,' he said, 'but my business is both serious and urgent.'

Without speaking, the actress sank gracefully into a luxurious arm-chair, indicating with a careless wave of her arm a seat for the Inspector in front of her. He obeyed her gesture and continued:

'I have been ordered, madame, to make an investigation into the death of the late Sir William Ponson of Luce Manor, not far from Luton. I understand that you are acquainted with his nephew, Mr Cosgrove Ponson?' His hostess nodded, still without speaking. Tanner thought her manner unnecessarily ungracious, and determined to give a hint of the iron which lurked beneath his velvet exterior.

'I deeply regret to have to inform you that there is reason to believe Sir William was murdered, and that grave suspicion rests on Mr Cosgrove.'

This time the mask of indifference was pierced.

'But how perfectly outrageous,' the lady cried, a flicker of anger passing over her expressive face, 'and stupid and cruel as well. How dare you come here and tell me such a thing?'

'Because I think you may help me to clear him. Please consider the facts. The medical evidence shows Sir William was murdered some time after 8.30 on the evening of Wednesday week. We know that Mr Cosgrove Ponson was financially in low water—in fact, was in debt for a very large sum, and under threat of exposure and ruin unless he paid up. We know also he benefited to a considerable extent under Sir William's will. Further, in the boathouse from which Sir William's body was set adrift, a cigarette end was found—one of a peculiar brand, but little smoked in England, but which Mr Ponson continually uses, and lastly, and this is what brings me to you today, Mr Ponson has been unable to account satisfactorily for his time on the evening in question. He says he was with you from 8.30 till 9.00, and what I want to ask you is, Can we get proof of that? I think you will appreciate that proof of that means proof of his innocence.'

Tanner had been unobtrusively watching his companion while he spoke, and her demeanour interested him keenly. While he was recounting the medical evidence and Cosgrove's financial position she had listened perfunctorily, as if bored by such trifles being brought to her notice. But when he mentioned the cigarette she started and a look first of fear and then of anger showed momentarily in her eyes. It seemed to Tanner she might have so acted if she knew Cosgrove was guilty—as if she was aware of and prepared for all he had to say except this about the cigarette, and that her anger was against Cosgrove for having smoked under such circumstances. She did not speak for some moments, and Tanner felt instinctively she had seen his little trap, and was considering a way out. At last she appeared to come to a conclusion, and replied in a quiet voice:

'What Mr Ponson has told you is quite true, or at least almost. He was at my room at the Follies for about half an hour that evening, but not quite at the hour you have mentioned. He came about half-past nine, and left at ten. I know the time because it is the only period in that play during which I am off the stage.'

She had avoided his trap anyway, and her answer confirmed Cosgrove's story. But Tanner recognised he was dealing with a very clever woman, and he was by no means so convinced of the truth of her statement as he was of that of the butler. He went on:

'Obviously, madame, if we have to go before a jury the more corroborative evidence we can get the better. Now, are there any other persons who might have seen Mr Ponson at the theatre, and who could be called to add their testimonies?'

'I don't know if anyone else actually saw Mr Ponson,' she answered, 'but I should think it likely. Probably the door-keeper did, or one of the other men. Have you made inquiries?'

'No, madame. Not yet.'

'Well, you had better do so,' and she got up to indicate that the interview was at an end.

Tanner found himself in the street with a baffled feeling of having handled the interview badly. But it was at least obvious that the lady's advice was good, and somewhat ruefully he drove back to the Follies.

Here he made exhaustive inquiries, but without any very satisfactory result. The stage door-keeper knew Cosgrove, and said he was a frequent visitor to Miss Belcher. He remembered he had come two or three evenings in the week in question at about 9.30, and stayed with the actress for about half an hour. But he could not be sure whether or not Wednesday was one of these evenings. Three or four other attendants had also seen him, but in no case had there been anything to attract their attention to him, and none of them could say on what nights he had been there. But Tanner had to admit to himself that he could hardly expect such information from persons who were not interested in Cosgrove's visit.

But on another point he got positive information. His inquiries established the fact that on the Wednesday night of the murder Miss Belcher had been on the stage at 9.15. She therefore could not have been masquerading as Mrs Franklyn's servant at the Old Ferry.

On the whole the Inspector felt that, in spite of his momentary suspicion of Miss Belcher's manner, he must fully accept the alibi. The evidence of Cosgrove's missing the 7.15 p.m. train, and travelling by the 10.30 was overwhelming. The butler's corroboration of his master's return to Knightsbridge was convincing. Though Tanner was not so sure of Miss Belcher's statement, it at least agreed with Cosgrove's. Further, the lady had not fallen into Tanner's little trap about the hour of the call and had disagreed with what he told her Cosgrove had said.

Then another point struck him. Cosgrove was at Knightsbridge between 7.45 and 8.00, and at King's Cross at 10.30. Was this evidence alone not sufficient? Would it have been possible for him to have visited Luce Manor in the interval? Suppose he had used a fast motor and gone by road?

Tanner did not think it could have been done. From London to Halford was thirty-five miles, and there and back made seventy. What speed could he reckon on? Considering how much of London would have to be traversed, and the amount of traffic to be expected on so important a road, Tanner felt sure not more than an average of thirty miles an hour at the outside. This would take two hours and twenty minutes at least, leaving from ten to twenty minutes. The motor never would have risked going up to Luce Manor, as it would have been heard—in fact, no motor did so. That meant that ten minutes must have been spent in going from the road to the boathouse, and another ten in returning. This even if it could be done at all, would leave no time in which to commit the murder, get out the boat and set the body and the oars adrift. Tanner considered it carefully, and at last came to the conclusion the thing would be utterly impossible. Indeed, he did not believe that an average of thirty miles an hour could be maintained. No, the alibi was complete. He felt he must unhesitatingly accept it.

Inspector Tanner was a depressed man as he walked slowly back to New Scotland Yard. Up to the present he saw that he had been on the wrong track—that all his time and trouble had been lost. He was now as far off solving the mystery, as when he started the inquiry, indeed further, for the real scent must now be cooler.

And Sergeant Longwell had been almost equally unsuccessful in his endeavour to trace the man who had made the fifth line of footprints on the river bank. With occasional assistance from Tanner the sergeant had made exhaustive inquiries in all the surrounding country, but without result. The only thing he had learnt which might have had a bearing on the matter was that a small, elderly man with a white goatee beard had taken the 5.47 a.m. train from St Albans to London, on the morning of the discovery of the crime. From Halford to St Albans was about fifteen miles, and Longwell's theory was that this man—if he were the suspect—had walked during the night to St Albans, thinking that at a large station a considerable distance from Luce Manor he would be more likely to escape observation. But there was no real reason to connect this early traveller with the visitor to the boathouse. His boots had not been observed. But even if it had been proved that he was indeed the wanted man, the detectives were no further on. For the traveller had vanished into thin air at St Albans, and no trace of him could be found either in London or anywhere else.

That day a note was received at the Yard from the Chief Constable at Halford, urging that, unless there was some strong reason for its further adjournment, the inquest should be completed. The delay, it was pointed out, was objectionable for several reasons, as well as being needlessly trying to the family. Rather bitterly Tanner wired his consent to the proposal, and later in the afternoon there was a message that the adjourned inquiry would take place at 12.00 noon next day, Saturday.

Twelve o'clock next day saw almost the same company assembled at the adjourned inquest in the long narrow room at Luce Manor, as had sat there on the morning following the discovery of the tragedy. But on this occasion a few additional persons were present. Some members of the outside public had gained admission on one pretext or another, while, as Tanner noted, both Austin and Cosgrove Ponson were now legally represented.

The proceedings were formal and uninteresting until the doctors were called, but the medical evidence produced a veritable sensation. In the face of it only one verdict was possible, and without leaving their seats the jury returned that of wilful murder against some person or persons unknown.

Both Austin and Cosgrove were evidently anxious and upset, and both showed relief when the proceedings were over. But, considering his interviews with them, and the inquiries he had made, Tanner did not think these emotions unnatural or suspicious.

Though the Inspector had hardly hoped to learn additional facts at the inquest, he was yet disappointed to find that not one single item of information had come out of which he was not already aware. Nor had any promising line of inquiry been suggested.

He was now of the opinion that the real clue to the tragedy must lie in the letter Sir William had received a week before his death, but as he could see no way of learning its contents, his thoughts had passed on to the deceased's visits to London. About these visits one or two points were rather intriguing.

Firstly, they had occurred almost immediately after the receipt of the letter, and it was at least possible that they were a result of it. Secondly, Sir William had travelled to town two days running, or at least two weekdays running. This was not in accordance with his habit and pointed to some special and unusual business. The third point Tanner thought most suggestive of all. Though it was Sir William's custom and preference to go to town by car, and his motor was available on these two occasions, yet he had travelled in each case by train. Why? Surely, thought Tanner, to enable him to make his calls in private—to avoid letting the chauffeur know where he went.

At all events, whether or not these conclusions were sound, Tanner decided the most promising clue left him was the following up of Sir William's movements in the city on these two days.

Accordingly, when the business of the inquest was over and he was once more free, he returned to the railway station at Halford. Here he was able after careful inquiries to confirm the statement made by Innes, the valet, as to the trains Sir William had travelled by on the two days. He went himself to town by the 4.32, determined that on Monday morning he would try to pick up the trail at St Pancras.

But before Monday morning his thoughts were running in an entirely different channel.

He had gone home on Sunday determined to enjoy a holiday. But Fate ruled otherwise. The grilling afternoon had hardly drawn to a close when a note was sent him from the Yard. It read:

'*Re* Ponson Case.—Halford sergeant phones important information come to hand. You are wanted to return immediately.'

Tanner caught the 7.30 train, and before nine was seated in the Halford Police Station, hearing the news. The sergeant was bubbling over with importance and excitement, and told his story with an air of thrilled impressiveness which considerably irritated his hearer.

'About four o'clock this afternoon a young woman came to the station and asked for me,' he began. 'She was a good-looking girl of about five-and-twenty. She gave her name as Lucy Penrose, and said she was typist and bookkeeper in Smithson's, the grocer's in Abbey Street. I didn't know her, and she explained that she lived three miles out in the country, and had only got this job since the beginning of the month. Then she said she had just read about the inquest in the evening paper, and that she knew something she thought she ought to tell.'

The sergeant paused, evidently delighted with the attention the London officer was giving him.

'She said,' he went on after a moment, 'that about half-past nine on the Wednesday evening of the murder, she and a young man called Herbert Potts were walking in the spinney belonging to Dr Graham, on the left bank of the river, and just opposite the Luce Manor boathouse. They saw a boat coming down the river with a man in it. He stopped at the boathouse, and seemed to try the water gate, but apparently couldn't get in, for after a moment he pulled on to the steps and went ashore, making the boat fast. In a couple of minutes he came back with another man and got in the boat again, and then went in through the water gate. The other man stood on the steps and watched him, and then he went round seemingly to the door of the boathouse. That was all they saw, but, sir, they knew the men.'

Again the sergeant paused to heighten his effect.

'Get on, man. Don't be so darned dramatic,' growled Tanner irritably. 'Who were they?'

'Mr Austin Ponson and Sir William!' The sergeant reached his climax with an air of triumph.

Tanner was genuinely surprised.

'Couldn't have been,' he said after a moment. 'I went into all that. Mr Austin was half-way to the Abbey ruins at that time.'

'She was quite certain, and she said the man Potts was certain too.'

'Have you seen him?'

'No, sir. He is a bookseller's assistant in London—to Evans & Hope, in Paternoster Row. His people live here, and he was down on a couple of days' holidays.'

Tanner noted the address.

'How was Mr Austin supposed to be dressed?'

'In bluish grey clothes that looked like flannel, and a white straw hat.'

'And Sir William?'

'In a black cape and felt hat.'

'They didn't see either of them leave the boathouse?'

'No, sir. They were passing on down the river towards the girl's home.'

Tanner was silent. If this news were true, though he could hardly credit it, the alibi must be a fake after all, and Austin must have duped him. And yet, how could it be a fake? He had tested it thoroughly, and he had been satisfied about it. He did not know what to think.

'Why did this girl not come forward before?' he asked.

'She didn't know till she read the account of the inquest that there was any question of foul play.'

Inspector Tanner was considerably perplexed. The more he thought over what he had just heard, the more disposed to believe it he became, and at the same time more puzzled about the alibi. But one fact at all events appeared to stand out clearly. If Austin had really been to the boathouse that night, it surely followed that he must be guilty of the murder? His presence there would not of course prove it, but would not the alibi? If he had merely omitted to mention the visit it would have been suggestive, but if he had invented an elaborate story to prove he was not there, it undoubtedly pointed to something serious.

But, as had always happened up to the present, his own next step was clear. He must see the girl and hear her statement himself, and afterwards visit Potts, the bookseller's assistant. If he was satisfied with their story he must once again tackle Austin's alibi and not drop it till he either found the flaw or was so convinced of its soundness as to conclude the new witnesses were lying.

Next morning he was early at the grocery establishment of Mr Thomas Smithson, in close conversation with a tall and rather pretty girl in a cream-coloured blouse and blue skirt. She repeated the sergeant's statement almost word for word, and all Tanner's efforts could neither shake her evidence nor add to it. She was quite sure the man in the boat was Austin; she had seen him scores of times; he was a well-known Halford figure. So was Sir William; she had seen him scores of times also. No, it was not too dark to see at that distance; her sight was excellent, and she was quite certain she had made no mistake.

She was very shamefaced about the cause of her presence on the river bank, and begged Tanner to respect her confidence. He promised readily, saying that unless absolutely unavoidable, her name would not be brought forward.

He returned to town by the next train, and drove to Paternoster Row. Here he had no difficulty in finding Herbert Potts. He was a man on the right side of thirty, with a dependable face, and a quiet, rather forceful manner. He seemed considerably annoyed that his excursion with Miss Penrose should have become known, fearing, as he said, that the girl would get talked about, and perhaps have to give evidence in court. But about the events on the night in question he corroborated her entirely. He also was positive the man in the boat was Austin. Though now employed in London, he was a Halford man and knew Austin's appearance beyond possibility of mistake. The Inspector left him, feeling that in the face of these two witnesses he could no longer doubt Austin had been at the boathouse, and therefore had faked his alibi.

But how? That was the question he must now set himself to solve.

It seemed clear that Austin's statement up to the time of his leaving the boat club pavilion, and after his arrival back there, was true. The testimony of the boatman, Brocklehurst, Miss Drew, and Austin's butler was overwhelming. The flaw therefore must lie in the evidence of what took place between those hours. Tanner went over this once again.

It hinged, as he had recognised before, on the shoes. And firstly, had the prints at the Abbey been made by those shoes? He had thought so at the time, and on reconsidering the matter he felt more certain than ever that he was right. A very trifling dint in the edge of one of the soles, evidently caused by striking a sharp-edged stone, was reproduced exactly in the clay. It was unthinkable that another pair of precisely similar shoes should have a precisely similar dint in the exact same place. No, when or by whom worn, Austin's shoes had made the tracks. So much was beyond question.

Then with regard to the time at which the prints had been made. On this point the evidence of the butler corroborated Austin's story. The butler had stated the shoes had been in Austin's dressing-room in his, the butler's, charge during the entire time from the Monday on which they were purchased till the Friday, with the single exception of this particular period on Wednesday evening. If this were true it followed that some person other than Austin wore the shoes, and made the tracks during this period. But was it true?

Tanner recalled point by point his interview with the butler. Invariably he reached his conclusions quite as much from the manner and bearing of the persons he interrogated as from their statement. And in this case he was forced to admit the butler seemed to speak as a perfectly honest man. The Inspector felt he did not possess sufficient intelligence to make his story sound as convincing as it had, unless he himself believed it to be true.

But might not the man have been mistaken?

Obviously the liability of humanity to err must be kept in view. At the same time it was difficult to see how a mistake could have occurred. The matter was not one of opinion, but of fact. Was Austin wearing the shoes when he went out and returned on the Wednesday evening? Were they clean before he started and muddy after he reached home? There did not seem to be any possibility of error on these points. More important still, were they worn at any other time? The butler had stated he always knew what shoes Austin was wearing, as all his master's footwear was in his charge. It seemed to Tanner that if Austin was away from the house for so long as a journey to the Abbey would involve, in dirty weather, the butler would expect a pair of shoes to have been soiled, and would therefore be bound to know if those in question had been worn.

But there was corroborative evidence which vastly strengthened the man's statement, and that was the apparent age of the footmarks. Tanner could not tell to an hour when prints were made, but he felt certain he could say to within twelve. And in the case of these particular marks at the Abbey their appearance told him unmistakably they must have been made on or about Wednesday night. That the shoes came in wet and muddy that night, and that on Thursday morning they had dried by just the amount that might reasonably have been expected, was also strongly corroborative.

The more Tanner pondered over the matter, the more he felt himself forced once more to the conclusion that the footprints at the Abbey were made on that Wednesday evening between the hours of nine and eleven. If Austin was now proved to have been at the boathouse between these hours, who then had made them?

And again, if so, what shoes had Austin worn at Luce Manor? On that night the butler had gone over all his footwear, and all except the shoes in question were there in Austin's room.

Tanner was genuinely puzzled. This whole matter of the shoes seemed so clear and straightforward, and yet, if Potts and Miss Penrose were to be believed, it was all a fake. As he sat smoking after lunch in the corner of a quiet restaurant he kept racking his brains to find the flaw. But he could get no light, and he did not see just where to look for it.

At last he decided he would try to trace Austin's movements, from the time of his visit to Luce Manor on the Sunday evening previous to the murder, right up to the time he handed over the shoes to him, Tanner, on the following Friday. If Austin had arranged for a confederate to make the tracks for him he must have had communications with him, and it was possible Tanner might thus learn his identity.

As he was in London, the Inspector thought he might as well begin with Austin's visit to town on the Monday previous to the murder. Of that, the only thing of which he knew was the purchase of the shoes. He had noted the maker's markings,

'Glimax   Hunt & Co.'

Messrs Hunt's was a very large firm, with perhaps a score or more of shops in the metropolis, and probably hundreds throughout the three kingdoms. 'Glimax' was one of the three or four 'lines' advertised in every paper. Tanner borrowed a directory and looked up their head office. Half an hour later he was seated with their manager.

Having introduced himself as an Inspector from Scotland Yard, he went on to business at once.

'I am endeavouring,' he said, 'to trace the movements of a man who, on Monday, the 5th, this day fortnight, purchased a pair of shoes from one of your shops —probably a West End branch. The shoes were marked Glimax B10735 over 789647S. Now, can you oblige me by suggesting how I might obtain a record of the sale?'

'With the best will in the world, I don't know that we can give you that information,' the manager returned slowly. 'We get weekly statements from all our branches which show the total sales of each class of shoe during the period. But, unfortunately for you, though fortunately for us,' the manager smiled deprecatingly, 'many shoes of the fitting in question would almost certainly be sold at each of our branches during each week. If, therefore, you were to go through our returns you would find yourself no further on—it would still mean inquiries at each individual branch. How do you propose to identify your man?'

'I have his photograph.'

'I am afraid you will have to depend on that. Some of the salesmen will probably remember him. Can I help you in any other way?'

'Two things, if you will be so good; to give me, first, a list of your West End branches and second, a note to your managers, asking them to assist me.'

'I will do both with pleasure.'

Ten minutes later Tanner reached the first branch. Here he saw the manager, presented his note, and explained his business. The official was extremely civil and brought the Inspector to each of the salesmen in turn. All gave him their careful attention, but none could recall Austin Ponson nor recollect the sale in question. With courteous thanks Tanner took his leave.

The second branch was not far away, and here the Inspector made similar inquiries. But here again without result.

Recognising that his quest was going to be tedious, he engaged a taxi and settled down to work systematically through the list. Progress was slow, and it was approaching six o'clock by the time he had reached the ninth branch. But here, just as he had decided, he would visit no more that evening, he had some luck.

In this shop, the second salesman he spoke to instantly recognised Austin's photograph, and recollected the purchase of the shoes.

'Yes,' he said, 'I remember the man perfectly. What drew my special attention to him was the very peculiar way he conducted the purchase. He came in and said he wanted a pair of Glimax B10735 over 789647S. He did not look at the shoes I brought him, except to check the number. I remarked that few gentlemen knew what they wanted so precisely as that, and he said he had had a pair of the same before which had suited him, and he simply wanted to replace them.'

'About what time was that?'

'Shortly after four, I should say.'

'And did he give his name?'

'Yes. I forget what it was, but I sent the shoes to the parcels office at St Pancras.'

In reply to a further question the man said he recalled the names of Ponson and Halford.

The Inspector was considerably puzzled by what he had heard, and that evening he lit a cigar and settled down to consider it. In the first place, Austin's statement that he had bought the shoes on that Monday was true. But how did he know their number? The butler, Tanner remembered, had said that his master had never had a similar pair. For a long time he pondered over the problem, but the only thing that seemed to him clear was that some trick had been played. But at last a possible solution occurred to him. What if there were two of them in it—Austin and

78

an accomplice? The accomplice buys a pair of shoes and sends Austin the number so that he may get a precisely similar pair. Then on the Wednesday night while Austin, wearing one pair, is at Luce Manor, the confederate, wearing the other, is making the tracks at the Abbey.

At first this seemed to Tanner to account for the facts, but then he recollected that the dent on the sole of one shoe proved that the pair which made the tracks at the Abbey was Austin's pair—the pair which had been in the butler's charge till he, Tanner, received it. Unless, therefore, Austin and his accomplice had exchanged shoes at the end of the excursion, this theory would not work.

Suddenly another idea came into the Inspector's mind, at which he slapped his thigh, and smiled to himself. 'Guess I'm on to it this time,' he muttered, as he went up to bed, well pleased with his day's work.

To test the soundness of his new supposition, he continued next morning the inquiry he had been making on the previous afternoon—interrogating the shoe shop salesmen for information as to Austin's purchases. He began with the tenth branch, as if he had discovered nothing at the ninth. But here his efforts met with no success. Nor did they at the eleventh, twelfth, and thirteenth. But at the fourteenth, with a feeling of pleased triumph, he discovered what he had hoped to find.

At this shop he inquired, as before, if any of the assistants recollected a man like that of the photo he showed having purchased a pair of shoes of the given number. At once he had an affirmative response. One salesman remembered Austin having called on the Monday in question, and after having been carefully fitted, having bought the shoes. The salesman had according to his usual custom handed Austin a card bearing the number of the shoes. He had offered to send the parcel, but Austin had said he was running for a train and would take it with him. The transaction had occurred about three o'clock.

'Bully for me!' thought Tanner as he drove to St Pancras, *en route* for Halford. 'See what a little imagination does!'

The theory he had evolved on the previous night now seemed not unlikely to be the truth. According to it, Austin had gone to town on the Monday and purchased two identical pairs of shoes. The first he had had fitted in the usual way in one shop; the second had been selected in another shop as being of the same number as the first. This had been rendered possible by carrying out the purchases in two different branch shops of the same firm. One pair he had bought openly giving his name and having the parcel sent to St Pancras; the other transaction he intended to remain a secret.

Arrived at his home, Austin had carried out the same tactics. One pair he had spoken of and given into his butler's charge; the other he had locked away privately. No one was supposed to know, and no one did know, that he had purchased more than one pair.

Let us call these two the known pair and the secret pair. On the evening of the murder, then, Austin puts on the known pair which the butler had in his charge, goes to Luce Manor, commits the murder, walks home through some muddy ground, gets the shoes wet, changes them on returning home, where they dry during the night and are cleaned by the butler next day, all exactly as the latter had stated. But at some other time, probably in the dead of Wednesday night, Austin gets up, puts on the other pair—the secret pair—and slipping out of his house unnoticed, makes the tracks at the Abbey. To make the deception more convincing he has previously dinted the sole of one of these 'secret' shoes, so that this dint will show on the prints at the Abbey. At some convenient opportunity when the butler is out of the way he himself cleans the secret pair, and then *changes them for the others*. The dinted pair which made the tracks at the Abbey thus become those in the butler's charge; the others, in which the murder was committed, are locked away by Austin, who doubtless takes an early opportunity of destroying them.

Tanner had to admit the ingenuity of the plan. To anyone not knowing there were two pairs of shoes in question, the alibi would be overwhelming.

But completely to prove this theory it would be necessary to show that Austin was at the Abbey at some time other than that he had stated. It was with this object Tanner was returning to Halford.

He made most persistent inquiries, but was unable to find any evidence on this point. None of the cottagers nor farm hands in the vicinity of the Abbey had seen Austin, either on the Wednesday evening or at any other time. Nor had any other stranger been observed. If, however, Austin had been to the Abbey in the middle of the night, as Tanner suspected, the failure to see him was not surprising, and did not invalidate the main conclusion. On the contrary, Tanner believed he had solved his problem. Austin, he felt, was guilty beyond a shadow of doubt.

And then Tanner saw that this solution cleared up another point by which he had been somewhat puzzled, namely, Austin's readiness, indeed almost eagerness, to tell of his visit to the Abbey. That, he now saw, had been a trap, and he, Tanner, had walked right into it. He saw Austin's motive now. From the latter's point of view it was necessary that Tanner should inspect the footprints while they were still fresh. If some days passed before suspicion was aroused, the marks would have become obliterated, and the alibi worthless. Austin was a cleverer man than the Inspector had given him credit for. By his manner he had deliberately roused the latter's suspicions so that his alibi might be established while the footprints were clear.

That evening Tanner made careful notes of the evidence he had accumulated against Austin Ponson. When the document was completed, it read:

1.   Austin never got on with Sir William.
2.   Though Sir William allowed him £1000 a year, this was a small sum compared to what he might equally easily have paid.
3.   Austin could not be making more than two or three hundred a year, so his total income could not much exceed £1200.
4.   He was living up to, or almost up to, this figure.
5.   Austin had become engaged to a girl to whom, as a daughter-in-law, there was every reason to believe Sir William objected. This girl had no dot.
6.   Unless he got an increased allowance Austin would find himself very pinched after marriage.

7.   Sir William had threatened that if the marriage came off, he would not only not increase the allowance, but might alter his will adversely to Austin.

8.   Austin would therefore be faced with the alternative of having his prospects ruined if his father lived, or, if he died, of receiving £150,000. Thus not only his own position and comfort were at stake, but that also of the girl he loved—a terrible temptation.

9.   Austin had an interview with Sir William on the Sunday night previous to the murder, at which, the two quarrelled about a lady—presumably Miss Drew.

10.   Austin had the requisite knowledge of Luce Manor and Sir William's ways to have accomplished the deed.

11.   Austin had on that Wednesday night rowed down the river and met Sir William at the Luce Manor boathouse.

12.   Austin had denied having been in the neighbourhood at the time.

13.   Austin had invented and carried out an elaborate plant with the object of proving an alibi. This alibi was a deliberate falsehood from beginning to end, and was prearranged.

As Tanner read over his document he felt that seldom had he investigated a clearer case, or got together more utterly damning evidence.

'The man's as good as hanged,' he said grimly to himself.

Next morning he laid his conclusions before his chief, with the result that an hour later he was again on his way to Halford, armed with a warrant for Austin Ponson's arrest.

He took the sergeant and a constable with him to the house, but left them waiting in the hall while he was shown into Austin's study. The latter was writing at his table.

'Hallo! Inspector,' he cried cheerily. 'And how are you getting on?'

Tanner ignored his outstretched hand, and as the other saw his visitor's face, his expression changed.

'Mr Austin Ponson, I am sorry to inform you I hold a warrant for your arrest on a charge of murdering your father, Sir William Ponson. I must also warn you that anything you may say may be used against you.'

Austin shrank back and collapsed into his chair as if he had been struck. His face grew ghastly, and little drops of moisture formed on his forehead. For some moments he sat motionless, then slowly he seemed somewhat to recover himself.

'All I can say, Inspector,' he answered earnestly, 'is that, before God, I am innocent. I am ready to go with you.'

The news spread like wildfire, and that evening the people of Halford had a fresh thrill and a new subject of conversation.

Chapter 9
Lois Drew Takes A Hand

Just about the time that the arrest of Austin Ponson was taking place, Miss Lois Drew entered her drawing-room, and sitting down at the old Sheraton desk near the window, became immersed in her household accounts.

The low ceilinged, green-tinted room was pleasantly cool on this hot, dusty morning. The bow window faced west, and so was shaded from the glare of the sun. The casements stood invitingly open to the warm, scent-laden air, which streamed gently in over the fragrant masses of colour in the flower beds without. The faint hum of honey-seeking insects fell soothingly and companionably on the ear. Now and then a sudden crescendo marked the swift passage of a bee, busily intent on its own affairs, while butterflies flitted aimlessly by with erratic, dancing movements. Beyond the garden a meadow stretched down to the river, in which cattle, immersed to the knees, stood motionless, enjoying the cool of the water. The surface of the reach was still and unruffled, and reflected as in a mirror the tree-covered slopes of the opposite bank. Restful and pleasant was the prospect without, and within, the whole atmosphere of the room breathed an equal contentment and peace.

And no less pleasant and restful to the eye was the figure of the girl at the desk. Though hardly anyone would have called her beautiful, she had what was of much greater importance—that elusive indefinable quality called charm. There was charm in her graceful movements, in the steady glance of her dark, lustrous eyes, in the ready smile which lit up her expressive face, and in the low, mellow tones of her musical voice. She bent over her task, working rapidly, carrying out the business of the moment as she did everything she undertook, quietly, unobtrusively, and efficiently.

She had lived what most girls of her age would have called a dull and pleasure-less life. Her mother, who had been the brains and the manager of the household, had died when she was fifteen, leaving the care of her kindly, idealistic, impractical father and her pretty, inconsequent younger sister on her hands. Almost unconsciously she had shouldered the burden, but a very real burden she soon found it. Though they lived comfortably, even well, they were far from being well off; indeed, before long the chronic strain of making ends meet became to her a veritable nightmare. But she carried on bravely with a smiling face, entirely forgetful of her own pleasure. If only her father could be spared worry, and her sister have as good an education and as much amusement as could be extracted from their circumstances. But if the strain had made her self-reliant and dependable, it had also somewhat aged her and given her a seriousness beyond her years. She had, however, her reward in the way her father, now a rapidly ageing man, idolised and leant on her, and in the exuberant affection of her sister.

She had on this bright summer morning just completed her accounts, having

82

with characteristic thoroughness at last run to earth a fugitive fivepence which for a considerable time had avoided capture. She was putting away her books when the elderly general servant brought in a note. It was addressed in Austin Ponson's square, masculine hand. With a sudden irrational feeling of foreboding she waited till the woman had left the room, then tore it open, and with a clutching at the heart read:

21st July.

'DEAR LOIS: I am writing this by the courtesy of Inspector Tanner of Scotland Yard, though he has warned me he will have to read it before sending it on. He tells me that some evidence has been received which throws suspicion of my father's murder on me, and that he is bound to arrest me. I do not yet know the details. This is just to say, dearest, that of course I see that under the circumstances there can be no question of an engagement between us. I will live in hope that if this trouble passes over, you will perhaps allow me once again to plead my cause, but if this should be good-bye, I can only say I am innocent of this awful charge, and beg you to think as kindly of me as you can.

'Always yours devotedly,

AUSTIN PONSON.'

For several minutes Lois Drew sat motionless, her white face hard and set, her horror-stricken eyes fastened on the fateful words. So the blow had fallen at last —the terrible blow that ever since the Inspector's visit she had feared day and night. Since the tragedy it had been as if some Dread Shade lurked, for the moment indeed in the background, but ready at any minute to step forward and intrude its baleful presence into Austin's life and hers. For never for a moment had it occurred to her to break off the engagement, and now, though Austin had written of its cancellation as an obvious and indeed an accomplished fact, she never really allowed her mind to harbour the idea. Had she not promised to marry him? Very well, that was enough. If he had wanted her when all things were well, would he not want her tenfold now when trouble had come? But though she did not seriously consider his proposal, subconsciously she was pleased that he had made it so promptly. And she did not resent the cold tone of his note. She realised his feelings were sacred to him. Neither he nor she could have them weighed and sifted by an Inspector of police.

As she sat, motionless in body and almost numb in mind, waiting unconsciously till the first rude shock should have somewhat passed over, she tried to consider the matter dispassionately. She knew that many persons arrested on suspicion were afterwards set at liberty, the charge against them breaking down on further investigation, and that of those actually brought to trial, a respectable percentage were acquitted. But she also knew that in a case like the present Scotland Yard would not order an arrest unless there were pretty strong grounds to go on. And this was particularly so where the accused had been under suspicion for some time, as she guessed from Tanner's visit to herself Austin had been. But she was a good friend. In all her cogitations never once did the possibility of her lover's guilt enter her thoughts. Of his innocence she was as certain as of her own existence.

As time passed, her mind became clearer, and her practical common sense reasserted itself. What, she wondered, was she to do? She was so ignorant of the law, so unversed in its usages, so unaware of its possibilities. But she felt one thing demanded her immediate care. That impossible idea of breaking the engagement must be put out of Austin's head without further delay. He must not be allowed to think for one moment that his trouble could make any difference to her. He must be made to feel she was not leaving him in the lurch.

But how was she to communicate with him?

She did not know whether he would be allowed to receive letters, but she fancied not. At all events there might be a delay in their delivery. She thought for a few moments, and then she took a sheet of paper and wrote as follows:

'DEAR MR TANNER: I have received the letter from Mr Ponson which you were good enough to permit him to write and I wish to convey to you my grateful thanks for your consideration. In case it should be contrary to the rules for him to receive my reply direct, I write to ask whether you could possibly see your way to convey to him this message—first, that I will not hear of our engagement being broken off; on the contrary, I am going to announce it immediately, and second, that though I know it is unnecessary to assure him of my absolute belief in him and in his innocence, I still wish to do so in the strongest manner possible.

'I thought you were exceedingly kind on the day you called here, and I am sure that if you can do me this great favour you will.

'Yours sincerely,

'LOIS DREW.'

She addressed the envelope to 'Inspector Tanner, Criminal Investigation Department, New Scotland Yard, London', marking it 'Personal'. Then putting on her hat, she walked quickly to the post office and dropped the letter into the receiver. She thought that many of the passers-by looked at her curiously, but she was too much absorbed in her own thoughts to care.

As she turned homewards it suddenly occurred to her that her cousin Jimmy might help her. Mr James Daunt was junior partner of a London firm of solicitors, a clever, and she believed, a rising man, and who would have all the knowledge of the possibilities of the case which she lacked. Moreover, Jimmy was a decent soul, and a good friend of her own. They had seen a lot of each other as children, and she felt he would help her if he could.

She turned into the local telephone office and put through a call. Mr James Daunt was in his office. If she came to town he could see her at five o'clock.

She travelled up by the 3.30 train, and at the hour named mounted the steps of the old house in Lincoln's Inn. She was soon in her cousin's room.

'Hallo old girl!' he greeted her when the door had closed. 'Jolly to see you. It's not often you take pity on a lonely old bachelor like this. Sit down, won't you?'

She sank back into a deep, leather-lined arm-chair. They talked commonplaces for a few moments, and then Lois referred to the object of her call. She found it much harder to begin than she had expected, but when her cousin understood she was really in trouble he dropped his somewhat breezy manner and became serious and sympathetic.

'Have you had tea?' he asked, interrupting her story.

'Not yet. I came direct from the station.'

'Then not a word till you've had it,' he declared. 'Come out to a quiet little place I know. We can talk there without interruption.'

Though she had not realised it, Lois was almost fainting for food. She had not eaten any lunch, and now the hot stimulant and the fresh rolls and butter did her more good than she could have thought possible. She smiled across at him.

'I believe I was dying of hunger,' she announced.

'Just like you,' he retorted, 'at your old games again. Always thinking of somebody else, and forgetting your own much more important self.'

'Well, you've probably saved my life. And now, Jimmy, I do want your help.'

'I know, old girl. I don't need to tell you I'll do everything I can. Just start in and let's have the whole story. You don't mind if I smoke?'

'Of course not. The first thing I have to tell you is—that I have become engaged to be married.'

'By Jove, you have!' cried Jimmy, jumping up and holding out his hand. 'I hadn't an inkling there was anything in the wind. Best possible congratulations, old girl. I think a cousinly salutation—' they were alone in an alcove, and he kissed her lightly on the cheek. 'And who's the lucky man, if it's not a secret?'

'Ah, there's no luck in it, Jimmy. That's what I've come about. It's Austin Ponson.'

'Austin Ponson? How do you mean no luck? Why, dear girl, I congratulate you again. I have heard of him, and always that he was a white man through and through.'

Tears trembled on Lois's long eyelashes. It took all her strength of will to speak in her normal tone.

'Dear Jimmy, you can't think what it means to me to hear you say that. You evidently don't know what has happened. He's in frightful trouble.'

Jimmy looked his question.

'He's just been arrested on the charge'—Lois's lip quivered in spite of herself—'of murdering his father.'

Her cousin whistled.

'Good Lord!' he cried, 'you don't say so? Poor old girl.'

'It's terrible. Oh, Jimmy, what are we to do?'

'It's damnable. But you musn't be downhearted. Many and many a man has been arrested for a crime he has known nothing about. Don't get upset till we're sure there is something to be upset about. Tell me the details.'

She told him all she knew; of Austin's visit at eleven on the fatal night, of the hoax that had been played on him, of their learning of Sir William's disappearance

85

the next day, of the inquest and its adjournment, of Tanner's visit to her, of the adjourned inquest, and of Austin's note, and her reply to it. He listened in silence till she had finished.

'And you have no idea what this new evidence is?' he asked at last.

'None whatever.'

'Our first step will be to find that out. I think I can do that. Then if you give me authority to act for you, I'll see him and hear what he has to say about it. That would probably be the quickest way to learn our defence.'

'Could I see him, Jimmy?'

Her cousin hesitated.

'I hardly think so,' he said slowly, 'at present. Later on if the case really goes to trial there should be no difficulty. Just for the immediate present I shouldn't make a move. You have done enough for him, writing that letter to the Inspector.'

Lois looked at him searchingly.

'Don't try to keep me away from him, Jimmy,' she pleaded.

'Of course not. But it would be difficult for you to get an order, and you better wait till we see how things go on. You probably wouldn't get two orders under any circumstances.'

'If you keep me from him, I'll never forgive you.'

'Dear girl, don't get notions. I wouldn't attempt it. But we're hardly so far on as that yet. There is his family to consider. Have you seen them?'

'No. Why should I?'

'Just that if they're going to undertake the defence I don't quite see where we come in. But we'll find that out.' He paused and then went on: 'Now, old girl, you've come to me for professional advice and you're going to get it. Don't think I'm trying to keep you away from Austin Ponson, but my advice to you is, don't make any announcement of your engagement for a day or two yet. You will only distract and worry Ponson, and you won't do any good. The thing to concentrate on is to get him out of the hands of the police. He'll want all his wits to help with that. He knows you're not going to drop him, and that will be enough to comfort him. Take my advice, Lois, and let things alone for the present.'

'But how can I see him or do anything for him if the engagement is not known?'

'What could you do if it was?'

'Well, I could at least take my share of arranging for his defence.'

'Aren't you doing that now? What more do you think you could do?'

'But how can you approach the family, acting for me, if it's not known that we're engaged?'

'Perfectly simply. I'll see him, explain the facts, and get *him* to employ me. That will give me ten times the authority that you could, and it will leave his mind at rest about you. Believe me, Lois, that's the thing to be done.'

'Oh, Jimmy, if you'll do that it would make just all the difference. How good you are!'

'Rubbish. But remember you've got to do your part—to sit tight and say nothing. I'll see all these people and arrange matters.'

'But you'll let me know how you get on?'

'Sure. I'll keep nothing back from you.'

He asked her some more questions, finally seeing her to St Pancras and putting her into the Halford train.

'By Jove,' he soliloquised as he left the station, 'here's a mess! Whatever happens'—he swore great oaths under his breath—'Lois must be kept out of it. As decent a girl as lives! That's the way with these extra good women—they *will* throw themselves away on rotters of all kinds. Heavens, what an idea! To announce an engagement with a man arrested for murder! And now first of all to nip that madness in the bud—*if* possible.' He hailed a taxi and was driven to Scotland Yard.

'Is Inspector Tanner in?' he asked. 'Private business.'

Tanner, it appeared, was just going home, but had not yet left. He returned to his room.

'My name,' began Jimmy, 'is Daunt—James Daunt, junior partner of Willington, Daunt & Daunt, Solicitors, of Lincoln's Inn.'

Tanner bowed.

'I know your firm, sir,' he said quietly.

'I called on behalf of my cousin, Miss Lois Drew, of Halford. You can no doubt guess my business?'

'You are going to act for Mr Ponson?'

'Not quite. At least I am not sure. It is my cousin I am really interested in. I want to ask your help, Mr Tanner. My cousin, who is a little—well, fond of her own way, has written you a letter, a compromising letter, one which should never have been written. You probably haven't received it yet, but in it she asks you to inform Mr Ponson that she holds him to the engagement that they had just fixed up, and is going to announce it at once. Now, Mr Tanner, you will see that this is quixotic and absurd, and it musn't be allowed. I have succeeded in getting her to promise to say nothing for the present, and what I want to ask you is to be so good as to respect her confidence, and keep her name out of it.'

Tanner looked somewhat distressed.

'I should be only too glad,' he answered, 'to do as you say, especially as I so greatly respected and admired what I saw of Miss Drew, if only it were possible. But I fear it won't be. I am afraid the engagement will be an integral part of the Crown case. But I may say that I shall not use Miss Drew's letter. Both she herself and Mr Ponson told me of the engagement.'

'You don't say so? And have you mentioned it to anyone else?'

'Only to my chief.'

'Well, you know the case against Mr Ponson, and I don't. I can only ask that you don't make the fact public until it is absolutely necessary.'

'That I will promise you with pleasure.'

'I am very grateful. And now there is another thing,' and Jimmy explained that he wanted to see Austin, and for what reason.

'I shall certainly raise no objection,' Tanner answered, 'but I'm afraid your application will have to go through the usual channel.'

'Of course. When is he to be brought before the magistrate?'

'Tomorrow at eleven.'

Two hours later the door of Austin's cell opened to admit the junior partner of Messrs Willington, Daunt & Daunt. Austin was sitting with his head on his hands and an expression of deep gloom on his face, but he rose with a look of inquiry as Jimmy entered.

'Mr Ponson?' said the latter as he introduced himself. 'I come on rather delicate business. It is on behalf of my cousin, Miss Lois Drew,' and he told of the interview which he had just had. Austin was much moved.

'God bless her!' he cried hoarsely. 'Isn't it unbelievable, even for her! But it must be stopped, Mr Daunt, at all costs it must be stopped. Her name must be kept out of it no matter what happens.'

Jimmy did not repeat what Tanner had told him.

'I'm glad you agree, Mr Ponson,' he said. 'Now another point. May I ask who is acting for you in this matter?'

Austin passed his hand, wearily over his forehead.

'I'm afraid I haven't arranged anything yet. You see, I only arrived here a few hours ago.'

'But who is your usual man of business?'

'Any little thing I have wanted done up to the present I have taken to Mr Hopkins, of Halford, and he was present at the adjourned inquest on my behalf. He is as straight as a die, but he is elderly, and I dare say out of date. I'm afraid he wouldn't be much use at this kind of thing. Wills and deeds are more in his line. I wonder, Mr Daunt, if I asked you to take it on would it draw attention to Lois?'

'It's rather a delicate matter as it looks like cadging for business, but for Lois's sake I should be glad to act for you. As for dragging in her name, I don't think half a dozen people in the world know we are cousins, and at Halford probably no one. Besides, you would not employ me, but the firm.'

'Then I do employ your firm—if you will be good enough to act. What is the first step?'

'The first legal step is to be present in court on your behalf tomorrow. Then I shall get hold of the case against you, after which we will put our heads together over your defence. But there is also your own family to consider. Have you any near relatives other than your mother, sister, and cousin?'

'None.'

'I presume you would like me to take them into our confidence?'

Austin agreed and they discussed the matter further, arranging terms and other details.

'Now, Mr Ponson,' said Jimmy when these were settled, 'I have to give you a very solemn warning. Your very life may depend on how you heed it. It is this. You must tell me the truth. I don't mean refrain from falsehood only, but tell me everything—*everything* you know. It is only fair to say that if you hold anything back I can no longer help you, and you may be signing your own death warrant. Do you realise that?'

'I certainly do. You need not be afraid. I'll be only too thankful to tell you. Now ask your questions.'

'You forget I know nothing of the case as yet. Just tell me the whole business from beginning to end and with all the details you can.'

Austin sat motionless for a moment as if collecting his thoughts, then, settling himself more comfortably, he began to speak.

He opened by explaining his relations with his father, and his mode of life in Halford, and then described his friendship with Lois Drew, culminating in his proposal and the engagement. He told of the note he had received on that fatal Wednesday evening, his taking the boat to the Old Ferry, the self-styled servant of Mrs Franklyn, her message, his walk to the Abbey, his visit to the Franklyns' house, and his call at the Drews. Then he recounted the circumstances of Sir William's death, the call from Innes, the inquiries at Dr Graham's, the search for and discovery of the body, the subsequent inquest, the interview with Tanner, the latter's questions, and the demand for the shoes, and finally, the medical evidence at the adjourned inquest, and his arrest. He stated he had no idea what the discovery was which led to this culmination.

It was clear to Jimmy Daunt that he must hear Tanner's side of it before he knew where they stood. Nothing more could be done that night. He therefore told his new client to keep his heart up, took his leave and went home.

The proceedings next morning were purely formal, evidence of arrest only being given. Austin was remanded for a week, bail being refused.

Daunt made it his business to see Lady Ponson, Enid, and Cosgrove, all of whom expressed themselves as being heartily in agreement with Austin's selection of advice. It was decided that if the case went on to trial, Sir Mortimer Byecroft, K.C., one of the most eminent criminal experts at the bar, should be retained for the defence.

When Daunt received the depositions of the crown witnesses, he saw at a glance that he was up against something very much stiffer than he had anticipated. The motive suggested for the crime was horribly adequate. In the face of Austin's story of his visit to the Abbey ruins, the evidence of Lucy Penrose and young Potts was almost overwhelmingly damaging. But when Daunt read of the purchase of the two identical pairs of shoes, and grasped the theory of the faked alibi which this seemed to support he was genuinely aghast. 'Heavens!' he thought, 'if the fellow hasn't an explanation of this, he's as guilty as sin!'

Accordingly, Daunt lost no time in again seeing his client, and at his interview he did not mince matters.

'Look here, Mr Ponson,' he said. 'There are two bad bits of evidence against you and I want to hear what you have to say about them. About 9.30 that night you tell me you were half-way to the Abbey. Is that so?'

'Certainly. I was on the path between the Abbey and the road.'

Daunt leant forward and watched the other keenly, as he spoke slowly and deliberately.

'Then how do you account for the fact that you were seen rowing a boat up to the Luce Manor boathouse at just that hour?'

Austin Ponson started and his face grew dead white. He sat motionless for several seconds gazing with terrified eyes, at his questioner, and apparently unable to speak.

'What's that you say?' he gasped at last, licking his dry lips. 'Impossible! I—I wasn't there.' He dropped his head into his hands while the sweat stood in drops on his forehead. Daunt waited silently. His doubts were becoming confirmed. The man surely was guilty.

Presently Austin raised his head.

'This is awful news,' he said hoarsely. 'I can only say I wasn't there. I swear it. There is a mistake. There must be. Who is supposed to have seen me? And from where?'

In Daunt's opinion the answer was unconvincing. The man's manner was shifty. Unless Jimmy was greatly mistaken he was lying. He replied somewhat coldly:

'Two people in Dr Graham's wood at the other side of the river are prepared to swear to it.'

'Two?' Austin groaned. 'My God! How can they? They must have seen someone else, and mistaken him for me.'

'Suppose it was proved there was no other boat down the river that night but yours. What will you say then?'

'What can I say? I don't understand it. That could not be proved—unless someone took my boat from the Old Ferry.' He sat up eagerly and a gleam came into his eye. 'Could that be it, Mr Daunt? Could whoever worked the trick on me have been watching at the Old Ferry, and have taken my boat when I went ashore? What do you think?'

This was an idea which had not occurred to Daunt, and he instantly saw that it might account for the whole thing. Suppose the real murderer, knowing of Austin's financial relations with his father, had seen how that fact could be used as the basis of a case against the son, and had added details to strengthen it. Suppose he had forged notes, getting Austin to bring a boat to the Old Ferry, and, leaving it there, go to the Abbey. Meanwhile he himself, made up to represent Austin, might have taken the boat to the boathouse, committed the murder and returned the boat to the Old Ferry before Austin arrived back? Daunt felt that this was a possibility which must not be overlooked. It might at any rate be a line of defence.

Then he remembered the shoes. No. If Austin had deliberately made a fake with the shoes, he must be guilty. He spoke again.

'Unfortunately, there is another very serious point. Your alibi depends on the fact that the prints made at the Abbey were made by shoes which it can be proved you were wearing on that Wednesday night and at no other time. Isn't that so?'

'That is so.'

'How many pairs of that kind of shoe had you?'

'One pair.'

'Then how do you explain the fact that you bought two pairs on the Monday before the murder?'

This time Austin showed no signs of embarrassment.

'I bought two—yes,' he answered readily, 'but I only brought one home. I lost the other.'

'Lost the other? Just how?'

'Very simply. I went that Monday to Hunt's shoe shop in Piccadilly and there I bought a pair of shoes. I had them carefully fitted, and was pleased with them. The shop-man gave me a card with their number, in case I should want to replace them. I took them with me, as I was hurrying to catch the 3.25 train from St Pancras. I had to call at a shop in Regent Street, and I walked there. But as I stepped off the footpath to cross the street, a lorry I hadn't seen came quickly up, and I had to jump back out of its way. I was startled, and I unfortunately dropped the shoes. As luck would have it they were run over by the lorry. A hawker picked them up and returned them, but one was badly torn, so, as they were no further use to me, I made him a present of them. That left me without any, so I decided to replace them. I noticed another of Messrs Hunt's shops close by, and I went in and asked for shoes of the number on the card. That saved me from a troublesome refitting. By the time my purchase was complete I was late for my train. I therefore waited till the 5.15. Does that make the matter clear?'

Daunt was relieved, but somewhat puzzled by what he had heard. Unquestionably, Austin's explanation was plausible, and he could see no reason why it should not be true. If the hawker who got the shoes could be found it would set this part of the matter at rest, but Daunt feared he would be untraceable. He felt doubtful and dissatisfied in his mind about the whole affair, but he saw that Austin's statements provided a line of defence, though whether the best available he was not yet certain.

Still turning the idea over in his mind he went down the next Saturday to Halford, to spend, on the earnest invitation of Lois, the weekend with the Drews.

Chapter 10
A Woman's Wit

After dinner on that Saturday evening, Lois Drew had a long conversation with her cousin, James Daunt. She waited until he was seated in the most comfortable chair in the drawing-room with his cigar well under way, and then she spoke of the subject next her heart.

'Tell me, Jimmy,' she begged, 'just what you *really* think. I want to understand exactly what we have to meet.'

He told her. Directly and without any attempt to gloss over the uglier facts, he told her all he knew. She listened in silence for the most part, but occasionally interjected shrewd, pertinent questions. Jimmy, who knew and respected his cousin's intellect, yet marvelled at her grip, her power of letting go irrelevant details, and the unhesitating way in which she went straight to the essential heart of the various points. When he had finished she remained silent for a considerable time.

'It seems to me then,' she said at last, 'that Austin's suggestion must be the truth—that the murderer forged the notes purporting to be from me, and which brought Austin to the Abbey that night, that he waited for Austin's arrival at the Old Ferry, that either he had an accomplice there or he himself was disguised as Mrs Franklyn's servant, that on Austin's leaving for the Abbey he made himself up to look like Austin, that he rowed to the boathouse, committed the murder, and returned the boat to the Old Ferry before Austin got back. What do you think, Jimmy?'

'It seems a possible defence.'

'It seems more than that; it seems to be what happened. If so, let us consider what that teaches us about the murderer. Several things, I think. Tell me if I go wrong. Firstly, he must have had a strong motive for Sir William's death. Secondly, he must have known all about the family—Sir William's habits, the lie of Luce Manor, the household arrangements, and that sort of thing. Thirdly, he must have been acquainted with Austin, and *his* house and habits, and fourthly, he must not only have been aware of my existence and friendship with Austin, but he must have had my handwriting to copy. Surely there can't be many persons in the world to whom all these conditions apply?'

'One would say not,' Daunt returned slowly. 'It's very unfortunate, of course, but you must see how the prosecution will use all these points you bring up— every one of them can be turned against Austin.'

'I know, but that's only wasting time. The fact that Austin's innocence rules him out surely makes the search for the real murderer easier?'

'Why, that is so, I suppose.' Daunt tried to make his voice cheery and sanguine.

'Very well. I came to that conclusion days ago. Now Jimmy, it's a horrible thing to say, but who is the only other person we know of that fits the conditions?'

Daunt looked up swiftly. It was suddenly evident to him that Lois was speaking with a more direct object than he had thought.

'I don't know, Lois,' he answered. 'Who?'

'Who but the cousin—Mr Cosgrove Ponson?'

'Good Heavens! That never occurred to me. But does he fill the bill?'

'I have thought so for some time, but it's a matter for you to find out. But just consider. Mr Cosgrove benefits by the will—Austin told me so. He knew Sir William and all about Luce Manor; he knew Austin and all about *him*; he was like Austin in appearance; and lastly he knew me—he has dined here with Austin.'

'Your handwriting?'

'I wrote to thank him for sending me the name of an English *pension* at Cannes—a friend of mine wanted to know.'

'When was that?'

'About two months ago.'

'Seems rather a long time. And when did he dine?'

'About a week before that. I happened to mention about the *pension*, and he said he had some addresses and would look them up.'

'And what kind of man is he personally?'

Lois did not reply for some moments.

'That's hardly a fair question,' she said at last. 'I have to admit taking a dislike to him. But it's not a question of my likes or dislikes. I think it is essential that you should find out something about him. Find out where he was on that Wednesday evening.'

Daunt smoked in silence. He was thinking that if Austin were out of the way as well as Sir William, Cosgrove's gains would not improbably be considerably increased. There might be something in this idea of Lois's after all. A few inquiries would do no harm at any rate.

'Well,' he said at last, 'I'll do as you say. I'll find out something about him.'

They continued the discussion, and it was arranged that as soon as any information was forthcoming, Lois would go to town, and they would have another talk.

As Sir William Ponson's will was to be one of the factors in the Crown case, Daunt had no difficulty in obtaining a copy. That, and a few judicious inquiries convinced him of the importance of Lois's suggestion. There seemed no question that Cosgrove's motive for the deed was at least as strong as Austin's.

For some time Daunt puzzled over the best way to get hold of his information. Then it occurred to him that so wideawake an official as an Inspector of Scotland Yard would certainly have foreseen and considered all that he and Lois had discussed. As Cosgrove had not been arrested, there must be some flaw in the case he was trying to make. He decided to see Tanner once more, in the hope of gaining some information.

With a man like Tanner there was nothing to be gained by any but the most direct methods. Daunt could ask for what he wanted, and either get it or be refused, but he felt he could not obtain it by a trick. To try his luck he called at the Yard and inquired for the Inspector.

'I want to get some information, Mr Tanner,' he said, when they had conversed for a few moments. 'I'm going to ask you for it in confidence, but you may not consider it proper to give it to me, and if so, there is of course no more to be said. It's not directly about the case.'

'What is it, sir?'

'It's this. In going into this matter it has struck me that the nephew, Cosgrove Ponson, had as much to gain by his uncle's death as the accused. It is obvious that that must have struck you also. I wondered if you would tell me why you acquitted him in your mind?'

'Now don't you get astray on that notion, Mr Daunt. It won't wash. I went into that, and I may tell you for your private information Cosgrove is as innocent as you are.'

'So I gathered from your action, in the matter, but if you could see your way to give me particulars, I should be greatly obliged. You see, it's Miss Drew. She's got it into her head Cosgrove was the man, and I'd like to be able to clear the thing up to her.'

Tanner thought for some moments.

'I'd like to oblige both you and Miss Drew,' he said, 'but I'm not just sure that I ought. However, as you say, it's not exactly on the case, and if you give me your word to keep the thing to yourself I'll tell you.'

'I promise most gratefully.'

'Very well. The man has an alibi,' and Tanner repeated Cosgrove's story of the visit to Montrose, the missing of the 7.15, the return to his rooms, the call at the theatre on Miss Belcher, and the final journey north by the 10.30. Then he explained how he had checked Cosgrove's statements, and produced his calculation of times and distances, showing that Cosgrove could not have motored to Luce Manor.

To Daunt the whole thing seemed utterly conclusive. Apart from the mere fact that it had satisfied Tanner—no mean test—he could not himself see any possibility of a flaw. With considerable apprehension of the disappointment Lois would feel, he telephoned to her and arranged their consultation for that evening.

She heard his story almost in silence. But she did not show the chagrin he expected.

'If the thing was obvious,' she said in answer to his comment, 'Cosgrove would have been arrested and not Austin. But I feel absolutely certain that that alibi of Cosgrove's is a fraud. He has tricked Inspector Tanner. How he has done it is what you've got to find out.'

'My dear girl,' Daunt remonstrated, 'it's all very well to talk like that, and I'll do my best of course, but you know, if Tanner with all his opportunities was taken in, it's not too likely I shall find the flaw.'

'It's quite likely,' she declared. 'Inspector Tanner was not specially looking for a flaw; you are. Don't you see—there must be a flaw. Look at it like this. A man resembling Austin was met by Sir William at the boathouse on that Wednesday night. It *must* have been Cosgrove, because no one else is sufficiently like Austin to be mistaken for him. No kind of facial make-up will meet the case, because Sir William himself evidently was satisfied. Therefore Cosgrove's alibi must be false. Don't you agree with me?'

'It seems reasonable,' Jimmy admitted. 'But the alibi certainly looks right enough too.'

'I admit that. It may be so good that we'll never find the flaw. But we must try. Oh, Jimmy,' she turned to him beseechingly, 'remember what is at stake—his life —both our lives. You will try, won't you?'

'Of course I'll try, and what's more, I expect to succeed,' Jimmy lied bravely. And he spoke in the same confident tone as, after dinner, he went to the station with her, and saw her off by the 9.30 to Halford. But his secret feelings were very different.

Two days later he had another call from Lois.

'You needn't be frightened,' she smiled at him; 'I am not going to haunt the office and make your life a burden to you. But I have been thinking over our problem. I want you, Jimmy, to begin an investigation. Will you?

'Why certainly, if I can. What is it?'

'If you haven't time yourself, and I don't expect you will have, employ a private detective. But get a good man who will do the work thoroughly.'

'Yes, yes. But what exactly is to be done?'

'This. The evidence seems to me overwhelming that Mr Cosgrove missed the 7.15 at King's Cross on that Wednesday night, and went to Montrose by the 10.30. But what did he do in between?'

Daunt was puzzled.

'I don't understand,' he said. 'We have the butler's and Miss Belcher's evidence to corroborate Cosgrove's own story there. I don't see that we can reasonably doubt he did what he said.'

'Don't you? But I do. Probably both these people were interested. Miss Belcher we know was—she was on too friendly terms not to be. And the butler may have been well paid to tell his story. Another thing makes me doubt Miss Belcher. You remember the conversation Mr Tanner overheard between her and Mr Cosgrove in the restaurant? They mentioned an alibi. Mr Tanner thought they were talking about Austin. I don't believe it. It was Mr Cosgrove's own alibi they were discussing. What do you think?'

'It's possible, of course,' Daunt answered slowly, 'but I question if we can be sure of it.' He began to think Lois had got an obsession.

'Well, whether or not is immaterial. What matters is that Mr Cosgrove's whereabouts after 7.30 has not been proved.'

'But you forget Tanner's time table. Cosgrove wouldn't have had time to go to Luce Manor between the trains.'

'Yes!' cried Lois excitedly, 'he would! That's the point I've been coming to. According to Mr Tanner's calculations he would have had time or almost time, to go to Luce Manor and back, but he wouldn't have had time to commit the murder. But Mr Tanner assumed he had first driven to his rooms. If he had gone direct from

King's Cross he would have had time for all.'

This was a new idea to Daunt, and he had to admit its possibility.

'It may be so certainly,' he answered, 'but how are we to prove it? That butler won't give himself away if he has lied.'

'I've thought of that, too, and there seems to be one way we might get at it. Mr Cosgrove said he took three drives during that time—first, from King's Cross to Knightsbridge; second, from Knightsbridge to the Empire; and third, from the Follies', to King's Cross. Could we not find the cabmen, or at least one of them?'

'By Jove, Lois, you should have been a detective,' Daunt said with half-unwilling admiration. 'I believe it's a good notion.'

'You see, if we were to search for these men thoroughly and fail to find them, it would greatly strengthen my theory. On the other hand, if we found them we would be sure of what we are up against, for if Mr Cosgrove took any one of the drives, his statement must be true. Will you try to find them, Jimmy? Or'—her eyes brightened eagerly—'let's do it together. Would you mind?

'Mind?' he echoed. 'Dear girl, what do you take me for? I'm ready to begin now—in collaboration with you, that is.'

'Dear Jimmy, you are so good. I can never thank you enough.'

'What utter rubbish. Now let's get to work. Have you made any plans?'

'I thought perhaps we could get lists from the taxi companies of the men on the various stands. Then I thought we could see all those on the stands nearest the three starting points. If it was none of these could we not send a letter to each driver in London—get some office supplies place to do it, you know? If this failed we might try newspaper advertisements.'

'Excellent. We could get the lists of the men through Tanner, if he would give them. I'll ring him up now.'

Inspector Tanner was at the Yard. On Daunt satisfying him as to the reason of the demand, he promised to have the information looked up and supplied.

The next day the lists came and the cousins set off to commence their investigations. They saw a number of the men on the stands in question, others at the depots and still others at their homes. After three strenuous days they had gone over them all. But they learnt nothing. None of the men had driven Cosgrove.

'It's hopeful,' Lois announced as they dined together that evening, 'but we must now try the circular.'

They drafted a letter offering a reward of £5 for information as to the identity of the man who had driven a fare answering to Cosgrove's description on any of the three trips in question. With this Daunt called to see Tanner on the following morning. He told him what they had done, and what they proposed, and asked for a complete list of the taxi and cab-drivers of London. Tanner, nothing loath to have his own conclusions verified, had the information made out. Then Daunt went to an office supplies firm in New Oxford Street, and arranged for a circular to be sent to each man on the list—several thousand.

Two days passed and there was no answer, but on the third day a taxi-driver giving his name as John Hoskins called at Daunt's office. Jimmy saw him at once.

'It was abaht this 'ere letter,' said the man. 'I guess I'm the man you want.'

'Yes? You drove a fare on one of those trips on that Wednesday evening?'

'Yes, sir. I were just passing out of King's Cross after setting down a lady and gent, when the gent 'e hails me, "Engaged?" 'e asks. "No, sir," I says. "174B Knightsbridge," 'e says. I drove 'im there, and that's all I knows abaht it.'

Daunt opened a drawer and took out half a dozen cabinet photographs, which, in unconscious imitation of Tanner, he had procured. One was of Cosgrove, the others of men as like Cosgrove as Jimmy could find.

'Is the man you drove among those?' he asked, handing them over.

The driver glanced over them and unhesitatingly picked out Cosgrove's.

'That's 'im, mister,' he said decisively.

'And what time did you pick him up?'

'Abaht 7.30. I left 'im in Knightsbridge at a quarter to eight.'

'That's all right, my man. It's what I wanted to know. If you give me your name and address I'll give you the five pounds.'

Jimmy telegraphed the news to Lois at Halford, using for the benefit of the postal officials a code on which they had previously agreed. The information, he feared, would be a heavy blow to her. She had so confidently made up her mind that Cosgrove was the guilty man, and here was proof—to Daunt it seemed final and conclusive proof—of his innocence. Even Lois herself had admitted that if Cosgrove had indeed returned to his rooms after leaving King's Cross, it would have been impossible for him to have visited Luce Manor—times and distances made that certain. Miss Belcher's confirmation of his visit to the Follies, and the discovery of the other two taxi drivers were therefore not required. As matters stood, Cosgrove's innocence was demonstrated.

So Daunt reasoned, but not so Lois Drew. As she tossed sleepless on her bed that night she racked her brains for some flaw in the case, some loophole that might save her lover. But the more she thought it over, the more hopeless it seemed. As dawn brightened slowly into day she had to admit herself beaten. And then, just as a delightful drowsiness began to creep over her restless, wearied body, an idea flashed into her mind. She remained motionless, hardly daring to breathe as its full significance gradually dawned upon her. When it did so all chance of sleep vanished. Her eyes became very bright, and she laughed contentedly to herself.

She travelled to town by an early train and was in Daunt's office soon after it opened. She received his condolences quietly, then startled him by saying demurely:

'I want you to send out another circular to the taxi-men, Jimmy. I have it here.'

The paper she handed him read:

'TEN POUNDS REWARD

'The above reward will be paid to the taxi driver who picked up a fare'—here followed a description of Cosgrove—'about 7.50 on Wednesday evening, 7th July, in or near Knightsbridge, on his identifying the man picked up from a photograph, and saying where he was set down. Apply—'

and here followed Jimmy's address.

'But my dear girl,' the latter objected, 'we have already sent that out, or practically that.'

'Never mind, Jimmy,' she said, with one of the brilliant smiles that lit up her face and made it momentarily beautiful. 'Do this for me, and don't ask questions.' Before he realized what she was going to do, she had kissed him lightly on the forehead, and with a whirl of skirts was gone.

'By Jove!' said Jimmy weakly to himself as the door closed. 'What bee has she got in her bonnet now? At any rate she might have waited and explained.' But he did what he had been asked, and two days later the new circular was in the hands of the taxi-men.

And it bore early fruit. Only a few hours after its distribution there was an answer. A small, sallow, rat-faced man in a peaked cap and leather coat called to see Daunt.

'You think you picked up the man described in the letter?' asked Jimmy, as he produced his six photographs. 'Was he one of these?'

Like his *confrère* of a day or two earlier, the man glanced over the cards and unhesitatingly drew out Cosgrove's portrait.

'That's 'im, mister,' he also said decisively.

'Where exactly did you pick him up?

'In Knightsbridge, not far from Piccadilly.'

'At what time?'

'About ten minutes to eight.'

'And where did you set him down?'

'Over thirty miles away—at a cross-roads away beyond Luton.'

James Daunt sprang excitedly to his feet.

'What?' he roared. 'Where did you say?' Here, surely, was the impossible! All were agreed that Cosgrove could not have made the run in the time, and yet, it now seemed, he had done so. And then the thought of the tremendous consequences of this discovery overwhelmed every other consideration. If Cosgrove had really been to Luce Manor, particularly after his own denial, he must unquestionably be guilty. And if he were guilty, Austin was innocent. Jimmy believed he now held the evidence which would save his client.

He thought rapidly for a few seconds.

'At what hour did you reach this cross-roads?' he asked.

'About quarter-past nine, sir. I remember noticing when I was making up the money.'

And the bogus servant met Austin at the Old Ferry about then! Truly this was a great find!

'Are you engaged within the next hour or two?' Jimmy went on.

'No, sir.'

'Very good. Will you drive me to this cross-roads? I'll make it worth your while.'

They stopped at a post office and Jimmy sent a telegram to Lois asking her to be at the end of the Old Ferry lane at midday. Then the run began.

As the vehicle slipped quickly through the traffic, Daunt chuckled with delight. Though he did not in the least understand how Cosgrove had managed it, it was at least evident that he had visited Luce Manor before taking the 10.30 to Montrose. And that, Daunt felt more than ever certain, meant his guilt and the breakdown of the case against Austin. Though, to do him justice, Jimmy's chief joy was the thought of the happiness this would bring to Lois, yet he was human enough to realise the kudos which must come to him personally from the skilful way he had unravelled the mystery. And yet, had he unravelled it? As he looked back he had to admit that every particle of credit must go to the girl. She it was who had suggested the steps which had led to success—she who had evidently guessed the solution which even now still eluded him.

In about an hour and a half they reached their destination, and Jimmy, who knew the district from his visits to the Drews, saw with satisfaction that the point was where the Halford-London road crossed that which passed over the river bridge above the Cranshaw Falls. From there to the Old Ferry was about ten minutes' smart walk, and, if the taxi-man's statement was correct, Cosgrove could therefore have reached Austin's boat about 9.25. It would take him ten minutes or more to row to the Luce Manor boathouse, so that he would arrive there, say, between 9.30 and 9.40. This was quite sufficiently in accordance with the statement of Lucy Penrose and young Potts that they had seen the boat arriving about half-past nine. Jimmy recognised delightedly that the whole thing was working in.

It was still about quarter to twelve, and Jimmy had the taxi run slowly on to the Old Ferry lane. Lois was already there, and he lost no time in putting her in possession of the facts.

'You guessed that this happened?' he queried.

'Yes. I suddenly thought of it in bed, the night before I came up to see you.'

'But I can't make head nor tail of it,' Jimmy confessed. 'Now it seems that Cosgrove must have been at the boathouse between half-past nine and ten, and yet he caught the 10.30 from King's Cross, where he couldn't have arrived till at least 11.30. The thing's an absolute puzzle to me. Can you see light?'

'Of course. He never caught the 10.30 at all.'

'But, my dear girl, he did—he must have. You forget the porter at Grantham and the dealer at Montrose.'

'Not at all. He travelled no doubt by the 10.30 from Grantham to Montrose. But that's a very different thing. I'll tell you, Jimmy, what's puzzling you. You haven't studied your Great Northern time table as I have. The 10.30 is not the only train in the day from London.'

Daunt waited.

'Well?' he said impatiently.

'Before that 10.30, as you might have known from Mr Tanner's story of his own movements, there runs a pick-up train. It leaves King's Cross at 10.00 and reaches Grantham at 12.28, ten minutes before the 10.30. And that train, Jimmy, stops at three or four stations. It stops'—she leant forward and whispered in his ear with an air of triumph—'*it stops at Hitchin at 10.45!*'

'And Hitchin is only six miles from here! Good Heavens, how stupid not to have seen that! Of course that's what he did! After the murder he motored to Hitchin and caught the relief train. Well, Lois, you deserve all you're going to get for thinking of it!'

'But we're not quite out of the wood yet,' the girl reminded him. 'We have to find out how he went from here to Hitchin.'

'Probably by the taxi,' suggested Daunt, and they returned to where the vehicle was waiting.

But his guess was incorrect. The driver assured them that on reaching the cross-roads Cosgrove had paid him off and he had returned at once to London.

'I thought of that first,' said Lois, 'then I thought not, that he would never have let any one man have so much information about his movements. Then I wondered if he wouldn't have arranged for a vehicle from Halford to pick him up, but I saw that wouldn't do either. At last I thought the most obvious and indeed the least suspicious plan would be to engage a car in Hitchin to run out for him. What do you think?'

'I believe you are right. Let's run over to Hitchin now and make inquiries.'

They reached the town in about quarter of an hour. There they paid off their taxi, having noted the man's name and address. Then after a hurried lunch they got to work.

At the first and second garages they drew blank, but at the third they had success. It appeared that late on the Monday evening before the murder, a man, whom the proprietor instantly identified from the photograph as Cosgrove, called and asked for a car to be sent to the same cross-roads near Luce Manor. It was to be there on the following Wednesday evening at 10.15, and was to wait for him and run him into Hitchin. He gave no explanation of his movements, but he turned up at the place a few minutes after the hour named, and was duly brought to Hitchin and set down near the George Hotel. Daunt had the driver sent for, and he stated he had seen his fare's face in the light of a street lamp when he was being paid, and he also unhesitatingly selected Cosgrove's photograph as that of the man.

'How far is it from the George Hotel to the station?' asked Daunt.

'Three minutes' walk, sir.'

Here at last was proof—utter and final proof. As the cousins left the garage Jimmy once more congratulated his companion on her success.

'But we're not finished yet, Jimmy,' she answered him. 'We have to find the woman—the false servant.'

'You think it couldn't have been Cosgrove?

Lois shook her head.

'He could never have deceived Austin. Besides, the hours don't work. Cosgrove could hardly have reached the Old Ferry till after Austin had left. In any case Cosgrove would never have had time to make up so well.'

'I agree with you. Then our next job is, *cherchez la femme*. Have you any ideas as to how we should start?'

'I don't know if you will agree with me,' Lois answered slowly, 'but I wonder if we should not take Mr Tanner into our confidence. He has been very straight and very kind all through, and I'm sure if he knew what we have learned he would take over the finding of the woman.'

'By Jove, Lois, I believe you are right in this as in everything else. I'll go and see him now. Would you care to come too?'

'No. I think you could do that best alone. I'll come to town with you and hear your report.'

They went up by the Great Northern, and Daunt drove to Scotland Yard. Inspector Tanner was out.

'I am the solicitor who is acting for Mr Austin Ponson—you know, the Halford murder—and I bring some very material information about the case. I should like to see someone in authority.'

He was asked to wait and presently was ushered into the presence of Chief Inspector Edgar. This official had followed the case with Tanner, and he heard Daunt's story with thinly veiled amazement.

'It's the most extraordinary case I have come across for many a year,' he exclaimed. 'That makes two suspects, and Tanner's off to Portugal after a third.'

'Good Lord! To Portugal?'

'Yes, with an extradition warrant and all complete. Well, Mr Daunt, I needn't say how grateful we are to you and Miss Drew for what you have done, and you may count on your information receiving the fullest and most careful attention. When Tanner gets back, perhaps you wouldn't mind calling in and having a chat over the matter with him?'

When Jimmy returned to Lois and told her of the Portuguese expedition she was as utterly amazed as he was. But there was no way of satisfying their curiosity, and they had unwillingly to content themselves to wait till Tanner's return.

Chapter 11
A Fresh Start

While Lois Drew and her cousin, James Daunt, were pursuing their researches into the movements of Cosgrove Ponson, Inspector Tanner had been far from idle. We may retrace our steps to the day of Austin's arrest, and follow the detective as he endeavours to complete his case against the accused.

Having reached London with his prisoner, and handed him over to the proper authorities, Tanner returned to the Yard and set to work on a statement of the evidence he was prepared to supply to the Crown Prosecutor.

But the more he considered this evidence, the less satisfied he became with it. Tanner was an ambitious as well as a naturally efficient man, and he hated giving over a case which was not complete in every detail. Here, though the facts he had learned undoubtedly made a powerful arraignment of Austin, they just stopped short of being conclusive. Always there was the possibility of a plant, with the accused as the innocent victim. At all events Tanner was sure a defence on these lines would be attempted, and he was not quite certain that he could meet it.

Another difficulty was his failure to discover the maker of the fifth set of tracks on the river bank. Until this man was identified, and his business there known, the affair would remain unsatisfactory.

Tanner determined he could not rest on his oars, but must continue his inquiries in the hope of making his case overwhelming.

He recalled the fact that he had intended to follow up Sir William Ponson's visits to London in the hope of finding that the latter's business in town had some connection with his death. His attention had been diverted into other channels by the unexpected information given by Lucy Penrose and young Potts of Austin's movements on the night of the murder. But now his mind reverted to the point, and he decided it remained his most promising clue. Without loss of time, therefore, he began to work on it.

He remembered that he had already learnt the trains by which the murdered man had travelled to town. He could thus start with the practical certainty that Sir William had arrived at St Pancras at 11.40 on the Saturday and the Monday before the crime.

By what means would the deceased leave the station? Tanner did not think a man of his position would walk or go by bus or tube. No, as his private car was not available he would take a taxi. 'I must find the man who drove him,' the Inspector thought.

He gave his bell a code ring, and instructed the assistant who answered to undertake the inquiry. From the constables on station duty the numbers of the vehicles which left on the arrival of the train in question could be obtained, and it would be a simple matter to find the drivers and learn by means of a photograph which of them had driven Sir William, and to what point.

But Tanner was by no means sanguine that such an inquiry would bear fruit. He believed that the deceased had not used his own car because he wished to cover his traces. And if so he would probably have avoided taking a taxi at the station. It would have been safer for him to have picked one up in the street outside. Tanner therefore felt he should if possible have another string to his bow. Where could such be found?

A second line of inquiry soon suggested itself. Sir William would not have passed the day without food. If Tanner could find where he lunched, it would give him another point of attack.

The Inspector had learned from Innes his master's usual restaurants, as well as the names of his two clubs. As all these were extremely expensive and exclusive, Tanner felt he might confine his researches to places of the same type.

He began at once. Driving to the first club, he made exhaustive inquiries. Sir William was a well-known figure there, and his death had caused some of the attendants to recall in conversation the occasion of his last visit. But this had been three weeks before the murder. The men were positive he had not been there either the Saturday or Monday in question.

At the second club Tanner received similar information. Here Sir William had not been seen for over two months prior to his death.

The Inspector then began on the restaurants. By the time he had visited the Carlton, the Savoy, and one or two others it was after eight o'clock. He therefore gave up for the night and, going home, busied himself in making out a list of other possible places at which he would inquire on the following day.

Next morning he was early at work. He was very thorough and painstaking, leaving no restaurant till he had interviewed every one who might conceivably help him, from the manager down to the cloakroom attendant. For a long time he had no luck. But at last in the late afternoon, when he had worked half down his list and visited no less than seventeen restaurants, he found what he wanted.

It was a small but expensive French place on the border of Soho, with an unobtrusive exterior, and a quiet, excellent service—a place frequented by a well-to-do but, Tanner somehow imagined, rather disreputable clientele. Here Sir William's photograph received instant recognition.

'But yes, monsieur,' the polite manager assured him. 'I remember this gentleman distinctly. He come here—let me see—about three weeks ago, I think. He come early and he ask for me. He wish a private room and lunch for three. Presently two other gentlemen join him. They lunch. After coffee he give orders that they be not disturbed. They stay there for ver' long time. Then they leave and this gentleman'—the manager tapped the photograph—'he pay for all.'

'Can you tell me what day that was?'

By looking up his records of the hire of the room the manager could. It was Monday the 5th July. Further inquiries elicited the information that Sir William had reached the restaurant about twelve, and had remained till three, when he left with his friends.

'Together?' asked Tanner.

'At the same time, monsieur, yes; but not in company. The old gentleman'—again the manager indicated the photograph—'he drive off in a taxi. The other two walk.'

'Now those other two. Would you kindly describe them.'

As he listened to the manager's reply, the Inspector got a sudden idea. He took from his pocket the half-dozen photographs he had used when tracing Cosgrove's movements, and asked the other if the two friends were among them. The manager glanced over them, then bowed and smiled.

'These are the gentlemen,' he declared, picking out those of Austin and Cosgrove.

Inspector Tanner was greatly surprised at the news. What, he wondered, could have been the business between these three, which was so secret that it could only be discussed in a private room of a somewhat shady foreign restaurant in Soho? Something dark and sinister, he feared. It was evident that all three had desired to keep the meeting a secret. Sir William had taken steps to cover his traces on the journey, and so probably had the other two. At least if they had not, they had practically denied being there. Both Austin and Cosgrove had stated explicitly that they had not seen Sir William on the day in question. Further, it must have been complicated business. Austin had been alone with his father for at least two hours on the previous evening—Tanner recollected that after dinner at Luce Manor on the Sunday the men had not joined the ladies in the drawing-room—and here, the very next day, an interview of three hours had been necessary. Or say two hours, excluding lunch. A lot of business could be put through in two hours. Tanner began to fear the whole affair was deeper and more complicated than he had at first supposed.

He questioned all of the staff who had come in contact with the three men, without result, until he came to the restaurant porter who had called the taxi. Here he had more luck than is usual in such inquiries. The taxi had been taken from a neighbouring rank, and the porter recollected the driver, whom he had called several times previously. He was an elderly, wizened man, clean-shaven and with white hair.

After slipping a coin into the porter's eager hand, Tanner walked to the rank. The driver of the third car answered the description. Tanner accosted him civilly, explaining who he was.

'On Monday the 5th instant, just three weeks ago,' he went on, 'about three in the afternoon, you were hailed by the porter at the Étoile over there. Your fare was this gentleman'—he showed Sir William's photograph. 'Do you remember it?'

The man looked at the card.

'Why yes, sir, I remembers 'im all right.'

'Where did you drive him to?'

'I'm blessed if I can remember the name, sir,' the driver answered slowly, 'It was to a little narrow street back of Gower Street. I 'adn't ever been there before. The old gent, 'e directs me there, and tells me to set 'im down at the corner, and so I does. 'E was standing there when I saw 'im last.'

'Could you find the place again?'

'I believe I could, sir.'

'Then drive me there,' said Tanner, entering the vehicle.

The district they reached was a miserable, decaying part of town. The streets were narrow—mere lanes, and the buildings high and unusually drab and grimy even for a London backwater. The houses had been good at one time, but the place had now degenerated into a slum. 'What in the name of wonder,' thought Tanner, as he stood looking round at the depressing prospect, 'could have brought Sir William here?'

He paid off his driver and began to investigate his surroundings. He was at a cross-roads, the broader street being labelled Dunlop Street, the other Pate's Lane. In Dunlop Street were a few shops—a bar at the corner, a tobacconist's, a grocer's—all small, mean, and dirty. Pate's Lane appeared entirely given up to tenement houses.

Tanner felt utterly at a loss. He could form no conception of Sir William's possible objective. Nor could he envisage any line of inquiry which might lead him to his goal. He seemed to be up against a blank wall, through which he could see no means of penetrating.

He wondered if a former servant or mill worker might not live in the neighbourhood, with whom the manufacturer might have had business. But if so, and if by some incredible chance Tanner were to hit on the person in question, he felt he would be no further on, and that all knowledge of Sir William's visit would almost certainly be concealed.

However, he would learn nothing by standing in the street, and he walked to the bar at the nearest corner and entered.

The landlord was a big, red-faced man with a bluff manner. Tanner, after ordering some ale, engaged him in conversation, deftly pumping him. But he learned nothing. The man had not seen Sir William, nor did the manufacturer's name convey anything to him.

Tanner tried each of the other three corner shops of the cross-roads, but again without result. Then, thinking that small tobacconists and news-agents sometimes act as mediums between persons who do not wish their connection to be known, he called at all the shops of these kinds in the immediate neighbourhood. Again he was disappointed, as he was also when he visited the pawnbroker's. By this time it was getting late, and he turned his steps homeward, intending to return on the next morning and begin a house-to-house visitation in the vicinity of the cross streets.

As he walked down the road towards Gower Street, he noticed three buildings which he thought looked more the kind of place for a rendezvous than any he had yet seen. Two were shabby and rather squalid looking restaurants, the third a building slightly larger and more pretentious than its neighbours. In faded letters it bore the legend 'Judd's Family & Commercial Hotel'. Tanner decided that, before beginning on the houses of Pate's Lane, he would try these three.

Next morning he drew blank in the first of the restaurants. A visit to the second was equally fruitless. But when he reached the hotel he had a stroke of luck.

A rather untidy porter was polishing the brass bell-push, and Tanner engaged him in conversation. Yes, he remembered a well-dressed old gentleman calling about half-past three on that Monday, three weeks earlier. He would recognise him if he saw him. Yes, he was sure that was his photograph. The gentleman had asked was a Mr Douglas staying in the hotel, and on being answered in the affirmative he had gone up to the latter's bedroom and remained with him for about half an hour. Then he had left, and that was all the porter knew.

'And what sort of a man was Mr Douglas?' Tanner asked.

'A small man, very small and thin,' the porter returned. 'Looked as 'ow a breath of wind would 'ave blown 'im away. Sort of scared too, I thought.'

Tanner pricked up his ears.

'What was he like in face?' he asked.

' 'E was getting on in years—maybe sixty or more, and 'e 'ad a small, grey goatee beard, and a moustache, and wore spectacles. 'E spoke like an American man and was a bit free with 'is langwidge, damning and cursing about everything.'

At last! Was this the man for whom he and Sergeant Longwell had been searching—the man who had made the fifth set of tracks at Luce Manor, and who had travelled from St Albans to London on the morning after the crime? With thinly veiled eagerness Tanner continued his questions.

'Who cleans the boots here?'

The porter looked interested.

'I do,' he replied, 'and why that?'

'Only this. Can you remember what sort of boots this man Douglas wore?'

'Well, they were small, like himself. Small boots like you'd expect a boy to wear.'

'With nails in the soles?'

'Just that. Guess, mister, you're a 'tec?'

Tanner nodded.

'From Scotland Yard,' he answered. 'I'm after that man Douglas, and if you can tell me anything about him, I'll make it worth your while.'

The man whistled.

'Gosh! but I just thought he was a wrong 'un. Wot's 'e been up to, mister?'

'Never mind now. Why did you think he was a wrong 'un?'

'W'y, 'e looked scared fit to die. 'E 'ad something worrying 'im, 'e 'ad.'

'All the time he was here?'

'No, the morning 'e left. 'E got 'is tea the night before a bit early—about 'alf five or thereabouts—and then went out, and 'e didn't come back till seven o'clock the next morning; walks in at seven o'clock all shaking and grey about the face and calls for brandy. Swallowed two large brandies nearly neat, 'e did. They pulled 'im together some, and then 'e pays 'is bill and 'ooks it.'

'Hooked it?'

'Yes, we never saw 'im no more after that.'

'And do you remember what day that was?'

'No, but I can get it for you at the office.'

The porter vanished for a moment to a room at the back.

' 'E left on Thursday morning, the 8th.'

'Did you notice anything about his boots that morning?'

'Yes. They were covered with mud—just covered. You couldn't but notice them. And the ends of 'is trousers too. 'E looked as if 'e 'ad been up to the knees in muddy water.'

Tanner was as nearly excited as his dignity would allow. There could be little doubt, he felt, that this Douglas was indeed the man of whom he was in search. The man's size—a small man would take short steps—the little, hobnailed boots, the wet and muddy trousers, the goatee beard—these points considered cumulatively, made the evidence of identity almost overwhelming. And in addition he had been out all the night of the tragedy, and had returned in the morning shaken and clamouring for brandy. Enough evidence to hang a man, Tanner thought with satisfaction. He turned again to the porter.

'What day did he come here first?'

'I looked that up when I went to the office. It was on the Friday evening before.'

'He left no address, I suppose?'

'Not 'im,' said the porter with a wink.

'How did he go away? Did he get a cab?'

'Keb?' returned the other disgustedly. 'Not 'im. 'E took 'is bag in 'is hand and just 'ooked it on 'is blooming feet.'

Tanner replied absently. He was thinking that a man who departed on foot from an hotel without leaving an address might not be so easy to trace. And the best description of his appearance he could get was too vague to be of much use. The porter had not noticed the colour of the man's eyes, if there was any scar or mark on his face or hands, the shape of his ears, any peculiarity in his gait—none of the matters on which identification depends. Tanner could only remind himself that a general hazy notion was better than no notion at all.

He went to the office and saw the proprietor. The latter was a tall weedy individual, dilapidated looking as his own hotel. But he spoke civilly, and exerted himself to answer the Inspector's questions, calling in various maids, and an untidy waiter for the latter's interrogations. Unfortunately, none of them could tell anything Tanner had not already learned.

The man had registered 'William Douglas, Fulham Street, Birmingham,' and with the proprietor's permission Tanner cut out and pocketed the leaf. Then he asked to see the room the visitor had occupied.

It was a small apartment on the fourth floor, supplied with the minimum of cheap, rickety furniture. The bed was not made up, and dust lay thick everywhere.

'It hasn't been occupied recently?'

'Not since Mr Douglas had it,' the proprietor admitted.

'I'll just take a look round, if you don't mind,' said Tanner. 'Don't let me keep you. I'll follow you to the office in a minute or two.'

Left to himself Inspector Tanner began one of his careful, painstaking examinations. The entire contents of the room were minutely inspected. Every inch of the carpet and the cracks between the floor boards were examined in the hope of finding some small object which might have been dropped. The drawers of the small wardrobe, the bedclothes, the dressing-table and washstand, all were gone through with the utmost care, but with no result. At last to complete his task the searcher turned his attention to the fireplace.

A broken Japanese fan was stuck in the old-fashioned grate, and only partially concealed a litter of matches, scraps of paper, bits of cord and other debris. Tanner lifted out the fan and began to go through the rubbish with the same scrupulous care. And then his perseverance was rewarded.

Among the papers he found the charred remains of an envelope which at once interested him. It was more than half burnt, a triangular portion with the stamp on one corner only remaining. As he picked it up it struck him it was of unusually good quality to find in a room of that description—thick, cream-laid paper, which only a well-to-do person would have used. A few letters at the end of each line of the address remained visible. But at these he hardly glanced at first, his attention being riveted on the postmark. The letters were slightly blurred, but still he could read it clearly—'HALFORD 4 pm 2 JY 20.'

As he looked at the large, firm calligraphy of the address, the suggestion this name conveyed to him was confirmed—the envelope had been written by Sir William Ponson. He examined the mutilated address. It contained four lines, and from three to five letters remained at the end of each. It was clearly not that of the hotel, and it therefore might, if decipherable, lead to the discovery of the man in question.

Tanner put the bit of burnt paper away in his pocket-book, and continued his search. But he could find nothing else of interest, and presently he took his leave.

From the nearest telephone call office he spoke to the chief of police at Birmingham, asking him to try to trace a William Douglas who lived in Fulham Street in that city, and he was not greatly surprised when that officer, after asking him to hold on for a moment, informed him that there was no street of that name in the town.

On reaching his office at the Yard the Inspector sat down at his desk, and taking the burnt fragment of the envelope from his pocket, set himself to try and puzzle out the address. The four lines ended in '—glas', '—ttage', '—rton', and '—von' respectively. Of these, the '—glas' at the end of the first line seemed unquestionably to be part of the name 'Douglas', and the Inspector was therefore not without hope that this was the man's real name.

Procuring another envelope of the same size, Tanner laid the charred fragment on the top, and endeavoured to estimate from the spacing of the '—glas', what had preceded it. It was probable that, as there was no 'Esq.', the line had commenced with 'Mr' but 'Mr' alone, or even 'Mr W.' or 'Mr Wm.' would not fill the line. Tanner tried to write 'Mr William Dou—' in Sir William's hand, and, as this seemed exactly the size of the required space, he assumed this had been the first line.

The '—ttage' at the end of the second line immediately suggested the word 'Cottage'. Writing in the 'Co—' in the same manner as the 'Mr William Dou—' he found there would be left before it space for a word of six or seven letters. Though his conclusions on this second line were admittedly only guesswork, he still felt fairly sure of his ground so far.

So many towns and villages ended with the letters '—rton', Tanner felt it useless to work at the third line. He therefore transferred his attention to the fourth, merely noting that as the third did not end in 'Street' or 'Road', the balance of probability was against the fourth line containing the name of a town. But this, of course, was by no means certain.

The fourth line ended in '—von', and, considering the suggestion made by the third line, Tanner determined to begin, by assuming this was the name of a county. He got down an atlas and went over all the counties in the three kingdoms. Two only ended in '—von'—Carnarvon and Devon. He tried spacing these in and found neither would suit. 'Devon' was out of the question, as the 'D' came after the 'n' of the third line, and 'Carnarvon', which fitted better, was still obviously too short.

He set to work then upon the towns. It was clear that as the name was the last in the address, the town must either be of considerable importance, or else lie close to Halford. Tanner chose the latter alternative first, and went over all the towns near Sir William's residence. He could find none to fit.

Sending for a Post Office Directory, in which towns with head offices—and therefore important—are printed in capitals, the Inspector laboriously ran his eye down the closely printed pages, searching for names in capital letters ending in '—von'. There were scores in '—ton', some in '—don', some in '—ven', and '—van', but he was amazed to find only two in '—von'—'Carnarvon' and 'Stratford-on-Avon'. Of these, while 'Carnarvon', as he had already found, seemed too short, 'Stratford-on-Avon' was clearly a good deal too long.

As he slowly pondered the matter, another idea occurred to him. 'Devon', he recollected, was rarely written alone, 'North' or 'South' was usually prefixed. To space out 'North De—' was the work of a moment. And then he felt more satisfied, for these letters seemed exactly to fill the required space.

While he fully realised that the evidence was by no means conclusive—in fact, was but slightly removed from a guess—he thought the probabilities of the last word being 'Devon' were such, that it would be worth while investigating on the basis of this assumption before trying any of the other names. The next question therefore became, What, if any, places in Devon ended in '—rton'?

He soon saw there were a number. Tiverton, Ashburton, Silverton, Merton, Halberton, Thorverton, Yelverton, Otterton, and Staverton he picked up at once from the atlas, and he felt sure there must be others, too small to be marked. His next step must therefore be to try if a small, elderly man with a grey beard, named William Douglas, lived in —Cottage, Tiverton, Ashburton, or one of the other places he had found.

He took a sheet of paper and drafted a letter to the chief of the local police at each of these places, asking him to forward the information with regard to his own neighbourhood.

Two days later he received a wire from Yelverton. 'William Douglas lives at Myrtle Cottage near Yelverton Station.' Tanner chuckled. He was getting on more rapidly than he could have hoped.

Chapter 12
A Stern Chase

When the 10.30 a.m. Riviera express pulled out of Paddington next morning, Inspector Tanner was occupying a corner seat in one of its first-class compartments. In his pocket was a warrant for the arrest of William Douglas, in case his investigations should indicate that such a step was desirable. He had determined that if his victim could not account satisfactorily for his actions on the night of the murder, or if his boots fitted the marks on the Cranshaw River bank, no other course would be possible.

Once again the Inspector was favoured with magnificent weather for his country ramble. Indeed, like the previous days, it was too hot, and as the train slipped swiftly through the sun-baked country, he moved into the corridor so as to make the most of the draught from the open windows. Each time that he had made this journey in the past he had enjoyed it, especially the portion between Exeter and Newton Abbott—down the estuary of the Exe, past Dawlish and Teignmouth with their queer spiky, red rocks, and precipitous little cliffs running out into the blue sea, then farther on inland again through the hilly, wooded country of South Devon, where one caught unexpected glimpses of tiny, nestling villages, and of narrow lanes, winding mysteriously, between mossy, flower-spangled banks under the cool shade of overhanging trees.

He reached Plymouth—the first stop since leaving Paddington—shortly before three. Changing at North Road, he boarded a branch line train after a short wait. A run of a few minutes brought him to Yelverton. Here he alighted, and when the Launceston and Princetown trains had rumbled off, he accosted the stationmaster.

'I am looking for a Mr William Douglas of Myrtle Cottage,' he said. 'Can you tell me where that is?'

The stationmaster could. Myrtle Cottage, it appeared, was half a mile away on the road to Dousland, and Tanner, having received directions as to his route, set off to walk.

The house was small and surrounded by trees, through which the gables showed picturesquely. It was set back some little distance from the road, a path leading through a not very well kept flower garden to the door. Mr Douglas was evidently an apiarist, for a row of wooden hives lined each side of the path, and the hum of the insects was audible even from the road. Along the side of the garden, and passing close to the gable of the house ran a lane, from which a large gate led to a yard in the rear. This gate, Tanner noticed, was standing open.

He walked up the path and knocked at the green-painted door. For some time there was no response, but after a second and more peremptory summons he heard footsteps approaching. The door was opened by a small man with grey hair and a beard trimmed short.

'Got him first shot,' thought Tanner, as he politely asked for Mr William Douglas.

The man threw the door open.

'Walk in, sir,' he said. 'My brother is upstairs. I'll call him.'

'Your brother?' asked Tanner sharply, as he followed his guide to a rather poorly furnished sitting room.

'Yes. I'm John. I've lived here for some years, but William is just back from America.'

Tanner nodded. He recollected the hotel porter had stated that William Douglas had spoken with an American accent, whereas this man clearly hailed from the north of England. Besides, the beard was different. The porter had mentioned a goatee, but the speaker's was cut to a tiny point.

'Sit down, sir,' said the man civilly. 'I'll send my brother down.'

He indicated a chair opposite the door, and Tanner took it. From where he sat he could see the foot of the staircase, and he watched John walk to it and leisurely ascend. Presently he heard him call 'William!'

A nasal voice answered, but the Inspector could not hear the words. John's voice, now more distant, mumbled something in reply, and there was a word, apparently of assent, from the other.

Tanner glanced round the room. Beside the easy chair in which he sat— leather lined, and very old and worn—there was not much that made for comfort. A deck chair stood with its back to one of the rather small windows. In front of the other window was a table on which lay a number of books, mostly dealing with bee keeping. The floor was covered by a carpet, the worn, threadbare condition of which was brought out pitilessly by the rays of the sun which struck obliquely across it. Tanner got up and began to poke about, but without taking his eye off the bottom of the stairs. William, it was evident, was in no hurry to come down.

Suddenly there came faintly the purr of a motor engine, and in a few seconds the sounds indicated that a car had started at no great distance away. It grew louder, and Tanner moved to the window. The sitting-room was in the gable beside the lane, and as the Inspector looked out he saw a small two-seater with one occupant pass out towards the road. But this occupant was a small man, and though his collar was turned up and his cap pulled down over his eyes, Tanner could see he had a grey beard.

He stood for a moment wondering how John had got downstairs without having been seen. Then, as the house seemed strangely quiet, an idea flashed into his mind, and he ran to the stairs and called, 'Anyone there?' There was no answer, and with a sudden feeling of foreboding, he raced up. Three rooms opened off a short landing, and the doors being open, he glanced into each in turn. They were all empty!

A casement window on the landing was open, and as Tanner looked out, he saw what had been done. About three feet below the sill was the roof of a low shed. Nothing could be easier than to step out of the window on to the roof, and drop to the ground. The open door of the outhouse to which led many wheel tracks showed where the motor had been kept.

Tanner swore savagely. Never before had he been so completely and so easily duped. It was now evident to him that William Douglas had recognised him approaching the house, and had invented a brother to enable him to hold the Inspector's attention while he bolted. And he had played his cards skilfully! Ruefully the Inspector had to admire the trick, though he surmised it had been worked out beforehand in view of just such an emergency.

'He'll not get far,' the angry man growled, as he prepared to follow. But, thinking a moment or two would now make little difference, he turned his steps instead to the kitchen. There on a shelf, as he had expected, were three or four pairs of boots. Drawing from his pocket a tracing of the marks on the Cranshaw River bank, he eagerly compared it with the soles. Those of the first pair he took up corresponded! Here was proof, if proof were required. William Douglas had been at the Luce Manor boathouse on the night of the murder!

Seizing a small handbag he had noticed in the sitting room, the Inspector packed the boots, then, after closing the windows, and locking the yard gates and the house doors, he hurried back along the road towards Yelverton. Inquiring for the local telephone call office, he rang up the Plymouth police authorities, describing, so far as he was able, the man and the car, and asking them to have a ring formed round the locality. Hastening on to the Yelverton police station, he told the sergeant what had occurred, and handing him the keys of the cottage, instructed him to take charge, and to make a thorough search of the premises.

He learned that a train left for Plymouth in a few minutes, and travelling by it, he soon reached the police headquarters of that city. Here he was met by a superintendent, and the two men discussed the affair in detail.

'I have done, I think, everything possible,' the Superintendent concluded. 'All the stations at a radius of about twenty miles or more have been advised, and the roads will be watched from Looe and Liskeard round by Launceston, Okehampton, and Moreton Hamstead, to Newton Abbott. All trains and steamers, as far as possible, will be examined before departure, and the railway people at the smaller stations will be advised. I don't think he'll make for Cornwall, you know. It's too much of a dead end. He will either go east in his car, or come to Plymouth and try the trains, or even more likely, the steamers.'

'That is my own view,' Tanner returned. 'I suppose there's nothing to be done now but wait for information?'

'I think we'll hear something before long. If you haven't had a meal, I should get it while you have the chance. The Dartmoor Arms, a few doors away, is quite good, and I'll send for you if there is news.'

As this seemed sound advice, Tanner followed it. But he had not finished his hastily served dinner when he was sent for. News had come in.

'I have a wire from the Tavistock men,' the Superintendent explained. 'A car answering your description has just been found abandoned in a lane about quarter of a mile on the Yelverton side of Tavistock. Evidently your man wouldn't risk taking it through the town.'

'Then he must be there himself.'

113

'Unless he got away by rail. What time did you say he left Yelverton?'

'About quarter-past four, or slightly later.'

'From Yelverton to Tavistock is not more than about five miles. He would do it easily in fifteen minutes. Say he would reach Tavistock between half past four and quarter to five.' The Superintendent picked up a Bradshaw. 'Here we are. By the Great Western there's a 5.27 for Plymouth and a 6.02 for Launceston. Now for the South-Western. There's a 5.22, and a 7.50 for Exeter. He's gone either by that 5.27 to Plymouth or the 5.22 to Exeter, and I should say the latter.'

'It seems likely. Would your men have reached the stations before those trains left?'

The Superintendent shook his head.

'It's just possible,' he answered, 'but I hardly think so. Your phone was received at '—he referred to a paper—'4.42. Orders were issued immediately, but considering telegraphic delays, they were probably not received at Tavistock till five or slightly after. The men would then have to be collected and instructed. They might have seen those trains out, but it's unlikely.'

'Well, I'll go on to Tavistock now anyway,' Tanner decided. 'I presume you will have those trains searched?'

'Of course. I issued a new set of orders immediately. Both trains will be carefully examined, and the country all about Tavistock will be scoured. We are well accustomed to that,' the Superintendent added with a grim smile.

'The Princetown convicts? I suppose you are,' answered Tanner, as with a brief word of farewell he withdrew.

There being no train by either line for some little time, Tanner took a car. As they climbed the long, slow incline to Yelverton, out of the relaxing, enervating Plymouth air, he felt himself growing fresher and more energetic. He was grimly determined not to rest till he had laid his hands on the man who had duped him. From merely professional, the matter had become personal. Tanner's pride was involved. No one, he swore, should play him such a trick and get off with it.

They slipped quietly through the fifteen or sixteen miles of charmingly wooded country, dropping into Tavistock as the shadows began to lengthen across the road. The sergeant had been advised of Tanner's arrival, and was expecting him. Together they ran back and examined the abandoned car. Though they found nothing directly helpful, Tanner felt sure it was the one he had seen from the sitting room at Myrtle Cottage.

He turned to his companion.

'Did you hear about this in time to examine the Plymouth and Exeter trains at 5.27 and 5.22?' he asked.

The other shook his head.

'No, sir, I'm sorry to say we did not. But I have since made inquiries. No one with a grey beard was seen at either station. At the Great Western Station four persons booked, all third single to Plymouth, but the clerk remembers one of these was a young sailor and the others women. At the South-Western Station two tickets were issued to Exeter, one a first to Major Reading, who lives here, the other a third

114

single to a little, elderly, clean-shaven man. Our men were there within ten minutes of the train's departure, so that's how the clerks remembered—between that and there being so few bookings.'

'A small, elderly, clean-shaven man, sergeant? Let us go round the Tavistock barbers.'

The sergeant looked up sharply.

'By Jove! sir, a likely enough ruse,' he cried. 'It won't take long to find out —there are only three.'

They ran back to the little town, and at the first barber's learned that a small, elderly man with a short grey beard and moustache had called at a few minutes before five, and had had his beard and moustache shaved off.

'Now to the telegraph office. We'll have him before long.'

The Inspector sent messages to Plymouth, to Exeter, and to some of the principal stations beyond, explaining that the bearded man of the previous wires had had himself shaved. Then he looked at his watch.

'Quarter to eight. Can I catch the 7.50? Phone to hold it while I run across.'

He jumped into the car and drove to the South-Western Station. There he caught the train for Exeter with a minute to spare.

He leaned back in the corner of a first-class compartment, and slowly drew out and lit a cigar, while he turned over in his mind the next step to be taken. He thought that at all events he should go on to Exeter. The 5.22 from Tavistock, by which Douglas had travelled, reached that city before his wire about the shaving had been sent out. Therefore it was hardly likely that the man would have been detained *en route*. Tanner, of course, recognised that a freshly shaven chin was unmistakable, but he did not think a village constable would have the sharpness to deduce what Douglas might have done, and act accordingly. But from Exeter in what direction would the quarry head?

There seemed two possibilities. Probably he would try either to reach London, or to get abroad. London, as Tanner knew, was perhaps the safest place in the world for a criminal to lie hidden. But many ill-doers had an overwhelming desire to put as great a distance as possible between themselves and the scene of their misdeeds. If Douglas were of this class he would try to get out of the country, and if, as the hotel porter had stated, he spoke like an American, would he not be likely to try to reach the country in which he might most easily pass for a native? There was, of course, no means of knowing, but at least it was clear that the approaches to London as well as the ports should be closely watched.

In any case, whatever the fugitive's goal, he would be almost certain to pass through Exeter. It was true he could double back to Plymouth, but the probabilities were he would keep away from the district in which he was known. As Tanner's train ran into St David's Station, Exeter, he felt sure his victim was not far before him.

A tall efficient looking sergeant of police was waiting on the platform. This man, sharply scrutinising the alighting travellers, promptly fixed on Tanner.

'Inspector Tanner, sir?' he questioned, and as the other nodded, continued, 'they phoned us from Plymouth you were coming through on this train. We have inquiries in hand both here and at Queen Street, the other station. So far we have heard nothing of your man.'

'What exactly are you doing?'

'We have a man at each station working the staffs—booking-clerks, ticket collectors, porters, refreshment rooms—the usual thing. Another man is going round the hotels, another the restaurants open at that hour, and another the garages, in case he might have gone on by car. Is there any other line you would wish taken up?'

'Why no, sergeant. I think you have covered all the ground. Have you advised your men that the fellow got shaved?'

'Some of them, sir; some of them we couldn't get hold of. We advise them as we can get in touch with them.'

Tanner nodded again.

'Well, we had better go to headquarters and wait for news.'

For a considerable time Tanner remained, chafing and impatient, until, just as eleven was booming from the town clocks, a constable appeared accompanied by a tall, fair-haired young man in a leather coat and breeches, and a peaked cap. The latter explained that he was a taxi owner, driving his own vehicle, and he believed he knew something that might be of value.

It appeared that he had been at St David's Station when Douglas's train had come in. He was engaged by a small, elderly, clean-shaven man with grey hair, dressed in a tweed overcoat and a cloth cap. The man seemed nervous and excited, and told him to drive to any ready-made clothes store which would be open at that hour. He took him to a shop in the poorer part of the town. The man went in, returning in a few minutes dressed in a soft, grey felt hat and a khaki coloured waterproof, and carrying a bundle. He re-entered the taxi and told the driver 'Queen Street Station as quick as you can.' He drove there, and the man paid him and hurried into the station, and that was all he knew.

'What time did you reach Queen Street?' asked Tanner.

'Going on to half-past seven.'

'We'd better go to Queen Street and find out what trains leave about that hour.'

Their visitor's car was waiting outside, and engaging it, they drove rapidly off.

For those who do not know Exeter, it may be explained that the Great Western and London and South-Western Railways, both running from London to Plymouth, form a gigantic figure 8, the centre where the lines cross being St David's Station, Exeter. In the same town, but a mile nearer London on the South-Western, is Queen Street Station. While therefore St David's is joint between the two Companies, Queen Street is South-Western only, and these facts seemed to indicate to Tanner the probability that Douglas was going for a South-Western train bound London-wards.

A glance at the time table at Queen Street supported this view. A train left for London at 7.32.

'Your constable saw the booking-clerk, I suppose?' Tanner asked.

'Yes, sir. But of course he gave the wrong description. He did not know the man had changed his cap and coat.'

'That's true,' Tanner assented. 'We had better see him again.'

The booking office was closed and the clerk had gone home. With considerable difficulty they obtained his address from a watchman. Then stepping into their waiting taxi, they were driven to it.

The house was in darkness, but their third thunderous knock produced a sleepy and indignant householder. Tanner, who was a past-master in the art, soothed his ruffled feelings, and he brought them in and civilly asked their business.

'You have been troubled about this before, I'm afraid,' the Inspector began. 'I shall explain the affair in a word and you'll see its importance. A murder has been committed, and we have traced the suspected man to Queen Street Station. He drove up in a great hurry just before half-past seven this evening, and we imagine he must have travelled by the 7.32. Now you will see why we want your help. If you can recall the man and recollect where he booked to, it would be of material assistance to us.'

'A clean-shaven man in a brownish cap and coat?' the clerk replied. 'But I have already answered that. I saw no one so dressed.'

'We have just discovered that he had bought a waterproof and a grey felt hat. Can you recall him now?'

The clerk made a sudden gesture.

'Why yes, I can,' he cried excitedly, 'I remarked him because he was in such a fuss, and I told him he was time enough. I should have thought of it when the constable asked me, but the description put me off.'

'Quite naturally,' Tanner assured him smoothly, 'but now if you can tell us where he booked to, you'll do us a very great service.'

'I can do so. His excitement drew my attention to him. He took a third single to Southampton.'

'Southampton! Just as I expected,' exclaimed Tanner. 'Making for the ships!'

The other nodded and Tanner went on:

'Where would he get to from there? Would he catch the night boat for Havre?'

'No,' answered the clerk as he fetched a time table and rapidly turned over the leaves. 'The 7.32 gets to Salisbury at 10.52, and there's a train on to Southampton Town at 11.00. It doesn't go to the Harbour. But the connection at Eastleigh is bad, and you don't get to Southampton till 12.30. The Havre boat leaves at 11.30.'

'And what time do you get to Eastleigh?'

'11.37'

'And from there to Southampton is how far?'

'About seven miles to the docks.'

'So that if he had taken a motor at Eastleigh he could have been there by midnight?'

'Yes, I should say about that.'

Tanner looked at his watch. It was five minutes to twelve. In from five to

117

thirty-five minutes Douglas would probably reach Southampton. Would there be time to intercept him there?

Hastily thanking the clerk, the two men jumped once more into their taxi and drove to the police station. There the Inspector hurried to the telephone to call up the Southampton police. But there was a delay in getting through. For thirty minutes he fumed and fretted. Then at half-past twelve he got his connection.

'I'm afraid the train will be in,' replied the distant voice, 'but if it's late we'll get your man if he's on it. If we miss him there, we'll go on to the Docks. There's a Union Castle liner due out at five o'clock. He may be going for that. What about the warrant?'

'Hold on a minute,' said Tanner, then turning to the sergeant, he spoke rapidly:

'A liner leaves Southampton at five for South Africa. Can I get there with a good car? There are no trains, of course?'

'None, sir. It's about a hundred miles and you should do thirty miles an hour —say three and a half hours. If you left here at 1.00, you should be there by 4.30.'

'I'll do that.' Then turning back to the telephone: 'I'm leaving here now by road for Southampton. You may expect me at the Union Castle berth about 4.30. I'll have the warrant.'

The taxi-driver they had been employing being unfamiliar with the surrounding country, they drove to the nearest garage and after some difficulty succeeded in knocking up a sleepy manager and hiring a powerful car and a man who knew the road, at least as far as Salisbury. But there were delays in getting away, and though the manager did his best, it was nearly half-past one when the big vehicle swung out of Exeter, eastward bound.

The night was fine but dark. As they purred swiftly along the smooth road, Tanner lay back on the comfortable cushions and let the cool air blow in on his heated forehead, while he took stock of the position.

He was perfectly aware that he might be on a wild-goose chase. The taking of the ticket to Southampton might have been a blind, and Douglas might not have done the obvious thing in making a bolt to the most convenient port. After the ruse the man had employed at Myrtle Cottage, Tanner felt he would not do the obvious thing unless he was impelled to it by some strong consideration. But such a consideration existed. There was the element of time. The man would realise that on such a journey he must inevitably be traced, but he would hardly imagine he could be traced in time. Before his pursuers could reach Southampton he would count on having been able to adopt a new personality, and put hundreds of miles of sea between himself and them. The more Tanner thought over this possibility, the more likely it seemed. If he were in Douglas's position it was the view he himself would have taken.

They were running well. Tanner watched the whirling hedges, lit up by the strong headlights, and blurred by the speed into quivering smudges, and judged they must be doing well on to forty miles an hour. It was, of course, breaking the law; moreover, it was by no means safe, but Tanner did not let such considerations weigh

118

against the chance of checkmating the man who had duped him. He had informed the chauffeur he would be responsible if there was trouble.

He fell to reckoning distances. He was not very well up in the geography of the district, but he knew there were two roads, north through Yeovil and Salisbury, and south through Dorchester and Poole. He imagined neither of these was quite direct, but he did not know if there was a good road lying between them.

In about half an hour they slackened for a town, after which the road rose for some miles. Then in half an hour more it fell again and they ran through another town, whose name appeared on several buildings—Chard. 'The Salisbury Road,' thought Tanner. Forty minutes later they left Yeovil behind and at 4.10, nearly three hours after leaving Exeter, they turned out of Salisbury on the Southampton road.

'Not bad going,' thought Tanner. 'If we can keep it up we should be at the boat at twenty to five.'

But alas! the driver's knowledge of the road which had served them so well up to Salisbury, now failed them. They had to reduce speed at cross roads and run more cautiously. Fortunately, it was now fairly light, or their progress would have been still slower.

Tanner, was getting nervous. It was going to be a near thing. He held his watch in his hand and counted the mile-posts as one after another they dropped behind. Now it was half-past four, and still they had nine miles to go.

At last they came to the town. But here matters instead of mending, grew much worse. Neither Tanner nor the driver knew the streets, and precious minutes were wasted trying to puzzle out the way from the rather inferior map the latter had brought.

Quarter to five. Tanner was in desperation. And then to his relief his eye fell on a policeman. It was the work of a moment to call him over, explain the situation, and get him up beside the driver. Then their troubles were over. The streets were empty and they made fine speed.

It wanted ten minutes to five as the car pulled up at the docks, and Tanner leaped out and raced to the berth of the great liner. A man whom he instantly recognised as a policeman in plain clothes stood near the bottom of each gangway, while a third was sauntering along the edge of the wharf beside the boat. Tanner spoke hurriedly to the latter.

'He's not on board, sir,' the man answered. 'We were here before he could have got down from the Town Station, and besides we made inquiries.'

'The other side of the ship?' queried the Inspector.

'We have a man rowing up and down.'

Tanner grunted.

'Who's in charge?' he asked.

'Sergeant Holmes. He went to phone the station. He'll be back directly.'

Tanner was woefully disappointed. He felt that if Douglas was not already aboard he would never risk it now. Had the man, he wondered, been sharper than he had counted on, and once again given him the slip? Fortunately, he had taken the obvious precaution of wiring all the stations at which the 7.32 stopped, so that, even if Douglas had alighted elsewhere, he would almost certainly be spotted. But had Douglas travelled by the 7.32 at all? Was his haste with the taxi and his purchase of the ticket another trick, and was he lying low in Exeter, intending still further to alter his appearance and make a bolt elsewhere? Or was he walking all night with the object of joining a train at some quite different station in the morning? Tanner could not guess.

Three minutes only remained and Tanner grew more and more anxious. It was now or never. Then, as the gangways were being hoisted, a sergeant of police appeared and went up to one of the plain clothes men. Tanner hurried forward.

'Mr Tanner, sir?' said the sergeant. 'I'm very sorry, sir, but you're late.'

'Late?' Tanner cried sharply. 'What do you mean, sergeant? There's plenty of time to go on board still.'

The sergeant shook his head.

'He's not there, sir. He's gone. I've just learnt that he left by the *Vaal River*. She sailed at four o'clock.'

'Damnation!' cried Tanner angrily. 'What were you thinking about, sergeant? How in hell did you let him slip through your fingers?'

'The man I sent down, sir, missed him. I can't imagine how he did it, but you'll hear what he has to say yourself. After I had all—'

'I'll see him,' said Tanner grimly. 'How did you find it out?'

'I posted the men, sir, first, then I went round them myself. I got to the *Vaal River's* berth as she was sheering out. I made inquiries at the office. There is no doubt the man booked.'

'Where to?'

'Tangier, sir.'

'H'm—Morocco, and there's no extradition from there. Where else does the boat call?'

'Lisbon, Marseilles, Naples, Suez, Delagoa Bay and Durban.'

'I'll get him at Lisbon. Show me the office.'

They hurried down to the East Africa Line Quay office. There Tanner interviewed the booking clerk and satisfied himself that Douglas really had sailed. He had booked under the name of Walter Donnell.

'Lisbon is the first call?' asked the Inspector.

'Yes. She's due there about six on Thursday morning.'

'And this is Tuesday. That's about a fifty hour run?'

'About that.'

'I must get there before her. How am I to do it?'

The clerk stared.

'I'm afraid you can't,' he answered slowly. 'She's not a specially fast boat, but there's no other leaving soon enough to pass her.'

'Overland?'

'No. There's not time. If you had caught the Havre boat last night you could have done it. You can't now.'

'Let me see the time table.'

The clerk produced a Continental Bradshaw.

'Here you are,' he said, turning to the 'Through Routes' on page 6. 'You see there are two trains a day from Paris to Lisbon. One, the ordinary, leaves Paris at 10.22 at night. It gets to Lisbon at 12.33 two nights later—that is, about a fifty hours' run. That's out of the question, and you'll see the other is too. It's a special fast train, the Sud Express, and it leaves Paris at 12.17 midday, and reaches Lisbon at 10.50 the following evening—that is thirty-four hours and a half. Now if you could catch that train today you'd be all right, but you couldn't. Even if you could catch the 8.00 a.m. from Victoria, which you couldn't. That would only bring you into Paris at 5.29—five hours late.'

'How long does your boat lie at Lisbon?'

'About four hours. She's due away about ten on Thursday morning.'

Tanner felt he was up against it. So far as he could see it was impossible for him to reach Lisbon before 10.50 on the Thursday night, and by that time the man he wanted would already have left some twelve hours. And if he missed him at Lisbon, he would miss him for good. He could never get him once he was ashore at Tangier. Nor was it any more possible for another officer from the Yard to go in his place.

Of course, there were the Portuguese police. Tanner had never been in Portugal, and knew nothing whatever about its police, but he had the not uncommon insular distrust of foreign efficiency. As he put it to himself, he would rather rely on himself any day than trust to any of these foreign chaps. But there seemed no other way.

Absently thanking the clerk, he walked with the sergeant back to his car and drove to the police station. As he dismounted an idea shot suddenly into his mind.

'Get the car ready for another run,' he shouted and hurrying to the telephone, put through a call to Scotland Yard.

'Yes, I'm Tanner,' he said, when the connection was made. 'The Ponson Case. That man Douglas I'm after got away on the *Vaal River*. Sailed from Southampton at four this morning. First call Lisbon. I must be there to meet him. It can only be done if I leave Paris at 12.17 today. None of the ordinary services would get me over in time. Can you arrange with the Air people to give me a plane?'

He was told to wait, and at six o'clock the reply came.

'The Deputy Chief has arranged for a fast plane to leave the drome near Petersfield as soon as possible. Get there at once and report to Major Forbes. Call at Hendon and we shall have French and Portuguese money for you, as well as the extradition warrant.'

Tanner was not long in reaching Petersfield, but there was a delay at the aerodrome, and he chafed impatiently as the precious minutes slipped away. It was not indeed till a little after seven that the actual start was made. The morning was clear at first, and they made good speed to Hendon, alighting and picking up the money and papers. But as they reached the coast they ran into a haze, which soon developed into a thick fog. The pilot did his best, going straight on by dead reckoning, but when in another hour they got through it, they found they had gone a good deal out of their course in a northerly direction. Tanner swore bitterly, for he found his margin of time was growing less and less. Finally they picked up the main line of the Northern Railway, and following it fairly closely, at last saw creeping up over the horizon the buildings of the capital.

'Down in ten minutes,' the pilot roared, and Tanner nodded as he looked his watch.

It was eleven minutes to twelve, and the Inspector recognised he would have to run for it. Soon they were above Argenteuil and crossing the great loops of the Seine, with St Cloud on the right and the vast city stretching away to the left. Now they were planing rapidly down, till with a gentle shock they alighted at the edge of the flying ground at Issy. Tanner leaped out and ran to the entrance as fast as the stiffness of his legs would allow. As he did so twelve sounded from the clock towers. He had seventeen minutes, the Gare Quai d'Orsay was two miles away, and there were no taxis within sight.

There was but one thing to do and Tanner did it. Some private cars were drawn up on the road just outside the flying ground. Tanner ran his eye hastily over them and selected one, a racing car from which a sporting looking man was just descending. The detective hailed him.

'Sir,' he panted, 'I have crossed by aeroplane from England to catch the 12.17 at the Gare Quai d'Orsay, and now I can't get a taxi. If you would run me till we meet a taxi, I just couldn't say how grateful I'd be.'

The man looked puzzled.

'I not speak Engleesh,' he said slowly, then adding interrogatively, 'You weesh—aller, aller—go—á la Gare Quai d'Orsay?'

Tanner nodded emphatically, and taking out his watch, ran his finger from the minute hand, which was now standing at five minutes past the hour, to seventeen minutes past. The man threw up his left hand to signify comprehension.

'Ah, oui,' he answered. 'Bon. Montez vite, monsieur. Chomp een.'

Tanner had obeyed the gesture before the man finished speaking, and the powerful car, swinging round, shot rapidly eastwards along the quais.

'Where you—allez—go?' jerked out the man as they tore along. Tanner understood.

'Lisbon,' he called.

'Ah, Lisbonne. Oui,' the man nodded.

Suddenly they came to a great building—Tanner did not know his Paris—and the car stopped abruptly. The man jumped out followed by his passenger. As they ran into the concourse of the huge Quai d'Orsay Station, the hands of the clock pointed to fifteen minutes past twelve. Two minutes to get the ticket! Without his new friend Tanner would have been utterly lost. The taking of a ticket seemed a complicated and interminable affair. But at last it was accomplished, and Tanner raced for the bridge across the low level tracks. But just before he reached the inclined plane descending to the platform, the ticket examiner slammed the gate. There was a voluble outcry from the sporting man, but for answer the official shrugged his shoulders and pointed to the roofs of the carriages. The train was already moving.

122

Once again Tanner swore bitterly, as he gazed at the disappearing vehicles. But his friend gave him no time for self-commiseration.

'Vite! Vite!' he cried, signing to the other to follow him, and rushing once more out of the station.

They threw themselves into the car, which started off at a furious pace eastwards. Then Tanner recollected that the terminus of the Paris-Orleans line had formerly been the Gare d'Austerlitz farther up the river, the Gare Quai d'Orsay being a new station at the end of a recently made extension. All trains, he farther remembered having read, stopped at the Gare d'Austerlitz to enable the electric engine which worked through the extension tunnel to be replaced by a steam locomotive. Evidently his friend thought he could overtake the train at the Austerlitz Station.

And he did—just. After wringing the hand of the man who had taken so much trouble to help him, he dashed to the platform and climbed into a carriage as the train began to move.

'Lord!' he said to himself as he wiped his forehead, 'only for that old sport I'd have missed it.'

Then began a long tedious journey. Though the train was rapid and luxurious, Tanner was pretty sick of it before he reached his destination. There was a restaurant car forward, and as they raced across the sunny country south of Paris, the Inspector did full justice to an excellent lunch.

After a time he grew wearied by the monotony of the flat lands, but the scenery became more interesting as they crossed the hills between Poitiers and Angoulême. Bordeaux was passed about seven o'clock, and as darkness fell they were traversing the dreary, desolate, sandy wastes and pine forests of Les Landes.

They reached Irun just before midnight, changing there into the broad-gauge carriages of Spain, and waiting for customs examination.

The moon rose as they passed through the rocky country north of Burgos, and it was daylight when they reached the latter town. Then on again through Valladolid to Medina, where the Madrid portion of the train branched off; through Salamanca of legendary fame, but now, for Spain, a considerable railway centre, then into Portugal, where the train hurtled along at considerably over thirty miles an hour. Finally, with brakes grinding, they descended the steep incline tunnelled beneath one of the seven hills on which Lisbon is built, and pulled up, twenty minutes late, in the Rocio Station.

When Tanner emerged into the brilliantly lighted streets and gazed down the splendid vista of the Avenida da Liberdade, he literally held his breath with amazement. The Portuguese he had always looked on as a lazy, good-for-nothing set, but this great new boulevard made him reconsider his opinion. He booked a room in the Avenida Palace Hotel, and then, crossing the Dom Pedro Square, walked down to the steamboat offices in the Rua da Alfandega.

The office was open—every one seemed to be on the move all night—and one of the clerks spoke English. The steamer, it appeared, was due about half-past six. Tanner took the clerk into his confidence, and the latter made arrangements for the Inspector to get aboard with the first boat from the shore.

At six o'clock Tanner was down on the Praça do Commercio, admiring in the brilliant sunlight the splendid river which flowed before him, and the charming setting of the town on its range of hills. In the river lay several steamers, some quite large, and all tugging at their anchors with their bows upstream. Down seawards, but inside the comparatively narrow mouth of the Tagus, a grey, two-funnelled boat was coming slowly up—the *Vaal River*—with, as Tanner hoped, William Douglas on board.

His friend the clerk arriving a moment later, the two men embarked on a motor launch. As the *Vaal River's* anchor fell with a mighty splash, they sheered alongside and made fast.

When the port authorities had gone aboard, Tanner was allowed to follow. He went straight to the captain, who was still on the bridge, and showing him his card, explained his business.

'And so Mr Walter Donnell's wanted for murder,' the captain commented. 'Guess he's aboard all right. I thought he had something on his mind. See the chief steward and you'll find him. What are you going to do with him?'

'Take him back to London.'

'Of course. But how?'

'I don't know. What would you advise?'

The captain pointed to a single-funnelled steamer of about 4000 tons lying not two hundred yards on their port quarter.

'That's the *Chrysostom*, a Booth liner, due out in about an hour. If you take my advice you'll get aboard and don't favour the shore with your presence. I'll run you over in the launch.'

Tanner thanked the man warmly.

'Guess that's all right,' he answered dryly. 'I'm as interested in getting him out of my ship as you are in taking him.'

Finding the chief steward, Tanner explained the matter in hand, adding that he wished to make the arrest as quietly as possible. The man seemed mildly interested and promised his help.

Douglas, alias Donnell, was, it appeared, still in his cabin, and the two went thither. He was in bed, and rose to open the door. When he saw Tanner his eyes started from his head with amazement, then his jaw dropped and his face went grey. Stepping quickly back, he collapsed on to the cabin sofa and sat staring helplessly.

'William Douglas or Walter Donnell,' Tanner said solemnly, 'I arrest you on a charge of being concerned in the death of the late Sir William Ponson, of Luce Manor, Halford. I have to warn you that anything you say will be used against you.'

The man made a desperate effort to pull himself together.

'My God!' he gasped. 'How did you trace me?' Then, Tanner not replying, he went on with pitiable earnestness:

'But you've made a mistake. I am innocent. I know the circumstances look bad, but I'm innocent, I swear it in God's name.'

'That will do,' said Tanner not unkindly. 'You'll have every chance to put

124

yourself right if you can do it. But you'll have to come back to London with me. And for your own sake, the less you say the better.'

For a moment the idea of making a desperate resistance seemed to cross the prisoner's mind. Then, apparently realising his hopeless position, he said quietly, 'I'll go with you. Let me pack my things.'

Tanner nodded, keeping a keen eye on the other's movements for fear he would attempt suicide. But such an idea did not seem to occur to him. He dressed and packed expeditiously enough, and then said he was ready to go.

The launch was waiting, and in a few minutes they stood on the deck of the *Chrysostom*, homeward bound. Presently the anchor was hoisted and the vessel, swinging round, commenced her 1200 mile trip to Liverpool.

Having explained his business to the captain and seen Douglas securely locked in a cabin, Tanner stood leaning on the rail, of the upper deck, watching the pleasantly situated town slip slowly astern. He could see the Cathedral of Belem standing, damaged, just as it was left by the earthquake of 1755. Then out of the mouth of the river and past the picturesque pleasure resort of Mont Estoril, with, just beyond it, the sleepy, old-world village of Cascaes till, rolling easily in the Atlantic swell, they turned northwards. The Burlings Islands, which they passed later in the day, were the last land they saw until, on the third morning, they awoke to find themselves lying in the Mersey. By midday Tanner and his prisoner were in London.

Chapter 13
Blackmail?

When Inspector Tanner reached his office in New Scotland Yard, he found an instruction from Chief Inspector Edgar, informing him that Mr James Daunt, of Lincoln's Inn, had important evidence to give him relative to the Ponson case. Accordingly, after he had made a formal report on his Portuguese expedition, he called up Jimmy and arranged a meeting. A few hours later he was seated in the solicitor's office, smoking one of the latter's best cigars.

'My Chief says you have something to tell me?' he began, after mutual greetings.

'Why yes,' Jimmy replied. 'Did your Chief tell you what it was?'

'Didn't see him. He's in Manchester.'

'I fancy you'll be surprised. You recollect you told me you had suspected Cosgrove Ponson, but that he had established an alibi and so must be innocent?'

Tanner nodded as he drew at his cigar.

'That's right,' he agreed.

'You were satisfied the alibi was sound?'

'Absolutely.'

'It's a fake,' said Jimmy quietly.

Tanner took his cigar out of his mouth and looked at the other.

'Get along now, Mr Daunt,' he answered. 'You're trying to pull my leg.'

'No. The thing's a fake right enough. Cosgrove was at the boathouse that night.'

Tanner stared incredulously.

'You seem in earnest,' he said slowly. 'But you've made a mistake. I went into it carefully. There's no doubt it's sound.'

'It's *you* that have made the mistake,' Daunt answered pleasantly, and he went on to tell the Inspector what he and Lois had done, and all they had discovered.

To say that Tanner was amazed and disappointed would be to understate the case. He was woefully chagrined.

'God bless my soul!' he cried, 'but that sort of takes a chap down. Here was I looking down on you and that splendid girl as a pair of meddling nuisances, and I'm blowed if you haven't had it over on me all the time.'

'Well,' said Jimmy, 'tit for tat.'

The Inspector eyed him almost aggressively.

'And what now?' he demanded.

'Why this. I've told you what we did about Cosgrove. Now you tell me what took you to Portugal.'

'Oh, that,' answered Tanner looking relieved. 'It's irregular, but I'm blessed if I care.' He re-lit his cigar, which in his agitation he had allowed to go out, and

126

beginning with the day of the adjourned inquest, he recounted his adventures in London and in Devon, the midnight run to Southampton, the flight to Paris, the journey to Lisbon, and finally the arrest of William Douglas. When he had finished, James Daunt was nearly as surprised and mystified as the Inspector had been a few minutes earlier.

' 'Pon my soul, a most extraordinary business,' he commented. 'There's Austin, first suspected, then cleared, then suspected again and arrested, and now cleared again. Then there's Cosgrove, first suspected, then cleared, and now suspected again. And now, here's a third man mixed up in the thing. I suppose the next thing that comes out will clear Douglas!'

'I don't think,' Tanner answered. 'But what do you mean by saying Austin is now cleared again? It's the first I've heard of that.'

'Why, Cosgrove was clearly impersonating him.'

'Not on your life,' said Tanner with decision. 'Mark my words, Mr Daunt, they were all there—Sir William and Austin and Cosgrove and Douglas. Every blooming one of them was there. See here,' he continued as the other showed signs of dissent, 'there's evidence against every one of them. Sir William was seen there. Austin was seen too, and there's no doubt he faked that business about the shoes. Yes, I know,' as Daunt would have spoken, 'his story about the shoes seems all right, and it's very clever, but it won't wash. He was seen there, and he was there. Then Cosgrove was there, for you've proved that. And lastly this man Douglas was there also, for I saw his footmarks on the boathouse floor. Yes, they were all there, and there's some conspiracy between them.'

Though Daunt had to admit this conclusion seemed sound, it was by no means what he wished the Inspector to arrive at. His business was to clear Austin, and while the bringing in of first Cosgrove and now this man Douglas had at the time seemed all to the good, it did not help if it merely led to a conspiracy charge. But Tanner's voice broke into his cogitations.

'You see,' the detective said, following on his own line of thought, 'they were together in London. Sir William, Austin, and Cosgrove lunched together—*both* Austin and Cosgrove denying it, mind you—and then immediately Sir William went to see Douglas. There was some business between the four of them. There's not a doubt of it.'

It gave Daunt a nasty shock to recall that Austin had to him also denied having seen Sir William on that Monday. If it could be proved that Austin had lied about this, as apparently it could, what reliance could be placed on any of his other statements?

There was silence for some moments, and then Daunt moved impatiently.

'Well, what are you going to do about it?' he asked.

'Get the names of that taxi-man and those other witnesses from you,' the Inspector answered promptly, 'and check over your conclusions about Cosgrove. Not that I doubt you, of course, but it's business. Then if I'm satisfied, I'll arrest him. Among his or Douglas's papers there'll be surely something to put us on the track.'

When Tanner had taken his leave Daunt sat motionless for some minutes, thinking over what he had just heard. And the more he thought, the less he liked the turn affairs had taken. All his doubts as to Austin's innocence had returned. If his client had really met Sir William on the Monday in question, why had he denied it? It would take an even more ingenious explanation to account for it than that he had given about the shoes.

To satisfy himself, when his work for the day was finished, Daunt put a photograph of Austin in his pocket and drove to the Étoile restaurant in Soho. But a few moments' inquiry was sufficient to convince him. Austin had been there beyond question, and therefore his statement to Daunt had been a direct falsehood.

Sorely puzzled as to what he should say to Lois, Jimmy Daunt returned to his rooms. There after much thought he decided he would see Austin next morning and tax him directly with the lie.

Another point had been worrying him. He recalled his surprise at the manner in which Austin had received the news of his and Lois's discovery that Cosgrove had been at the boathouse on the fatal night. Austin had professed incredulity, but all the same had seemed terribly shocked. He had ridiculed their idea that Cosgrove could have been impersonating him, and utterly refused to sanction a defence on these lines.

At the time Daunt had put this down to cousinly affection, but in the light of Tanner's theories it seemed to take on a more sinister interpretation. What if Tanner were right, and both cousins were involved in the murder? Would not that make a horribly complete explanation of Austin's attitude? Might the latter not fear that the bringing in of Cosgrove might be a step towards the elucidation of the whole affair? It was therefore with foreboding that Daunt set out next morning to see his client.

He had determined to try a little test. He conversed at first as on previous visits, and then when the other's mind was occupied and he was off his guard, he said suddenly, but as carelessly as he could, 'By the way, William Douglas has been arrested.'

The effect on Austin surpassed his most gloomy prognostications. Surprised out of himself, the accused man started back, his face paled and he gave vent to an exclamation of what seemed to Daunt to be veritable consternation. Then rapidly controlling himself, he tried to simulate indifference.

'William Douglas?' he repeated questioningly, 'I have heard my father speak of him. An old gardener, wasn't he? What on earth has he been doing?'

Daunt felt instinctively the reply did not ring true.

'That's what I've come to ask you,' he retorted. 'What were you and he doing at the boathouse on that Wednesday night?'

'My dear fellow,' Austin answered—he was evidently shaken, but still spoke with a certain dignity—'you forget yourself. You have no right to ask me such a question.'

'Then I withdraw it and ask you another. You told me, I think, that the Sunday evening when you dined at Luce Manor was the last occasion on which you saw Sir William alive?'

'Certainly.'

'And you repeat that now?'

'Why, of course I do.'

Daunt leant forward and spoke impressively.

'Then how do you explain your having lunched with him on the next day at the Étoile in Soho?'

Again Austin started. Daunt was sure that the shot had told. But the other only said:

'It seems to me you have mistaken the side you're on. Are you taking prosecuting counsel's place?'

'Good Lord, Ponson, don't play with words,' cried the solicitor angrily. 'It's far too serious. If I'm to act for you, I must have an explanation of these things. Why have you denied being there when you were?'

'Who says I was?'

'Everyone concerned. The manager, two waiters, the porter—all agree. There's no mistake. I saw them myself. Tanner knows all about your lunch there with Sir William and Cosgrove, and about Sir William's visit afterwards to Douglas.'

Austin was pale, and a look of positive dread showed for a moment in his eyes. But he preserved his calmness and only replied:

'They were mistaken. I was not there.'

Daunt dropped his detached air, and spoke with all the earnestness at his command.

'Look here, Ponson,' he said. 'What the truth in this wretched business is I don't know, but I do know that for you to go on like this means a certain verdict of "Guilty". That's as sure as you're sitting there. If you don't care about yourself, for God's sake think of that girl that's giving up her all for you. You must tell her the truth—in common honour you must tell her. Your actions must look suspicious to her as well as others. If you can explain them, for Heaven's sake do so, and if not, don't let her commit herself too far to get out.'

Austin slowly raised his head and smiled unhappily.

'You're a good fellow, Daunt,' he said. 'God knows I'm ten times more anxious for Lois than for myself. But all I can tell you is to repeat what I have already said; I was not there. There must be some ghastly mistake.'

Daunt felt his anger rising.

'It's a mistake that will cost you your life if you don't rectify it,' he answered sharply. 'If you can't be open with me I must give up the case.'

'Then you don't believe me?'

'Believe you? How can I believe you? I show your photograph to four separate men at that cafe and all identify you without hesitation. But see here'—he spoke as if a new idea had occurred to him—'the thing can be easily settled. If you weren't at the cafe with Sir William where were you? Tell me that?'

'I lunched that day at the Savoy.'

'For three hours?'

'Well, no. I sat and smoked in the lounge. Then I got one or two things— tobacco and those two pairs of shoes.'

Jimmy Daunt did not believe him, but all the persuasion of which he was a master failed to induce Austin, whatever he might or might not know, to supplement or vary his statement. But the latter consistently scouted the idea that the trial could end in a conviction, stoutly maintaining that there was no evidence to lead to such a conclusion.

At last Jimmy took his leave, intensely dissatisfied with the result of the interview. As had been arranged between them, he sent a wire to Lois asking her to come to town that afternoon, though he looked forward to the meeting with anything but pleasure.

It was nearly five when she arrived. He greeted her with no hint that his news was bad, and as before insisted on an immediate visit to the quiet restaurant. Over a cup of tea he told her all of Tanner's adventures and discoveries, with the single exception of his learning of the meeting between Sir William, Austin, and Cosgrove at the Étoile restaurant. But when they had returned to his office, he became more serious.

'I'm frightfully sorry, Lois,' he began, after seeing that she was comfortably seated, 'but I haven't told you all the news yet, and I'm afraid the rest of it is not too good.'

Her expressive face became clouded and anxious, but she did not speak. Then Daunt told her as gently as he could of the lunch at the Étoile, and Tanner's theories resulting therefrom.

'But that's not such bad news,' she said with evident relief. 'Inspector Tanner must have made a mistake. Austin said he didn't see his father after the Sunday evening.'

Daunt moved uneasily. It was a confoundedly awkward job, and he wished he was through with it.

'Dear Lois, it sounds a perfectly horrible thing to say, but that is just the difficulty. In spite of Austin's denial, Tanner is convinced the meeting took place. I believed he was mistaken, so I went down to the restaurant myself. I took Austin's photograph, and the manager, two waiters, and the porter recognised it instantly. All four are prepared to swear Austin was there.'

'Did you tell Austin?'

'Yes. He stuck to his denial.'

Daunt had expected and feared an outbreak from Lois on hearing the news, but though her face showed extreme pain, she spoke very quietly.

'There is no reason to suppose the four men in the cafe are dishonest. They couldn't have been bought to swear this?'

'It's possible, I suppose, but I fear there's no evidence of it, and even if it were true, we would never get evidence.'

'In that case, as Austin wasn't there, they must have been mistaken.'

She looked steadily in Jimmy's eyes as if challenging him to contest her statement. He marvelled at the faith a good woman will show in the man she loves, and he felt if Austin had by word or deed deceived her, hanging would be too good for him. He hesitated in replying, and she went on:

'You understand what I mean? Austin was supposed to have been seen at the boathouse, and as he wasn't there we deduced an impersonator. We find, in my opinion, the same thing here—probably the same man.'

'In the boathouse case we imagined Cosgrove was the impersonator. Here it could not be Cosgrove, as he was present also.'

She nodded.

'That is true certainly. Tell me honestly, Jimmy, what you think yourself.'

Jimmy hedged.

'It's not what I think, Lois, or for the matter of that, what you think, or even what Tanner thinks; it's what the jury will think; and as you've asked me the direct question, I must tell you I greatly fear they will disbelieve Austin.'

'I fear so too,' she answered quietly. He felt she was conscious he had not answered her question, and was thankful she was going to let it pass. But his relief was short-lived.

'You thought he was'—she hesitated for a moment—'not telling you all he might?'

Jimmy hated doing business in opposition to a clever woman. Again and again he had found that except for their own purposes they seldom considered either his words or actions, but always his quite private and secret thoughts. He realised that Lois knew exactly what was in his mind regarding Austin.

'To be strictly truthful,' he answered, 'I admit he did give me the impression that he was holding something back. But of course it was only an impression, and I may have been wrong.'

She nodded slowly and then said, 'I think, Jimmy, I must see him myself.'

This was what her cousin had feared, and he felt he must exert all his powers of diplomacy to prevent it.

'Well, you know, Lois,' he answered truthfully, 'I had that in my mind. I hardly liked to suggest it. But undoubtedly if he does know anything, he would tell you when he mightn't tell me.'

She looked at him in unveiled surprise, but only said:

'Can you arrange an interview for tomorrow?'

'I would try if you thought that would be best. But I was going to suggest waiting until Tanner has investigated the affairs of Douglas. He believes, and I agree with him, that there was some private business between Douglas and Sir William, which, if we knew it, would clear up the whole affair.'

'Ah,' said Lois comprehendingly.

'If Austin,' Jimmy went on desperately, 'is really holding anything back, we may take it he has a good reason for doing so. Unless it becomes really necessary—and it has not, so far—it would be better not to try to force his confidence. He will tell us when he thinks it right.'

'Really, Jimmy,' Lois smiled faintly, 'you are quite coming on. I don't say you have persuaded me, but I will agree to postpone my visit—shall we say for a week?'

'When Tanner returns from Devonshire I shall see him, and let you know his report immediately,' returned the relieved but suspicious Daunt.

They continued discussing the affair for some time. Jimmy could see that in spite of the brave face Lois put on things, she was deeply worried and despondent. Never had he admired her more. He marvelled at her belief in Austin, her assurance that he, Jimmy, was doing the utmost possible, her fairness to Tanner, and her utter and absolute forgetfulness of herself. As he saw her to the train he felt his resolution strengthened, to spare himself neither time nor money to bring about the result she desired.

When Tanner left Daunt's office on the previous day, he returned at once to the Yard. First he arranged for Cosgrove to be shadowed, in case that gentleman, learning of Douglas's arrest, might consider discretion the better part of valour and disappear. Then he busied himself in re-examining the witnesses of Cosgrove's movements on the night of the murder, which the efforts of Lois and Daunt had unearthed. When he had heard their statements he had to admit himself convinced of the cousin's duplicity.

After a consultation with his chief a warrant was issued, and Tanner went to the flat in Knightsbridge and executed it. When cautioned, Cosgrove made no statement beyond earnestly and emphatically protesting his innocence, and declaring that a terrible mistake had been made.

A detailed search of the flat revealed one or two things which Tanner had not already known. As he had suspected on the occasion of his first visit, Cosgrove had a second desk for his more private papers. In the dressing-room was an old Sheraton escritoire, and there the Inspector found complete information about his prisoner's finances. The latter appeared even more involved than Tanner had suspected, which of course strengthened the motive for the murder, and therefore the case against the accused.

But this was not all. The motive had been stronger than any merely financial embarrassment could have made it. In the same desk was a bundle of letters from the actress at the Follies, Miss Betty Belcher. These showed that Cosgrove's relations with her had been extremely intimate. For a considerable time he had evidently been pressing her to marry him, and in one letter, dated about three weeks before Sir William's death, she had openly admitted she loved him and would marry him if only he were rich. 'You know, Cos.,' the rather cynical letter went on, 'it would be absurd for me to think of marrying a poor man. I have been too long accustomed to all that money gives to contemplate any other kind of life. If you had a fortune—well, I might consider it, but as things are you must see it would be out of the question.'

'He must have been far gone to want to marry her after that,' mused Tanner, 'but he evidently did, for here a week later is another letter in the same strain.'

He filed the papers in the Cosgrove dossier, from which they duly found their way into the hands of the public prosecutor.

The next item on Tanner's list was a similar search in Douglas's cottage, and on this business the detective found himself once more seated in the 10.30 a.m. from Paddington, on his second journey to Devonshire.

He thought he was beginning to get some kind of grasp of the case. It was evident that Austin and Cosgrove, separately and individually, had each the two strongest motives known to weak humanity for desiring Sir William Ponson's death. In each case there was the direct want of money. But in each case also, to this crude desire was added the more subtle and infinitely more powerful consideration that the money was for the loved one. Neither man could accomplish the marriage upon which he had set his heart, and live afterwards in the way he wished, without more money, and by Sir William's death this money could alone be obtained.

So much was obvious, but the facts seemed to permit a further conclusion. Suppose these two, knowing of each other's position, had conspired together to commit the crime which would relieve the necessities of both? In some way not yet clear they had lured Sir William to the boathouse, met him there, committed the murder, and arranged the matter of the boat to create the impression of accident. In case suspicion should be aroused, each had worked out a false but ingenious alibi.

Tanner felt himself so far on fairly firm ground, but when he came to consider Douglas and the part he had played in the affair, he had to confess himself absolutely at sea. However, the search on which he was now engaged might throw some light on that.

He reached Yelverton at the same time as on his first visit, and went at once to the police station. The sergeant had got together some information for him. Douglas, it appeared, had come to the neighbourhood some seven years previously from, the sergeant believed, New York. He had taken a ten-year lease of Myrtle Cottage, had engaged an elderly housekeeper who was still with him, and had settled down to a quiet existence of gardening and bee farming. That he had some money was obvious, but he was not well off, and seemingly had at first found it difficult to make ends meet. But during the last four years his prospects appeared to have improved, as he had carried out a number of alterations to the house, had purchased a small car, and generally seemed to have taken things more easily. The sergeant, after Tanner had left on the day of the attempted arrest, had made a careful search of the house, but without finding anything suspicious. He had then admitted the housekeeper, who had been visiting friends in Princetown, and she had been living there since. Douglas had not borne a very lofty reputation in the neighbourhood. He was morose and ill-tempered, and drank more than was good for him. But he kept himself to himself and there had been no open disputes with his neighbours.

So much Tanner knew when he reached the house to conduct his own examination.

A lengthy interrogation of the housekeeper led to nothing fresh. And then began another of those exhaustive searches to which Tanner was so well accustomed, and which always bored him so exceedingly.

He found nothing of interest till he came to examine Douglas's papers, but from them he learned a good deal of the man's life. Douglas had been, it was evident, a clerk in the Pennsylvania Railroad Terminal in New York, there being letters on railway paper and photographs of groups of employees, as well as a testimonial from the head of the office. This was dated seven years earlier, and referred to Douglas's service of twenty-one years. The man must therefore have held the position since

1892. Of his life since settling in Devonshire there were records, principally connected with bee-keeping, but of his history before his connection with the Pennsylvania Railroad Tanner could discover nothing.

'He is surely either an Englishman or a wonderful mimic,' thought the Inspector, as he recalled the north-country accent with which the man had spoken on the day of his bolt for liberty.

The search dragged on, and at last, as it was nearly concluded, Tanner made three finds, though none of them seemed of much value. The first was that when examining with a mirror the blotting paper on Douglas's desk, he saw that an envelope had been addressed to Sir William Ponson. Unfortunately, in spite of his careful efforts he could trace nothing of the letter presumably sent therein, but the marks were a still further proof of the relations which had obtained between the two men.

The second discovery appeared at first sight of even less importance, and Tanner noted it principally as being the only thing he had yet come on which, it seemed possible, might refer to Douglas's early life. In an old and apparently little used book on American passenger rates, the leaves of which the Inspector was painfully turning over in the hope that some old letter might be therein concealed, he came on a photograph. Evidently of considerable age, it was faded to a light brown and discoloured as if at some time it had been wet. It was a view of a tombstone and grave with a building—presumably the porch of a church—in the background. A lich-gate showed in the farther distance, while on the stone the inscription appeared as dark, broken lines, the only word decipherable being the first—'Sacred.' Tanner put the photograph in his pocket with the idea that this might represent Douglas's family burying ground, which, if traceable, might throw light on his birthplace. At the same time he felt that such information, even if obtainable, could not help much in his quest.

The third find was that in an engagement book or diary there was a reference to the visit to London, and to certain calls to be paid there. On the space for the Thursday before the murder was written 'London, 10.25 train, Judd's Hotel, Dunlop Street.' On the next space, for Friday, was an entry, 'Insurance Co., 77B Gracechurch St.' There was a list of articles—probably purchases—'Collars, handkerchiefs, *The Apiarist*, by S. Wilson Holmes,' and some other items. Last, but not least, for the evening of the murder there was 'X—9.30 p.m.'

This last entry set Tanner puzzling. 'X,' he presumed, stood for the Luce Manor boathouse, and its use seemed to show the same desire for secrecy about his visit there as had been noticeable with the others who had been present. But Tanner had to confess that this entry did not square with the theory that the murder had been its object—at least on Douglas's part. It was inconceivable that a man about to commit such a crime should have required a reminder of the hour of the deed. Every detail of the plan would have been seared into his brain. Was the suggestion of this entry, wondered the Inspector, not that Douglas had been made a tool of by the cousins? If the man should make that case this would certainly be corroborative evidence. Tanner attached some weight to the point, as he felt it was too subtle to have been designed.

Having seen from the papers that Douglas had an account in the Plymouth branch of the Western Counties Bank, Tanner next day called on the manager. Here, after a study of the accused's finances, he made an interesting discovery. At intervals during the last four years Douglas had lodged sums of money—invariably in notes, so he was told—and what particularly intrigued the Inspector's imagination was the fact that each such lodgment had taken place a few days after the drawing of an 'X' cheque by Sir William Ponson, and in each case it was for just a trifle less than the amount of that cheque. It seemed evident that Sir William had been paying Douglas these sums, and the method of lodging showed the latter equally eager to keep the transactions secret. What service, mused Tanner, could Douglas have possibly done Sir William to have merited such a return?

It was an anxious and disappointed Inspector who that afternoon stepped into the London train at Millbay Station, Plymouth. He had been hoping for great things from his search of Douglas's rooms, and he had found practically nothing—only an old photograph and the address of an insurance company in London. And neither of these seemed the slightest use. Could anything be learned by tracing that tombstone or calling at that insurance office? He did not think so.

But more than once he had learnt the folly of neglecting any clue, no matter how slight. Therefore on arrival in London he prepared a circular to be sent to every police station in England. It bore a reproduction of the photograph, together with a paragraph asking if the recipient could identify the place and send in a note of its whereabouts, as well as a copy of the inscription on the tombstone.

Next morning he set out for 77B Gracechurch Street.

A suite of offices on the second floor of a large building bore the legend 'The Associated Insurance Company, Limited,' and Tanner, entering, asked for the manager. After a short delay he was shown into the presence of a tall, gaunt man, with iron-grey hair, and tired looking eyes. Tanner introduced himself as an Inspector from the Yard.

'I have called, sir,' he went on, 'with reference to a man named William Douglas, a small, elderly man with a grey beard, who lives near Yelverton in Devon. I understand that he has had some dealings recently with your Company. I imagine, but am not certain, that he came here on Friday, the 2nd of July last.'

'I cannot recall the man myself,' the manager returned. 'What is the precise point in question?'

'We have had to arrest him on a serious charge—in fact, that of murder. I am endeavouring to trace his recent history and movements. I want to know if he did call, and if so, on what business.'

The manager pressed twice a button on his desk. An elderly clerk answered.

'Mr Jones, do you recall our doing any business recently with a man called William Douglas from Devonshire?'

'Yes, sir,' the clerk replied. 'We were in correspondence about an annuity, but the matter fell through.'

'This gentleman is Mr Tanner, an Inspector from Scotland Yard. You might let him have all the particulars he wants.' Then to Tanner, 'If, sir, you will go with Mr Jones, he will tell you everything he can.'

Mr Jones led the way to a smaller office, and waved his visitor to a chair.

'William Douglas?' he said, bending over a vertical file. 'Here we are, Mr Tanner.'

He withdrew a folder, and settling himself at his desk, took out some papers.

'Here is the first letter. You will see it is an application from William Douglas of Myrtle Cottage, Yelverton, South Devon, for particulars of annuities. He wanted to purchase one which would bring him in £500 a year. Here is our reply enclosing the information and a form for him to fill in, and here is the form which he returned to us duly filled. You will notice he is aged sixty-six. We then wrote him this letter explaining that the annuity would cost him £4600, and asking his further instructions. He replied, as you see, to proceed with the matter, and he would send on the cheque in due course. We prepared the necessary documents, but received no further communication from Mr Douglas until about ten days later we had this note stating that he regretted the trouble he had given, but that he found himself unable to proceed with the matter at present. And so it stands.'

'Then Douglas didn't call here?'

'No.'

Tanner was considerably puzzled by this information. As he walked slowly along the Embankment back to the Yard, he racked his brains to understand Douglas's motive or plan. What had been the ex-clerk's idea? The figures of his bank account showed that at no time since he came to live at Yelverton had he had more than £600 to his credit. As he could not possibly have paid the four thousand odd himself, where did he expect to raise it?

And then a sudden idea flashed into the Inspector's mind. Sir William Ponson had been paying Douglas sums ranging from £100 to £400 at intervals during the last four years. These sums were all paid by cheques marked 'X' on the block. On the day before his death Sir William had written an 'X' cheque for £3000. This cheque had never been cashed.

Was there not a connection? Had that £3000 'X' cheque of Sir William's not been written for the purpose of paying for Douglas's annuity? It certainly looked like it. And had the sudden death of Sir William not prevented its being cashed?

Of course, the amounts did not tally—the cheque was for £3000, while the price of the annuity was £4600. But it was obvious that these sums might represent the different opinions the two men held of what was due. Possibly also negotiations were in progress between them on the point. This was of course guesswork, but at least it would explain the facts.

The Inspector walked like a man in a dream as he concentrated his thoughts on the whole circumstances. There seemed just one link of his chain missing—some one point which, if he could find it, would flood the whole of these mysterious happenings with light and make the disconnected facts he had learnt fall into their places like the closing pieces of a jigsaw puzzle. And then suddenly he wondered if he had not got it, as another and more sinister idea occurred to him.

What if the business were blackmail? It had a nasty enough look. Could Douglas have got hold of something discreditable in Sir William's life, and could the latter be paying for his silence?

The more Tanner thought over it, the more likely this theory seemed. It would explain the facts generally, as well as the secrecy with which both parties had acted. And yet there were difficulties. This annuity business was a difficulty. From Douglas's point of view it was easy enough to understand. If the blackmailer thought his receipts were precarious, or if time was reducing or about to reduce the value of the secret, it would be a natural step for him to try to convert his vanishing doles into a fixed and certain income. But Sir William's motive would be different. His only hold on the preservation of his secret was the expectation on Douglas's part of sums yet to be paid. If the manufacturer agreed to the annuity his hold would be gone. That he should do so was inconceivable to Tanner. And yet apparently he had. He had at least written the £3000 cheque.

But the second difficulty to the blackmail theory was more serious. The wrong man had been murdered! If Douglas had been the victim it would have fitted in well enough. It would have been argued that Sir William had taken a desperate remedy to escape from an intolerable situation. But Sir William's death would have been the last thing Douglas could have desired. He would never have cut off the source of his income. No; attractive as the blackmail theory had seemed at first, Tanner found its difficulties rather overwhelming.

He had by this time reached the Yard, and sitting down at his desk, he lit a cigar, and continued his ruminations.

Suppose again that blackmail had been levied, where did Austin and Cosgrove come in? They must in this case obviously have taken sides. Either they must have been assisting Sir William to extricate himself, or else they must have been party to the blackmail.

But as Tanner pondered these alternatives, he could not see how either would meet the facts. If the cousins were acting for their relative, they obviously would not have murdered him—it was a contradiction in terms. Here again the wrong man had been killed.

On the other hand, it was difficult to see how they could have been in league with Douglas against Sir William. Anything discreditable to the manufacturer would react on both the son and nephew, and their threat to make the matter public would therefore hardly be convincing. For their own sakes the cousins would be as anxious as Sir William to keep the thing quiet. It was also clear to Tanner that they would never have put themselves in the power of a man like Douglas. If they had wished to murder Sir William for his money, they would have done so at some time when Douglas would not have witnessed the crime.

So far had Tanner progressed when he realised his argument really was that Sir William could not have been murdered at all! He swore angrily, and went back to see the point from which he had started. Blackmail. It would seem, then, that blackmail could not be the explanation. And yet . . . It was an attractive theory . . .

Some days later, rather to Tanner's surprise, he received from a sergeant of police in the north of England an answer to his circular about the photograph. It read:

'SIR: We have found the churchyard illustrated in your view attached. It belongs to the Parish Church of Tynwick, a village six miles south-east of Gateshead. The headstone is still standing. It bears the inscription—"Sacred to the memory of John Dale, aged 53, who departed this life on 4th September 1871, and of Eleanor, his beloved wife, who entered into rest on 25th March 1890, at the age of 67.' "

'Gateshead? Dale?' thought the Inspector. 'Those names sound familiar.'

He turned to his notes of the case. And then he got rather a thrill. Gateshead was the place from which Sir William had come to Luce Manor. It was there the deceased gentleman had been born and had spent his life, and where the ironworks he had owned was situated.

And Dale? This was more interesting still. Dale was the name of his wife's first husband! He had married a Mrs Ethel Dale. Here at last was a connection between the manufacturer and William Douglas.

But after all was it not a very slender one? What exactly did it amount to? That Douglas had in his possession a photograph of the grave of a man and woman of the same name as Lady Ponson's first husband, and who lived somewhere in the same locality. Not much to go upon, and yet it was suggestive, and where there had been nothing before, Tanner welcomed it eagerly. Who knew what it mightn't lead to? He determined he must go to Tynwick and make inquiries.

The shades of evening were falling when Inspector Tanner reached Newcastle. He had not been favoured with his usual travelling weather. For the first time since he started work on the Ponson case, the skies had remained all day grey and leaden, and the rain had poured ceaselessly and hopelessly down. It had not been possible to open the carriage windows, and he was tired from so long breathing the stuffy atmosphere of the train.

It was too late to do anything that night, but the next morning, which fortunately was fine, he took the train to Tynwick. It was a village of about five hundred inhabitants, an attractive little place, with pleasant creeper-covered cottages, separated from the road by narrow gardens, all ablaze with colour. In the centre was the church, and strolling slowly into the churchyard, Tanner had no difficulty in identifying the spot from which the photograph had been taken. As the sergeant had said, the headstone was still standing, and Tanner paused and re-read the inscription of which he already had received a copy.

Close by the churchyard and connected with it by a gate in the dividing wall, stood an old, grey stone house—evidently the vicarage. Tanner pushed open the gate, and walking slowly up to the door, knocked.

'Could I see the vicar for a few moments?' he asked courteously, as the door was opened by a trim maid.

He was shown into a comfortable study, and there after a few moments he was joined by an elderly man, clean shaven, white haired, and kindly looking.

'Good morning,' said the latter. 'You wished to see me?'

Tanner rose and bowed.

'Yes, sir,' he answered, 'for a moment.'

'Sit down, won't you?' His host waved him to an arm-chair and seated himself at his desk.

'My business, sir,' went on Tanner, 'is, I expect, of a rather unusual kind for you to deal with. My name is Tanner—Inspector Tanner of New Scotland Yard, and I have come to ask your kind help in obtaining some information of which I am in need.'

If the clergyman was surprised he did not show it.

'And what is the nature of the information?' he asked. Tanner took the photograph from his pocket.

'We have had,' he explained, 'to arrest a man on suspicion of a serious crime —murder, in fact. The only clue to his antecedents we have is this photograph. You will see it represents part of your churchyard, and the headstone in the foreground is in memory of John Dale and his wife, Eleanor. We thought if we could find out something about these Dales, it might help us.'

'Is Dale the name of your suspect?'

'No, sir, he is called Douglas, but of course that may not be his real name.'

The clergyman thought for a few moments.

'I fear I cannot tell you very much,' he said at last. 'When I came here thirteen years ago there was no one of that name in the parish. I do remember hearing of the family you mention, but they had moved some years previously.'

'You don't know to where?'

'Unfortunately I do not.'

'Perhaps, sir, some of your remaining parishioners could tell me?'

'That's what I was going to suggest.' The clergyman again paused. 'There is a family called Clayton living close by, gentlemen farmers, who have been here for generations. Old Mr Clayton is well over seventy, but still remains hale and hearty— a wonderful man for his age. I should think that if anyone could give you your information, he could. He'll probably be at home now, and if you like, I'll go down with you and introduce you.'

'I should be more than grateful.'

'Come then,' said the vicar, leading the way.

The Claytons lived on the outskirts of the village in a charming little creeper-covered house, standing in small but perfectly kept grounds. As the two men passed up the rose-bordered path to the door, they were hailed from the lawn behind. An old gentleman with a full white beard, a grey felt hat, and a tweed suit was approaching.

'Mornin', vicar,' he cried cheerily.

'How are you, Mr Clayton? Beautiful morning. Can we have a word with you?'

'Delighted, I'm sure. Come in here. It's always better out of doors than in, eh, Vicar?'

He shook hands with the clergyman, and turned expectantly to Tanner.

'May I introduce Mr Tanner? Mr Tanner has just called with me in search of some information which I unfortunately was unable to give him, but which I thought you possibly might.'

'I had better introduce myself more fully, Mr Clayton,' said Tanner. 'I am a detective officer from Scotland Yard, and I am trying to trace a family named Dale, who, I understand, formerly lived here.'

Mr Clayton led the way to a delightfully situated arbour, and waved his guests to easy chairs, but the vicar excused himself on the ground that his part in the affair was complete. On his departure Tanner produced the photograph and explained his business to his host.

'The Dales? Yes, I knew them well. They lived at the other end of the village for many years, until indeed John Dale, the father, died. Then they moved into Gateshead. They weren't left too well off, I'm afraid. But I don't know that any of them are alive now.'

'What did the family consist of?'

'The mother and two sons. She died some years after her husband—you have the date on your inscription.'

'And can you tell me anything about the sons?'

'Yes, I remember them well. They were very like each other—good looking, with taking manners, well dressed and all that, but a couple of rotters at heart. They were always out for what they could get, and there was drink and gambling and worse. When they cleared out they weren't much loss.'

'Place too hot to hold them?'

'In Edward's case, I think so. Edward was the younger. He was in debt heavily, I know, and he slipped off quietly one night to the States, and was never heard of again.'

'And the other?'

'The elder brother, Tom, was a bad lot too. He had a tragic end. He was drowned. But I don't think anyone mourned for him. He had well-nigh broken his young wife's heart in the three years they were married.'

Tanner was like a bloodhound on a hot scent. This was very interesting. He remembered that Sir William Ponson had married a Mrs Dale from this part of the country, whose husband had been drowned on his way to Canada. It looked like as if the Tom Dale of whom Mr Clayton had been speaking might have been this man.

'What was the business of the Dale brothers?' he asked.

'They were both in the same firm—the Eagle Ironworks. You know it maybe —in Gateshead? It was Peter Howard's then. I remember young Ponson joining it— poor fellow, he's gone now—it was he that made it. When he started as office boy there was just one small shed and about a dozen men, and now it's a company employing over a thousand hands. A wonderful change.'

'Wonderful indeed, Mr Clayton.'

'Ay. A man of my years can look back over great changes. That's more than a young fellow like you can do, eh, Mr Tanner?'

'It's true, sir. And you say Tom was drowned?'

'Yes. He got a sudden call. He was in the *Numidian*. You wouldn't remember about her?'

'I don't think so.'

'No, it would be before your time. A terrible business it was. The *Numidian* was a big boat, big for those times, I mean. She was running from Glasgow to Quebec, and she struck a berg. Went down off the banks in a few minutes. Nearly every soul on board was lost, and Tom Dale was one of them. A sudden call, it was.'

'A terrible affair. I do remember hearing of it.'

'Ay, no doubt. A sudden call for Tom, that it was.'

'You said he nearly broke a good woman's heart, Mr Clayton?'

'Ay, and so he did. Little Ethel Osborne was fool enough to marry him. And it wasn't long till she was sorry for it. They say she saw him drunk for the first time the night after the wedding. But it wasn't the last, not by a long chalk. He was a bad boy all through, was Tom.'

'Then his death must have been something of a release to her?'

'Yes, poor soul. But she had more sense the second time.'

'The second time?'

141

'Ay, she did what she ought to have done at the start—married young William Ponson.'

'Never neglect the smallest clue!' thought Tanner triumphantly, as he recalled his doubt of the wisdom of following up the photograph. The connection between Douglas and Sir William was strengthening. Doubtless he was on the right track at last, and maybe if he questioned him skilfully, this old man would let something drop which would give away the secret.

Mr Clayton was glad to talk—the old gentleman seemed lonely—and presently the whole story came out. Substantially it was the same as that Tanner had already heard from Mr Arbuthnot, the late manufacturer's lawyer. Mr Clayton told of William Ponson's start in life as office-boy in the Eagle Ironworks of John Howard; of his rapid rise to the position, first of manager, then partner, and finally of sole owner; of his taking his brother John, Cosgrove's father, into the concern; of their extraordinary prosperity; of William's municipal life, culminating in his knighthood, and of John's death, followed by Sir William's sale of the business, and retirement to Luce Manor.

With all of this Tanner was familiar, but he found Mr Clayton was able to give him rather more details of the manufacturer's family affairs than he had yet learnt.

It seemed that when the deceased knight was aged seven-and-twenty, he had fallen deeply in love with a Miss Ethel Osborne, the daughter of a Gateshead doctor. Miss Osborne was a pretty, though not very brilliant girl of some twenty summers, with a placid, pleasure-loving disposition, and a little money. The Dale brothers at this time held positions in the firm, Tom, the elder being a traveller, and his brother Edward a clerk. Tom was a handsome youth with rather fascinating manners. He was considerably below middle height, had delicate features, small and beautifully shaped hands and feet, and dark, passionate eyes.

When William Ponson began to press his attentions on Ethel Osborne, he soon found he had a rival in Tom Dale. For a long time the young lady was unable to decide between her two admirers. For Ponson she had more respect, and she felt that as his wife she would have an assured position and a comfortable home. But Ponson was 'stodgy.' His thoughts were centred in his work, and his own advancement, and he had forsworn that lighter side of life—theatres, dances, excursions—which the young girl found so attractive. With Dale she believed her prospects might be less secure, but life would certainly be pleasanter. He seemed to understand her, and respond to her moods better than the other, and he was a delightful companion. And who shall blame her if she sacrificed material prosperity to the joy of life, rather, who shall not praise her?

In due time she married Dale, and at once, on the very self-same day, her disillusionment began. That night, as has already been mentioned, he returned drunk to the Scottish hotel at which they were to spend the honeymoon. And that was only the first occasion of many. Soon she learned of an entanglement with a barmaid which had been going on at the very time of the wedding. It was not long before their numerous quarrels led to an open rupture, and Dale made no secret to his wife of the fact that he had married her for her money. Matters went from bad to worse, till debt began to fasten on them its horrid shackles, and ruin stared them in the face. The one alleviating circumstance was that there had been no children from the marriage.

All this William Ponson watched, grieving for Ethel, but of course helpless. Then it became necessary for the firm to send a representative to Canada, and the choice fell on their traveller, Tom Dale. Whether or not Ponson had any say in this decision was not known, but at all events Dale sailed for Quebec in the *Numidian*. As will be remembered, the vessel was lost off the coast of Newfoundland, a mere handful of her complement being saved. Dale's name was amongst the lost. Ethel Dale therefore found herself not only without assets, but called upon to meet a considerable crop of debts. Her father having died since her marriage, she was thus absolutely destitute.

It was believed to be owing to William Ponson's efforts that a small pension was granted her by the firm, and the debts were wiped out by a presentation from some of the employees. She took a small house, and by letting rooms contrived to make a living.

William Ponson, though he had acted throughout in a strictly honourable manner, had never ceased to love Ethel. He bided his time for over two years, then, calling on the widow, he told her of his love and boldly pressed his suit. She then realised that she had loved him all along, and though at first she refused to consider his proposal, his steady insistence wore down her opposition and in 1887, five years after he had first loved her, he obtained his desire, and they were married. The trouble through which she had passed had profoundly modified her character, sobering her and bringing out all that was best in her, and her life with William Ponson, though quiet, had been truly happy. Two children were born, Austin and Enid.

'And you said the other Dale went to the States, I think?' asked Tanner, when he had learnt the above facts.

'Edward? Yes, he got into difficulties too. He was a born gambler. He was owing money everywhere, and the place got too hot for him. He went to the States shortly after Tom was married.'

Tanner felt he had done well. Almost first shot he had found this Mr Clayton and obtained information which must prove of the utmost value. But he had stayed chatting to and pumping the old man for an unconscionable time, and he began to express his thanks, preparatory to taking his leave. And then an idea flashed into his mind, and he sat motionless for some moments, thinking.

'What was the Dale brother, Edward, like in appearance?' he asked, trying to keep the eagerness out of his voice.

'Like enough to his brother Tom, but not so good looking, nor with such good manners by a long chalk. But passably well looking for all that.'

'But was he a small man?'

'Small? Ay, that he was—like Tom. Both were small men.'

Could it be? Edward Dale, a little man with small hands and feet, knowing all about William Ponson's youth—knowing probably a good deal more than Mr

Clayton had told or perhaps knew—Edward Dale, a clerk, had gone to America and disappeared. William Douglas, a little man with small hands and feet, and apparently knowing intimate facts about Sir William Ponson—William Douglas, a clerk, had come from America, his youthful history being unknown. Could they be one and the same?

The more Tanner thought over this theory, the more likely it seemed. As he sat smoking with Mr Clayton in the pleasant garden, he went over in his mind all that he had learnt of each man, and was unable to recall anything inconsistent with the hypothesis.

But how could he test it? He must make sure. But how?

There was of course one obvious possibility. Mr Clayton, if confronted with Douglas, might recognise him as Edward Dale. Or Douglas might recognise Mr Clayton, and so give himself away. It was not a certainty, but it would be worth trying. The Inspector turned to his host.

'I believe, sir,' he said, 'that if I told you just what was troubling me, you might be able to help me out, if you would. I was asking you about Edward Dale, but I did not tell you much about the man we arrested. In the first place, Douglas, as he says his name is, came to England from New York, where he was employed as a clerk in the Pennsylvania Railway for several years. We have traced his movements back to 1892, previous to which we can discover nothing whatever about him. Now, you tell me Edward Dale left for the States about the year 1882, and has since been lost sight of. That is coincidence Number One.'

Mr Clayton nodded without speaking. He was listening with eager attention.

'Next,' continued Tanner, 'I did not tell you whose murder the man Douglas was suspected of. It was that of Sir William Ponson.'

'God bless my soul!' cried the other, 'you don't say so? A terrible affair that. And you think you've got the man, do you? All I can say is, I'd like to see him hanged.'

'It seems clear from various things,' Tanner went on, 'that the trouble originated before Douglas went to America. Now Edward Dale knew Sir William in those days. That is coincidence Number Two.'

'You said, I think, that Douglas's history could not be traced before he became a clerk in the Pennsylvania Railway? How then do you know he left England prior to that?'

'We don't absolutely know, but we think it for two reasons: first, he can speak with a North of England accent, and secondly, that in an old book of his we found the photograph of the Dales' grave.'

The other nodded.

'That photograph,' continued Tanner, 'is coincidence Number Three. Few men would have such a photograph unless it represented something connected with their own families. And coincidence Number Four, Mr Clayton, is this. Douglas is a very short man with very small hands and feet.'

'God bless my soul!' Mr Clayton exclaimed again. 'But this is most interesting. Go on, Mr Tanner.'

'Well, sir, that leads me up to a very obvious question. You must have guessed it. You have known Dale intimately in the past; could you identify him now?

Tanner sat back in his chair and drew at his cigar. The other did not answer for a moment. Then as he slowly refilled his pipe, he said hesitatingly:

'I hardly like to say. Thirty-eight years is a long time, and a man might change a lot during it. I think I would recognise Edward if I saw him, but I couldn't be sure.'

'Then, sir, my second question follows naturally. Will you come up to London and try?'

The other smiled.

'It's a long journey for a man of my years,' he said, 'but I imagine I have no choice. You Scotland Yard people are so autocratic.'

Tanner smiled in his turn.

'If you will come at our expense, sir, you will confer a great favour on us. Do you prefer day or night travel?'

'Day. When would you like me to go?'

'The sooner the better, sir. Tomorrow, if it would be convenient.'

'One day is much like another to me. I will go tomorrow, if you like.'

They sat on for some time longer smoking and chatting. In spite of his years Mr Clayton's mind remained active and vigorous, and he had kept himself well abreast of recent events. He evidently enjoyed exchanging ideas with the Inspector, and the latter exerted himself to entertain the old gentleman, relating several of the adventures he had met with in his professional career.

In the afternoon Tanner called at the Eagle Works. But there he got no help. The firm's official records did not go back far enough to include the Dales' names, and none of the office staff recalled the brothers' affairs.

On the following day the Inspector and Mr Clayton travelled up to town together, and the former saw his new friend to an hotel. The interview with Douglas was to take place next morning.

Inspector Tanner delighted in a dramatic situation, especially when he was the *deus ex machina*. In the present instance he thought he was sufficiently sure of his ground to risk an audience. After consulting his chief, he accordingly rang up James Daunt.

'I think I am on to a clue at last,' he said. 'As you and Miss Drew are interested and have helped so much I will stretch a point from strict etiquette and invite you both to be present while we test it tomorrow. . . . Yes, here at the Yard at eleven o'clock.'

At the time appointed a little group sat in the Inspector's room. There was first of all Miss Drew, dressed quietly in a navy blue coat and skirt, and a small hat. Her kindly, dependable face was pale and somewhat drawn, as if the strain of the last few weeks had taken its toll of her. But she was calm and pleasantly courteous as usual, and did not betray by word or deed the anxiety which was gnawing at her heart.

Jimmy Daunt, who sat beside her, seemed the more nervous of the two. He was extremely dissatisfied at the way his case was going, and eagerly anxious to learn in what direction the Inspector's fresh information would tend.

Mr Clayton, who sat next to Daunt, was anxious too. He devoutly hoped that after all the fuss and trouble of his visit to London, he should be able to give a decided opinion—to say definitely whether the man he was to see was or was not Dale.

On the other side of Tanner sat Chief Inspector Edgar. On Tanner reporting what he proposed to do, the latter had expressed a desire to be present. He it was who had suggested having the meeting at the Yard, in order to avoid the necessity of Miss Drew's visiting the prison. But he took no part in the proceedings, Tanner conducting all the business.

When the visitors had been introduced to each other, Tanner rose, and bowing to Miss Drew and her cousin, said:

'I have taken the liberty of asking you to be present this morning, as I know the keen interest you take in this case. Following a certain line of inquiry, with the details of which I need not now trouble you, I had the good fortune to come across Mr Clayton here. From what he told me there seemed a reasonable probability that the man whom I arrested in Portugal, and who gave his name as William Douglas, was not so named at all, but was a certain Edward Dale, a clerk in the late Sir William Ponson's Ironworks, who emigrated to the States in the year 1882. Mr Clayton has been good enough to come up all the way from Newcastle to put this theory to the test. I propose now to confront Douglas with Mr Clayton, so as to see whether the two men recognise each other. I may add that if Douglas has to admit he is Dale, it is more than possible he may make a statement explaining the whole affair. Now, Mr Clayton, might I ask you to sit here at my desk with your head bent as if writing, and when I sign to you, to move round so that Douglas may see your face suddenly.'

A roll top desk was placed at right angles to the wall beside the large double window, and Mr Clayton crossed over and sat down on the swing chair, bending forward as if to write. Anyone entering would see only his stooped shoulders, and the back of his head, but when he swung round his features would be fully lighted from the window. The others placed themselves with their backs to the light, and in view of the door. When he was satisfied as to the position of each, Tanner pressed a bell and a sergeant of the police entered.

'You may bring him in now.'

The man withdrew, closing the door, and silence came down on the little group. To Lois Drew such scenes were new, and on her expressive features there was a look of compassion for the unhappy man for whom the trap was set, and whose life might depend on his actions during the next few moments. To her the whole business was evidently extremely distasteful, and it was not hard to conclude that only the possibility of helping her lover had induced her to continue to take part in it.

Tanner's emotions were evidently far otherwise. The eagerness of the hunter showed in his eyes, and his whole body seemed on the stretch. He was by no means a cruel man, but he had pitted his wits against the other, and the issue between them

146

was now about to be joined.

A knock came to the door, it was thrown open, and William Douglas entered.

The man seemed to have aged since Tanner had first seen him at his house at Yelverton. His face was paler, his hair seemed greyer, and he was even smaller and more stooped. Innocent or guilty, he was already paying for his connection with the crime.

'Take a seat, Mr Douglas,' said Tanner, moving forward and placing a chair where the full light from the window shone on the other's face. 'I have asked you to meet my friends here, to discuss some points about this case. But I have to repeat my warning that you are not bound to make any statement or to answer any questions you may be asked unless you choose. This lady is Miss Drew, a friend of the Ponson family; this gentleman,' he indicated Daunt, 'is Mr Austin Ponson's solicitor, and this,' he waved his other hand, 'is Chief Inspector Edgar. I think you already know our friend at the desk.'

As Tanner spoke he signed to Mr Clayton, who swung round suddenly and faced Douglas.

The latter had seemed very much mystified by the whole proceedings. His eyes had followed Tanner's gestures as each member of the party had been mentioned, and he had made each a slight bow. But when he saw Mr Clayton's face he remained as if turned to stone. At first for a moment he seemed puzzled and doubtful, then his eyes fixed themselves in a tense stare on the other's features, his face grew slowly pale and drops of sweat formed on his forehead. Then, as if some second thought had passed through his mind, an expression of something like relief showed in his eyes. So he sat, staring, motionless.

But if the effect of the meeting on Douglas was disconcerting, it was as nothing to that produced on Mr Clayton. On first seeing the newcomer, he too looked puzzled and doubtful. Then gradually an expression of utter astonishment spread over his features. He literally gasped, and seemed so overwhelmed with amazement as to be bereft of the power of speech.

The surprise on the countenances of the two chief actors in the scene was reflected faintly on the faces of Lois Drew and the solicitor. But on Tanner's there was triumph. If the girl and her cousin had not realised what was happening, he had. His plan had succeeded. That these two knew each other was established beyond any possibility of denial. It was as if each had shouted his recognition of the other aloud. He spoke quietly to the suspected man.

'So you really are Edward Dale?'

The words seemed to restore the power of movement to Mr Clayton.

'No,' he almost shouted in his excitement. 'It's not Edward Dale. It's Tom!'

Tanner jumped as if struck in the face.

'What?' he stammered. 'What's that you say? Tom? But—but—I thought—'

His voice trailed away into silence as the meaning of this discovery began to penetrate into his mind. Tom Dale was lost in the *Numidian* disaster thirty-five years before—so he had been told, and so every one had believed. But every one must have been wrong. If this were Tom, he must have escaped from the wreck. He must have escaped and he must have concealed his escape. Why? Why should he conceal it? Why, to get rid of his wife, of course. It was a case of desertion. He had had all her money; he hated her. Of course that was it. He would take the opportunity to change his name and make a bid for freedom. But his wife—And then Tanner gasped in his turn as he saw the further consequences involved. His wife had married Sir William Ponson, thinking her first husband was dead. But now it was clear that had been no marriage at all. Lady Ponson was Lady Ponson no longer, but Mrs Tom Dale —the wife of the drunken ex-clerk and suspected blackmailer! Sir William was not married. Austin and Enid were illegitimate! No wonder Sir William submitted to blackmail rather than allow such a scandal to become public. As innocent in the matter as the babes unborn, Sir William and the woman he had considered his wife, as well as his son and daughter, would have had to pay as dear as if the whole affair had been deliberate.

Tanner glanced at Mr Clayton. His excitement had subsided, and a look of fierce indignation against Dale was showing on his face. Tanner spoke.

'I suppose there can be no mistake?'

'Mistake?' the other burst out. 'Man alive, look at him. By heaven I wish there was a mistake!'

'We had better bring him up to Gateshead, and see if anyone else will confirm your identification.'

There was an interruption from the prisoner.

'You needn't trouble,' he said sadly. 'I admit it. I am Tom Dale.'

'You escaped from the *Numidian*?'

'I escaped. I was picked up by a fishing smack and taken into Gloucester. I was on board four days before we got in, and I had plenty of time to make my plans. I don't pretend I wasn't wrong, but I wasn't so bad as you think. I dare say you won't believe me, but I did it for Ethel's sake. She was tied to me, and I knew I was a bad egg and had all but ruined her. And what's more, I knew I would ruin her outright if I went back to her. So I deserted her. But all I rid her of was trouble. I thought I would give her another chance with her life, and I did. I swore she would never know. And if I did go wrong, she at least has had her life happy since because of it.'

The man spoke simply, and with a certain dignity which impressed his hearers.

'How did you conceal your identity?' Tanner asked.

'Very easily. I had made friends on the voyage with another passenger. He had told me he was alone in the world. I saw him drown. I took his name.'

'And then you came here and blackmailed the man you had injured?'

Dale nodded his head slowly.

'I admit that too,' he said sorrowfully. 'I most bitterly regret it, but I must admit it. I do not want to make any excuses for that, but here again the facts are not quite so black as they look. When I had been out there about thirty years I got a longing for the old country. I had made a little money in the States, and I left my job and came over to England. I was afraid to go back to Gateshead, so I looked around and took that cottage in Devonshire. Then one day in London I met Ponson—I didn't know he had a handle to his name then. He recognised me, and there was a scene. I thought he would have killed me in the street. Then I got him into a bar, and we took a private room and had it out. I understood he had a right to have a down on me for deserting Ethel, but at first I couldn't understand why he was so absolutely mad. Then I learnt. I hadn't known what had happened to Ethel, for I was too much afraid of arousing suspicion as to who I was, to go back to Gateshead or make any inquiries. He threatened me so wildly I got afraid for my life, and then I saw how I could turn the tables on him. I told him that so far from me being in his power, he was in mine. I told him I would make the affair public myself, and that if I could be punished I would take it, and he could have the scandal. He blustered at first, then gradually he saw his position, and then he crawled. He offered to make the thing a business proposition. He would pay for my silence. He pressed his offer on me, and I accepted it at last. And I have at least kept my word. Not a whisper of the affair has passed my lips. But I admit taking the money. I was very hard up, and it meant a lot to me. You don't understand, gentlemen, how much a few pounds means to a poor man. And with all his thousands he didn't miss it. Not any more than you would miss a penny if you dropped it. I took it and I admit I pressed him for more.'

'Was that what you went to the Luce Manor boathouse for on the night of the murder?'

Chief Inspector Edgar moved suddenly.

'Come, Tanner, that won't do,' he advised, and then to Dale: 'You needn't answer that unless you like.'

Dale hesitated. To the others it seemed as if he was on the verge of a confession. Then he bowed to Edgar.

'Thank you,' he said. 'I had perhaps better consult my solicitor first.'

Tanner looked annoyed, but he controlled himself and again addressed the prisoner.

'Then you don't wish to make any statement?'

'No. Not at present, at any rate.'

Tanner nodded and rang his bell. The same sergeant re-entered and signed to Dale to follow him. Then, including the whole party in a slight bow, the latter rose from his chair and the two men left the room.

The silence which fell when the door was closed lasted a full thirty seconds, and then Daunt broke it.

'Well, Inspector, this has been very interesting, but I'm hanged if I can make head or tail of it. Maybe you'd explain to Miss Drew and me what it's all about.'

Chief Inspector Edgar rose.

'I think that's all I'm concerned in,' he said, and turning to Mr Clayton, he invited him to smoke a cigar in his room.

When Tanner was left alone with the cousins, he realised that he had an extremely unpleasant task to perform. Miss Drew, as the affianced wife of Austin Ponson, was personally interested in the story. Though from his knowledge of her he thought she would not place so great importance on the unfortunate occurrence as might a shallower and more conventional woman, yet the news could not be otherwise than a shock to her. He wished someone else had the telling of it.

But no purpose would be saved by delay. The sooner he began, the sooner the unwelcome job would be over.

Asking Miss Drew's permission, he passed his cigar case to Daunt, then drew forward his chair and began to speak.

'I am afraid the story I have to tell you will come rather as a shock to you,' he said, as he examined the end of his cigar. 'This man Dale had been blackmailing Sir William Ponson for the last four years. There was an exceedingly unfortunate secret in Sir William's life—unknown to him until he learnt it from Dale at that time, four years ago. Sir William was in no wise to blame for what had taken place. So far as I can learn, he had acted with scrupulous honour all through. The fault was Dale's and Dale's only. But to make it clear I must tell you from the beginning.'

The cousins remained almost motionless while the Inspector related the details of his journey north, and the facts he had there learnt; the family history of the Dales; how the brothers came across Sir William in the Eagle Ironworks; the rivalry between Ponson and Tom Dale for the hand of the pretty Ethel Osborne; Tom's success in the contest; the unhappy married life of the young couple; Tom's mission to Canada; the loss of the *Numidian*, and his presumed death; Sir William's marriage with Mrs Dale, and the birth of Austin and Enid; Tom Dale's return to England; and finally the blackmailing, culminating in the presumed negotiations for the purchase of the annuity.

'But the murder?' asked Daunt when at last the Inspector paused. 'What about that?'

'The murder unfortunately remains as great a mystery as ever,' Tanner answered slowly; 'indeed, even more so,' and he explained his difficulty about, as he expressed it, the wrong man having been killed.

The two men discussed the affair for some minutes further, Miss Drew remaining silent. When they got up to take their leave her eyes were very bright, and there was an expression on her face the Inspector could not quite fathom.

'Mr Tanner,' she said as she held out her hand, 'I would like to thank you for the way you told your story.'

Outside the Yard she dismissed Daunt.

'I am going to write to Austin,' she announced. 'I shall leave the letter at your office shortly after lunch, then, like a dear man, you will take it to him immediately, and bring me the answer.'

'Of course, I will, old girl,' Daunt answered her as they parted.

That same evening Daunt paid his promised visit to Austin Ponson. He found his client seated despondently in his cell, his head resting on his hands. Like Dale, he had aged since his arrest. His face was pale and drawn, his eyes weary, and as he moved his head a suspicion of grey showed at his temples. His manner had lost its old ease and lightness, and it was evident that the crisis through which he was passing would leave its mark on him for many a day to come.

'I have something for you, Mr Ponson,' the solicitor said as he sat down and felt in his pocket for Lois's letter. 'You are to let me have an answer.'

Austin's eyes lit up as he saw the handwriting, and he seized the note with eagerness. To let him read it in peace, Daunt drew some papers from his pocket and began to study them. But he hadn't done so for many seconds when an exclamation drew his attention back to the other.

Austin Ponson had risen to his feet and was excitedly pacing the cell. He was a transformed man. A smile was on his lips, his eyes were shining, and his face had a rapt and beatific expression, like that of a man who sees a vision of angels.

'My Heavens!' he cried, '*What* a girl! She's beyond anything I could have imagined. One in a thousand millions! I can hardly realise it. I tell you, Daunt, if I never get out of this hell again, it's been worth it. It would be worth any suffering to get such a letter. Tell her—But you can't tell her. Nor I. No one could ever tell her what I feel.'

He paused and looked at the other, then resumed his hurried pacing.

'I swear that if I get out of this place, I'll make it up to her. I'll live for her day and night, and for nothing else. She'll never regret what she has done—that is,' he sank into his chair and the dejected look returned to his face, 'if I ever do get out.'

'You forget, Mr Ponson, that I don't know what's in your note.'

Austin stared.

'You don't?' he queried in surprise. 'Why, she tells me the whole thing's out —that Tom Dale has been found, and that she knows about my father's marriage and my birth. And'—his face lit up and he spoke triumphantly—'she says she doesn't mind—that it will make no difference to'—he paused as if for a word, then concluded—'her feelings towards me. What do you think of that?'

'I congratulate you very heartily, Mr Ponson,' Daunt replied, though with a mental reservation. 'But I can assure you that so far as I am aware, the whole thing is anything but "out". It is true the identity of William Douglas with Tom Dale has been discovered, and the effect his existence has on the validity of your father's marriage is known. But that is all. No explanation of the murder has yet come to light. And, after all, that is really what matters.'

'Has Dale admitted his identity?'

'Yes.'

'And has he made no statement about what took place in the boathouse?'

'None. But, Mr Ponson, that remark implies to me that you were there yourself and know.'

Austin looked sharply at the speaker.

'I didn't say so,' he answered dryly, 'but—stop, let me think a moment.'

For some minutes silence reigned in the gloomy cell. To Daunt it had seemed as if his client was on the verge of a confession, and he wondered if one more sordid story was to be added to the list of those to which the grey walls of this grim apartment had in all probability listened. Austin sat motionless, his mind evidently engrossed with some problem, the solution of which eluded him. But at last he seemed to find it. Straightening himself up, he faced the solicitor.

'This news you have brought makes a tremendous difference to me,' he said. 'From my point of view there is no longer any reason why the events of that tragic night should not be known. I have remained silent for two reasons. First, because of my mother. The thought of her learning that she was still the wife of that drunken scoundrel was more than I could bear. You'll understand my feelings—the whole thing is so painful I hate to speak of it. Then there was another reason. I made the unforgivable blunder of being afraid to tell Miss Drew. I have paid for that already, and every bit of that payment I deserve ten times over. I distrusted her. I thought if the circumstances of my birth came out she might have nothing more to do with me. And I just couldn't risk that. You see, it was not as if there had been any deliberate evil on my parents' part. Both were utterly innocent, and even ignorant that anything was wrong. Therefore I could not see that I was called upon to chance the wrecking of my happiness on what was after all a mere technical matter only. God forgive me, I did not intend to tell that angel. I feared the stigma would remain. Well, I have suffered for it. As I ought to have known, she was above a petty feeling of that sort. I should have told her the moment I knew of the matter myself. I should have told Tanner everything at the start. Much trouble would have been saved. And now it may be too late. I may not be believed.'

'I don't know, of course, what you propose to tell,' said Daunt as the other paused, 'but as your legal adviser I should warn you to be very careful of what you say to anyone. If you care to tell your story to me, I shall be pleased to advise you as to what, if any of it, should be made public.'

'I suppose that would be wisest,' Austin returned, 'but I have quite made up my mind. From the first I decided to tell all I knew if the secret of my parentage came out. That was the only reason for my silence. Indeed, I was coming to the conclusion I must tell in any case, even if I myself had to reveal it. I appreciate your offer and under other circumstances would gladly avail myself of your advice, but whatever the consequences, I am going to tell. But I by no means wish the affair to be made public. I want most of all to tell Miss Drew, I would like to tell you, and I must tell Tanner. If you will help me by making this possible, I will be for ever your debtor. One other thing, I should like Cosgrove to know my decision. It is only due to him. Can you arrange these matters?'

'I think so. But I cannot but feel you may be making a mistake in not first taking, I don't say my advice, but the advice of some legal man. I cannot move you on that point?'

'My dear fellow,' said Austin warmly, 'there is no one whose advice I would take more readily than yours. But in this case we need not discuss it. If you will not help me to the interview I want, I will send for Tanner and tell him here.'

Daunt saw there was no more to be said. He waited till Austin had written his reply to Lois—a lengthy and complicated proceeding—then, promising he would see Tanner without delay, he left the cell.

Inspector Tanner was keenly interested by the news.

'At last!' he exclaimed in a satisfied tone. 'We shall get the truth this time. He's getting frightened. He'll not bluff us any more.'

'I don't see that you've any right to say that,' Daunt returned hotly. 'It will be time enough to accuse him of lying when you hear what he has to say.'

Tanner smiled.

'Very good, Mr Daunt. I'll not say a word—till then.'

It was arranged that the proceedings of that morning should be repeated next day. Austin would be brought to Scotland Yard, and there in the presence of Lois, Daunt, Tanner, and a stenographer, he could make his statement.

At eleven o'clock next day Lois and Jimmy Daunt drove up to the Yard, and were shown without delay to Tanner's room. There they met the Inspector and his Chief, Mr Edgar, who had expressed a wish to be present on this occasion also. At the desk was a shorthand writer.

It was cool in the grey walled room. The open window allowed a current of fresh air to flow gently in, carrying with it the subdued hum of the great city without. In the sunny courtyard the sparrows were twittering angrily, while a bluebottle buzzed endlessly up and down the window pane. The little group, after the first brief greetings, sat silent. Expectancy showed on every face, but whereas Tanner's and the Chief Inspector's also indicated satisfaction, uneasiness was marked on Daunt's and positive apprehension on Lois's. To her at least, the coming meeting with her lover was obviously no light ordeal. On it, as was evident to them all, largely depended the future happiness of both.

They had not waited long before a knock came to the door and a sergeant of police admitted Austin Ponson. The young man was dressed in a suit of navy blue, and bore himself quietly and with some dignity. In the bright light of the room the lines of suffering showed more clearly on his face, and his eyes looked still more weary.

Instantly on entering they swept over those present, fixing themselves immediately on Lois. In spite of an evident effort for self control, the light of an absolute adoration shone in them for a moment, then he withdrew them, bowed generally to the company, and sat down.

But this was not enough for Lois. She sprang to her feet, and going over to him, held out her hand. He rose and clasped it, and though neither would trust themselves to speak, they saw that in each other's eyes which satisfied them.

Tanner with some delicacy busied himself for a few moments in giving directions to the stenographer, then turning to the others, he spoke.

'I don't think it is necessary, Miss Drew and gentlemen, for me to explain our presence here. Last night Mr Daunt intimated to me that Mr Ponson had a communication to make, at which he wished Miss Drew, Mr Daunt, and myself to be present. This meeting has therefore been arranged. I have only to make known to you, Mr Ponson, Chief Inspector Edgar'—he indicated his colleague—'and to ask you to proceed with your statement. It is, of course, understood by you that you make it voluntarily and that it may be used against you?'

'I understand that right enough, Inspector,' began Austin, 'and I wish to say I have no quarrel with your treatment of me. You have been fair all through.'

He paused, settled himself more comfortably in his chair, and went on:

'The only thing I should like to ask is whether my cousin, Cosgrove, has been told that I am going to make this statement?'

'He has been told,' Tanner answered.

'And may I learn if he was satisfied?'

'He seemed so.'

'Thank you. I am not quite sure how much of my story you know, but I shall tell you everything. When I have finished I shall have a request to make of you—that you will keep what I am about to tell private—but I do not know whether or not you will find that possible.'

Tanner nodded without speaking.

'Of my early life,' went on Austin, 'I do not think I need say much. I expect'—he looked at Tanner—'you know all about it. You know that, while we never had an open breach, my father and I did not pull well together. We looked at things from such different points of view that our intercourse only produced irritation. My father wished me to read for the bar with the idea of entering Parliament, and trying for a seat in the Ministry. I was not ambitious in that direction, but preferred literary work, and scientific research. Therefore, as you no doubt are aware, I found it irksome at home, and I set up my own establishment in Halford. But that we remained good friends was proved by my father's moving to Luce Manor at my suggestion. With my mother I was always in sympathy. She was easy-going, and deferred without protest to my father's decisions, but never at any time was there the slightest cloud between us. So things had gone on for years, and so they went on until this terrible business began.'

Austin moved nervously in his chair, glancing quickly round the little group.

'On Sunday, 4th July,' he resumed, 'occurred the first event of this unhappy tragedy, so far as I was concerned. I received by that morning's post a letter from my father, saying he wished to see me on very private business, and asking me to dine and spend that evening with him. He directed me to destroy his letter, and not refer to the matter to anyone.

'Considerably surprised, I burnt the note, and duly went out to Luce Manor in time for dinner. When the meal was over my father and I retired to his study, and there when our cigars were alight, he said he had a very grievous and terrible secret

154

to impart to me which would doubtless give me considerable pain. He locked the door, then sitting down he told me what I believe you already know.

' "My boy," he said, "we have not perhaps pulled it off together as well as I could have wished, and when you hear what I have to tell you, I fear you may be tempted to think more bitterly of me than I deserve. But I can assure you on my honour, that in this terrible affair I acted in perfectly good faith all through. Until four years ago I was as ignorant as you are still that there was anything wrong."

' "I don't understand," I said.

' "No," he answered, "but you will soon."

'Then he told me of his early life, and that of the two Dales; of his falling in love with my mother, Ethel Osborne; of the rivalry between himself and Tom Dale for her hand; of Dale's success; of the miserable married life of the couple; of Dale's mission to Canada, and of his presumed death in the *Numidian* disaster, and of my father's own marriage with the widow. All this I had known more or less vaguely before, and I could not understand why my father recited the circumstances in such detail. But he soon made it clear to me.

' "As you know," he went on, "your dear mother and I have lived happily together ever since. She had her time of suffering, but thank God, she has enjoyed her after-life, and please God, she shall never learn what I am about to tell you."

" 'Some four years ago," continued my father, "I happened to be in London, and walking down Cheapside I met a man whose face seemed vaguely familiar. He was short and slight, with small features, rather delicately moulded, white hair, and a short goatee beard. He saw me at the same time, and his eyes fixed themselves on my face with an expression of almost incredulous recognition. For a few seconds we stood facing each other, while I racked my brains to recall his identity. And then suddenly I knew him. It was Tom Dale!"

'My father paused, but for some seconds I did not grasp the full meaning of his statement. Then gradually its significance dawned on me. I need not repeat it. You have heard what it involved. I was appalled and horrified. Though upset on my own account, I ask you to believe that what distressed me most was its possible effect on my mother and sister. Of my mother I just couldn't bear to think, and it also hurt me beyond words to believe that any such secret should have power to throw a shadow over Enid's life.'

'Did you speak to your father on this particular point?' Tanner interjected.

'Speak? I should rather think so. I was beside myself with horror.'

'Can you recollect the exact words you used?'

Austin considered.

'I hardly think so,' he said at last, 'though every detail of the scene is fixed in my memory; I said as the thing began to dawn on me, "And my mother—it can't be that she—?" I did not wish to speak the words, and my father completed my sentence for me. "Yes," he said, "there's no escape from it; she is the wife of that drunken ruffian." Then I cried, "Good Heavens! She can't be," or something to that effect, and he answered that it was only too true.'

'Might the words you used have been, "My God, sir, she isn't?" '

'Yes, I believe those were the words. That was the sense anyway.'

'Continue, please.'

'It appeared that upon their recognition there was a scene between my father and Dale. Eventually, however, they took a private room at a neighbouring bar, and there talked the matter over. Then to my father's amazement it came out that Dale had not known of my mother's second marriage. But when the latter realised how matters stood, his manner changed. He said it was my father, and not himself, who had come within the reach of the law, and that if the affair became known, even if my father escaped imprisonment, he would still have public opinion to reckon with. Was he prepared to face the scandal?

'My father was not. His good name and that of his family were very precious to him. In his agitation he did a weak thing. He offered to buy Dale's silence.

'My father then told of his negotiations with Dale, with the details of which I think I need hardly trouble you. Suffice it to say that Dale put on the screw and got several hundreds that year. But that did not satisfy him. His demands grew more and more outrageous till at last my father came to the conclusion that some step must be taken to rid himself of the incubus.

' "It is not the actual money he is now getting," said my father, "it is the uncertainty under which I am living that is making me ill. He will continue to bleed me, and after I am gone he will bleed your mother and yourself, and perhaps Enid. Besides, we don't know if he really will preserve the secret. I have been thinking for some time that I must tell you and Cosgrove the whole story, so that we may devise some plan to protect ourselves, but now events have been precipitated by a fresh demand from Dale. Read that."

'My father handed me a letter headed "Myrtle Cottage, Yelverton, South Devon". It was from Dale, and in it he said the existing arrangements with my father were unsatisfactory, that instead of a hundred or two now and then, he would rather have one large sum which should close the account between them. He demanded my father should buy him an annuity which should bring him in £500 a year for life. In peremptory words he required an immediate answer, adding that he was coming to town that day and would stay in a small hotel near Gower Street, where my father could see him.

'That letter had come on the previous Thursday, and on the Saturday—that was the day before our interview—my father had gone to town and seen Dale. The man, it seemed, had been more truculent and overbearing than ever before, and had presented what amounted to an ultimatum. Either he would have the money for his annuity, or he would tell. After a long wrangle my father had promised to consider the matter until the following Monday, when he would see Dale again and let him know his decision.

'My father went on to say he would willingly pay the demand to be rid of the whole business, but his difficulty was, of course, that he had no guarantee the payment would rid him of it. He would still be, to precisely the same extent, in Dale's power.

'He continued that he felt that as Cosgrove and I were also interested in the

156

affair, the time had now come to take us into his confidence, in order to see if some joint action could not be taken to bring the matter to an end. He had not yet spoken to Cosgrove, but he suggested that on the following day, Monday, we should both go to town and have an interview with my cousin, after which he could go on and see Dale. We decided to travel separately, to meet at a little French restaurant in Soho, and to keep the matter perfectly private.'

Austin once again paused and glanced round the little group. He was speaking quietly, but there was a ring of truth in his voice. Tanner, who sat checking his every statement in the light of what he had himself learnt, and watching like a lynx for discrepancies, had to admit to himself that the story they were hearing was consistent with the facts. If Austin could explain away all the damaging points in an equally convincing manner, the Inspector felt that the case against him might easily collapse.

'Early next morning I made the appointment with Cosgrove by telephone,' Austin resumed, 'and by different trains my father and I went to town. We took a private room at the restaurant, and there my father told Cosgrove. He was not so upset as I had been, and recommended refusing to meet Dale and letting him do his worst. Though the matter did not affect Cosgrove so closely as it did me, I would have agreed to this proposal, but for my mother and sister. After all, I thought, my father has plenty of money. He will not feel what he may give to this Dale, and there can be no doubt it would be better for all concerned if the affair remained a secret.

'The question then became, "How could we ensure that a further payment would really have the desired effect?"

'My father had a plan—a wild, unpractical, even farcical plan—or so it struck me at first. He said that as we could not adopt the only infallible scheme to silence Dale—to murder him—we must be content with one which promised at least a reasonable chance of success. He said the man was a coward, and that we must work on that. If we could frighten him enough we would get what we wanted, and by his plan he thought we could frighten him so much that he would not dare to reveal what he knew. The plan was as follows:

'My father was to see Dale the same afternoon, hand him £100 as a pledge of good faith, and promise to pay the annuity, though not for the amount claimed. The refusal was to be made more or less doubtfully so as to convey the impression to Dale's mind that he had only to negotiate further and he would get what he wanted. In fact, the interview was to terminate with the principle agreed on, but the precise sum unsettled.

' "But why do that?" interrupted Cosgrove. "If you pay the lump sum you lose your hold on him."

' "I think not," returned my father. "It is part of my scheme that he should have a strong temptation to fall in with our wishes, and the annuity will provide that."

'Cosgrove nodded, and my father went on with his explanation.

'Dale was to be told to get further figures from the insurance company, giving the cost of annuities for smaller annual amounts. At the same time another meeting would be arranged at which the matter would be settled and the money paid. My father was to explain to him that he didn't want to make any more mysterious visits to town, and that Dale must therefore bring the information to Luce Manor. To keep the visit secret he was not to come to the house, but was to be at the boathouse at 9.30 in the evening, where my father would slip out and meet him. Owing to the fact that my mother and sister were going away on a visit on the following day, Tuesday, the meeting was provisionally fixed for Wednesday.

'Without letting Dale know, Cosgrove and I were also to be at the boathouse, and with our support my father was to take a strong line with Dale. The following proposition would be made him. My father would recognise the value of the secret, and would pay Dale, through some agency which would conceal his identity, a sum to the insurance company which would bring Dale in an annuity of about a pound a working day—say £320 per annum. This he would do on condition that Dale would give us an incriminating weapon against himself, which would take the value out of his secret, but which would not be used if he held his tongue. He was to sign a document stating that he was Edward Dale, not Tom; that he admitted having blackmailed my father by falsely representing himself as Tom; that he further admitted my father's power and right to send him to penal servitude, but that he begged that on this full admission of guilt, coupled with an immediate and total cessation of all annoyance, my father would refrain from ruining and embittering the closing years of his life.

' "He'll never sign," Cosgrove interrupted again.

' "Wait a moment," my father answered, and he went on to explain that if Dale refused to sign, he was to be threatened with immediate death by being tied up, gagged, and drowned in the water basin in the boathouse, it being explained to him that, after being unbound, his body would be sent down over the falls, whereby his death would be put down to accident.

'I was amazed at my father seriously suggesting such a proceeding, and I felt strongly opposed to it.

' "No, no," I cried, "we can't do that," and Cosgrove nodded his agreement.

' "Why not?" my father queried, and set himself to overcome our scruples. He argued that if our objection was to making the man sign a false statement, we must remember it was only a bluff, and said that for the sake of my mother and sister we must be willing to do what we might otherwise reasonably object to. If, on the other hand, we were considering Dale's feelings, we should not forget we were suggesting no harm to him—on the contrary we were about to offer him a large sum of money. The intention was not to injure him, but to prevent him injuring us.

' "It's not that," said Cosgrove. "I don't give a fig for the false statement, nor the man's feelings either. As you say, he more than deserves far worse treatment than what you suggest. Nor do I care if the thing brings us within reach of the law—I would risk that for my aunt, and so would we all. But I don't like your plan because it will not work."

' "Why not?" asked my father.

' "Why not?" Cosgrove repeated. "Because Dale has only to inform the police of the whole affair. He would be believed. How would we account for our meeting here, to take one point only?"

' "Ah," my father rejoined, "you always go too fast. I meet that difficulty in two ways. If Dale informed, I would say he signed the confession when I saw him in London—I shall see him this afternoon—under my threat of otherwise immediately exposing his blackmail to the police. Secondly, alibis are easy to fake. Each of the three of us must work out a false alibi, so that we can deny the meeting in the boathouse *in toto*."

' "No, no, I don't like it," Cosgrove demurred.

' "None of us like it," answered my father, "and I admit my plan is far from perfect. But can you suggest anything better?"

'I was even more strongly against the whole business than Cosgrove, and both of us began raising objections to it. We argued that even if we obtained the false confession, it would not ensure our immunity from annoyance. To this my father replied that that was where Dale's cowardly nature came in. The man would not be sure how the confession would affect him if it fell into the hands of the police, and he would be afraid to risk its becoming known.

'We discussed the matter at great length, but neither Cosgrove nor I had an alternative proposal to offer, and at last my father persuaded us against our better judgment to fall in with his.

'I need not weary you by telling you all the arguments used, but at last the details were settled and we turned to the consideration of the false alibis.

'In my father's case it was considered sufficient that there should be no evidence of the visit, lest overmuch proof of our statements should show an element of design. Owing to my mother and sister being from home, he would in the evening be left alone in his study, from which he could slip down to the river with the practical certainty of his absence being unnoticed.

'Cosgrove and I worked out the plans which, I believe, you know. Cosgrove's required the help of his friend, Miss Belcher. Mine was dependent on footprints, and I proposed to report the alleged hoax played on me to the local police, so that these marks might be observed by them while still fresh.

'Our plans had taken nearly three hours to work out, and we parted at the restaurant door. Later in the evening my father telephoned—we had arranged club calls—that Wednesday night would suit Dale.'

Again Austin paused and moved uneasily, and again Tanner had to admit to himself that so far the story they were hearing, while utterly unexpected and extraordinary, bore the impress of truth. Up to the present he had been unable to detect any inconsistency between it and the facts he had himself learnt. He was coming to the opinion that they were about to hear the truth of the tragedy itself, and he set himself to listen with renewed concentration as Austin resumed:

'I bought the two pairs of shoes I required for my alibi, on that Monday afternoon. At home I locked one pair away, and took care the attention of my man should be called to the other. Then on the Wednesday evening I wrote the forged note from Miss Drew, and dropped it into the letter box on my hall door, where my man found it as I had intended.

'Putting on the new shoes of which my man had had charge, I got a boat and rowed down to the boathouse. My statement about the hoax was obviously false, and the evidence of that girl and her lover in Dr Graham's wood was true.'

It was evident that this admission, made in the calm matter-of-fact way in which Austin was speaking, came as a considerable shock to Lois Drew. But she made no remark, listening motionless and intent to what was coming—as indeed were they all.

'The water gate was closed, and as I did not want Dale to see my boat and perhaps take fright, I went into the boathouse to open it. My father was there already, and he opened the gate, and I took the boat in. Presently Cosgrove turned up. He had motored from London.

'We waited for a few moments and then Dale arrived. Directly he entered Cosgrove slipped behind him and locked the door, putting the key in his pocket. Dale was obviously taken aback when he saw three persons waiting for him, and when he observed the door being locked he got very white and frightened looking. But my father spoke to him quietly.

' "You need not be afraid, Dale," he said. "If you are reasonable, no harm will befall you. These are my son and nephew, who are as much interested in the affair as I am. We are going to make you a proposal, but I am afraid we are not going to give you the option of declining it."

'My father then explained clearly and quietly that he was willing to pay well for the preservation of the secret, and promised to purchase an annuity which would bring Dale in £320 a year for life. Dale interrupted that it was £500 he wanted, but my father replied that £320 was the sum he had decided on. I think it was the quiet, final way my father spoke, as if the reopening of the matter was by his decision made impossible, that first gave Dale a hint of what he was up against.

'My father went on to point out that on his side he required an end of the annoyance, and explained about the confession. Dale then blustered and said he would see us all in a warm place before he signed. My father, still speaking very gently, said we would give him five minutes to make up his mind. He took a revolver from his pocket—he had previously shown us it was unloaded—and pointing it at Dale warned him that if he tried any tricks he would instantly be shot. And so we waited, my father calm and placid though keeping a wary eye on the other, Cosgrove nervous and smoking cigarette after cigarette, while I, also a little excited, kept pacing up and down the edge of the basin.

'At long last the five minutes was up and my father spoke.

' "Well, Dale?" he queried.

'The man showed his teeth like an animal.

' "I'll see you in Hades first," he snarled.

'At a sign from my father Cosgrove and I sprang forward and seized the blackmailer. He was, as you know, small and elderly, and weakened from drink, and he was like a child in our hands. I held him while Cosgrove tied his hands and feet, in each case with silk handkerchiefs which would leave no mark on the skin. He grew very white, and a look of terror shone in his eyes, but he would not give way, and we felt that we had still failed to make him believe we were in earnest. My father tried to frighten him still further. He spoke again in a matter-of-fact tone.

' "You think, Dale, we're not going to carry the thing through? I can assure you all the details have been carefully worked out. If you do not sign we shall make that anchor"—he indicated that belonging to the largest boat which was standing in the corner with its rope attached—"fast to your shoulders and lower you into the basin. After ten minutes we'll pull your body up, take off the handkerchiefs, carry your body out in the boat and slip it overboard where it will be swept down over the falls. There will be nothing to indicate your death was not an accident. Then I may tell you for your information we have all arranged carefully planned false alibis, so that we can prove we were not here tonight at all. On the other hand, if you sign, you get your freedom, and here"—my father took a paper from his pocket and held it so that Dale could read it—"is a cheque for £3000 for your annuity. So now, do you still refuse?"

' "Your scheme won't wash," growled Dale. "No one would believe I would sign such a confession except under compulsion."

' "Quite right," my father answered. "We wouldn't suggest that you did it of your own free will. I would explain that the compulsion I employed was a threat to hand you over to the police. Come now, we can't spend the night here. Will you sign or will you not?"

'Dale did not move.

' "Very well. Gag him and get the anchor on," said my father.

'Cosgrove gagged him, while I brought over the anchor, and the two of us then made it fast to Dale's shoulders.

'Now over with him.

'We lifted our victim towards the edge. We intended really to duck him if he remained obdurate. But he didn't. He couldn't stand any more. Furiously he nodded his head.

' "Stop," said my father, and to Dale: "Do you agree?"

'The little man again nodded.

'We released him, and bringing him over to a shelf at the side of the room, gave him paper and ink and a draft of the confession, and ordered him to copy and sign it.

'The man was shivering with fright and rage, but he did as he was told. At last we had a weapon, which, we believed, would save us from further annoyance.

' "Don't imagine you can report this to the police," my father warned him. "You would not be believed against our word and alibis, but we could prove the blackmail, and you would go to penal servitude. And now," he went on, "we'll deal as straight with you in the matter of payment. Here is a bearer cheque for £3000, which I hand to Mr Cosgrove Ponson. You and he can go up to town tonight, and he will cash it in the morning and hand you the money, seeing that you pay it into your bank and then send a cheque for it to the insurance company. The transaction will not therefore be traceable to me, as if any question arises Mr Cosgrove and I will swear the money was a gift from me to him to help to pay a pressing debt. That, I think, is everything."

'It was just quarter to ten. The whole business had only taken little more than ten minutes, and now nothing remained but to slip away quietly from the boathouse and establish our alibis. And then suddenly occurred that frightful business which robbed my father of his life, and has caused all this sorrow and suffering and trouble to the remainder of us.'

For the first time since he began to speak, Austin showed signs of emotion. He moved uneasily and seemed to find it difficult to continue. But he pulled himself together, and it was with a breathless interest that the others listened as he resumed.

'I suppose you know the plan of the boathouse?' He paused, and Tanner nodded. 'Then I needn't describe it. Before the tragedy my father and Dale were standing facing each other at the angle of the L-shaped wharf, that is, close beside the corner of the basin. Cosgrove and I had been beside Dale, but on the conclusion of the business we had moved away. Cosgrove had unlocked the door and gone out to see that no one was in the vicinity, and I was engaged in raising the water gate preparatory to getting out my boat.

'My father was holding the confession in his hand, and it was probably the sight of it that gave Dale the idea that he might recover his lost hold on us. Presumably he thought he could seize the paper and bolt with it before either Cosgrove or I could stop him. However, be that as it may, I saw Dale suddenly spring forward and attempt to snatch the paper from my father's hand. My father stepped quickly back. But as he did so, his heel caught in the rope by which my boat was moored, and he fell backwards, his head striking the granolithic floor with terrible force. He never moved again. We rushed forward, but he was dead.'

Austin paused and wiped the perspiration from his forehead, while his hearers sat motionless, amazed beyond speech at this unexpected *dénouement*. So this was the explanation of all these mysteries! No murder had been committed. The affair was an accident! If this story were true, the case against all these men would break down.

But was it true? Tanner, at least, had his doubts. These men had shown considerable ingenuity in constructing false alibis. Maybe this story also was only a clever invention. But on the whole the Inspector was inclined to believe it. It certainly rang true, and it was consistent with what he had otherwise learnt.

Austin had waited a moment, but now he continued:

'I need hardly say we were speechless from consternation. Our first thought was to run for help—Cosgrove to Luce Manor, while I took my boat across for Dr Graham. But this, we saw, would involve disclosing the secret, and we hurriedly consulted in the hope of finding a way of avoiding the revelation. And then it flashed across our minds what a dreadful position we ourselves occupied. Might we not be suspected of murder? Here we had come secretly to the boathouse, having devised elaborate alibis to prove ourselves elsewhere. Though these alibis were not completed, enough had been done to make the whole business exceedingly fishy. We recollected that both Cosgrove and I not only stood to gain fortunes by the death, but were also, both of us, in special need of money at the moment. Then it was known I did not get on well with my father . . .

'I need not elaborate the case; no doubt, Mr Tanner, you considered these matters before you arrested us. All I have to say is that we became panic-stricken and lost our heads. We made an appalling blunder. Instead of going for help and telling the truth, we decided to arrange the circumstances to suggest accident, and trust to our alibis in case suspicion should be aroused. It was so easy, for the plan had already been worked out to frighten Dale. We talked it over quickly, and thought we might improve on it.

'We saw at once that it would seem much more natural if we suggested that my father had taken out a boat of which he had lost control, and had been carried over the falls. The injuries the body would get in the rapids below, would, we imagined, account for the bruise on the back of the head. By throwing the oars into the water nearer the other side of the river, they would not go ashore with the boat, indicating that my father had lost them, and thus explaining the accident.

'The only thing unaccounted for was the motive which had caused my father to take out a boat at this hour. To meet this difficulty I made an entry in a small engagement book I found in his pocket, "Graham, 9.00 p.m." I hoped it would be assumed he wished to make a private call on the doctor.

'There is little more to be told. We lifted the body into one of my father's boats, and I towed it out and set it adrift, dropping the oars in some distance away. Then I returned to the Halford Clubhouse, knocked up the attendant, and called on Miss Drew, all as you know. About three in the morning I put on the shoes I had kept hidden, slipped out of the house and made the tracks to the Abbey ruin, returning without my absence having been noticed. I put the shoes back in their hiding-place and next day, having sent my man on an errand, I cleaned them and changed them for the other pair. This latter pair I afterwards destroyed. The pair which had made the traces at the Abbey (the sole of one of which I had marked) was thus left in my man's charge, and he was prepared to swear—quite honestly—that they had only been out of his possession at the time of the alleged hoax. Is there anything else you wish to know?'

Tanner asked a few questions, all of which Austin answered with the utmost readiness. Then, after receiving an assurance that his statement would receive the most careful attention of the authorities, the meeting came to an end. Austin was led out, and after a few words of conversation, Lois and Daunt took their leave.

Chapter 16
Conclusion

The doubts which Inspector Tanner had experienced as to the truth of Austin's statement were short-lived. After a careful consideration of the story, Austin was subjected to a most searching examination on small details—such points and so many of them as no trio of conspirators could possibly have foreseen and provided for. Cosgrove, who made a statement similar to Austin's, was also tested upon these points, and his answers convinced the authorities that at last the truth was known. At his request the false confession of blackmail, signed 'Edward Dale,' was given up by Miss Belcher, to whom it had been handed for safety. But what cleared the last shreds of doubt from the minds of those concerned was the statement of Dale. Not only did his testimony agree with that of the others, both generally and on the small matters in question, but he went further than either of them. He confessed fully that his action had been the cause of the tragedy, stating, which neither of the others, had done, that he had actually pushed Sir William back. He swore most positively he had no idea of injuring the manufacturer, nor had he noticed the rope or thought about the other's tripping.

It was clear to the authorities that with any ordinary jury the defence would win, and indeed, both Tanner, his Chief, and the Crown Prosecutor themselves believed the explanation given by the three prisoners. The case against Austin and Cosgrove was therefore unconditionally withdrawn, and they were set at liberty.

Against Dale the matter was not so clear, a charge of manslaughter being considered. At last, however, it was decided he could not be proved guilty of this, his only punishable offence being blackmail. But as Austin and Cosgrove resolutely refused to prosecute, the charge was not proceeded with, and Dale also was set free. The cousins even agreed to pay him the £320 a year he had been promised, though they would not purchase for him the annuity.

All the cases thus collapsing, the Yard authorities did not consider it necessary to make known the illegality of Sir William's marriage, and the secret was therefore preserved.

A few weeks, later two announcements were to be seen in the fashionable papers. First came:

'PONSON—DREW. Dec. 29, 1920, at St George's, Hanover Square, by the Rev. Sydney Smallwood, cousin of the bride, Austin Herbert, son of the late Sir William Ponson of Luce Manor, Halford, to Lois Evelyn, eldest daughter of Arthur Drew, of Elm Cottage, Halford.'

Below it was another announcement:

'PONSON—BELCHER. Dec. 29, 1920 at St George's, Hanover Square, by the Rev. Sydney Smallwood, Cosgrove Seaton, son of the late John Ponson of Oaklands, Gateshead, to Elizabeth Clare (Betty), youngest daughter of the late Rev.

Stanford Belcher, of St Aiden's Rectory, Nottingham.'

THE END

www.ingramcontent.com/pod-product-compliance
Lightning Source LLC
Chambersburg PA
CBHW030301130626
46549CB00002B/638